# *Dancing in the Trap*

===============================================

by James Whelpley

2019

PUBLISHER'S NOTE

This novel is a work of fiction. Names,
characters, places and incidents are either the
product of the author's imagination or are used
fictitiously and any resemblance to actual
persons, living or deceased, events, or locales
is entirely coincidental.

For my wife, Jackie, my best friend, the bedrock and wellspring of all the best things in my life.

To a group of fellow writers to whom I owe the completion of this work. Deborah Ellison, Terry Baklas, Don Burquist, Donna Heath, Patrick Parker, and Lewis Sarkozi. Thank you.

# One

I read the letter from Paris, standing at the kitchen sink of my third-floor walk-up, over a glass of beer and a bottle of Palmolive. It was written to a man named Samuel Dile, written, I supposed, by a woman. The stationary was tinted pink, pulpy like craft paper, and smelled better than anything had a right to. The letter lamented that Sam's time in Paris was too short, insisted that he would be missed, and demanded a good sum of money. It was blackmail penned in letters so long and smooth they could have hailed a cab.

After ten years in the merchant marine, I'd held on to enough money to start a business, teaching first-date couples and kids with their weekend-fathers to scuttle dinghies around the harbor. That's where I met Andrew Grey. It was raining on the docks the day I kept his forty-foot Catalina, *Pig Iron*, from trading paint with a local sloop. He said thanks over a beer and a lobster roll, then a few more beers. Grey seemed as amiable and good-natured as you'd expect a guy with his kind of dough to be, but never are. Instead of listing all the things he owned, he asked me about my merchant days, and I recounted all the ports I'd seen for him, twice.

He asked for my business card, certain I had one. It read Mickey Fairfax, Sailing Instruction & Boat Rental, contained the shop address, phone number, and a few fraternal nautical symbols. From his yacht, I knew Grey had seen better specimen than the thin card-stock and bumpy lettering, which he ran his thumb over like braille. He grinned at its flimsiness and I thought he might use it to wipe his mouth. Instead, he tucked the card in his wallet and we shook hands.

Two months later, I was sitting in my shop listening to the radiator when Grey strolled in. He looked much as he had the day we'd met, as if on sabbatical from a Campari ad. His ash blonde saddle brush crew cut was made whiter by his sun-baked skin. His mustache matched a pair of thick blonde brows, over eyes set deep in his face, if they were in there at all. A red polo and light gray pants stretched like canvas over his mahogany frame. In his wake was another man, wrapped in a bad facsimile of Grey's yachting attire. Purchased for the occasion, the thin leather laces of his deck shoes were still too stiff to stay tied. I pictured a closet somewhere full of double-breasted suits bent in the shape of a fire hydrant.

Grey asked if I remembered him. I said I did as I shook his hand. I didn't hob-nob with many so many millionaires that I couldn't keep them straight.

"I'd like you to meet my friend, Sam." That was our entire introduction before, "Go ahead, Sam. Ask him."

His name was Samuel Dile and he had recently returned from Paris. He confessed this to me as Grey thumbed a two-man lifeboat suspended from my shop ceiling. A week ago, Dile said, he had received a letter demanding money. I wondered why Grey had brought this man to me, but Dile came to the point rather quickly.

"I want you to go to Paris for me and deliver the money."

I made a dumb face. "I teach people to sail."

"I can't go, I just got back! What would I tell my wife?" he erupted. He insisted he needed someone he could trust, and that Grey had vouched for me. I scanned the shop again for Grey who had taken a long oar from the wall and stood with it on his shoulder like a cricket bat. His jaw grinned from where I thought his teeth should be.

"Paris is a long way," I said, "my bookie will worry."

Dile didn't laugh. He was staring at my mouth waiting for a ping-pong ball with the word "Yes" to pop out of it.

I had the distinct feeling that *no,* wouldn't have closed the matter, so I tried different words. "Who's blackmailing you, Mr. Dile?"

You could have heard a pin sneeze.

Samuel Dile was an older man, but not old, shorter, but not short, and paunchy but, not fat. Male-pattern baldness had left a token ring of hair around his head that accentuated his plucked scalp. His eye-glasses were from a past decade, and his small mouth was just wide enough for his mustache to escape Hitler comparisons. His story, *Man Steps Out on Wife*, had failed to pique my interest or my pluck at my heart strings.

It was Grey who broke the silence, "I thought you could use a change," then after a pause, "and the money." He had raised his voice needlessly to call across the empty shop. Business at the harbor was slow and time between clients was lengthening faster than I could tighten my belt. Maybe Dile was in the same boat. Maybe Dile didn't have yachting clothes because he didn't have a yacht. Grey's endorsement aside, maybe I was just someone Sam Dile could afford to trust.

The little man stood in front of me, reddening. Tight-lipped as he'd been about the details, he'd spilled his guts to a complete stranger. He was an open wound, and so far, I was an empty box of Band-Aids. Grey's hand on his shoulder startled then stayed him, and a normal color returned to Dile's cheeks. With his friend righted, Grey swung around and beamed at me. "So, will you do it?"

* * *

It was raining outside the Port Authority and I was standing on the curb when a car screeched to a halt in front of me. It was the aggressive round-about driving of a European. The red Alfa Romeo looked as if it had been packed in salt and shipped from Italy. Grey's personal assistant, Shabin, rolled down her window, and addressed me from the idling car. She was an Egyptian woman in her forties, educated in London, compact, conservative, and refined as an English sugar cube. Her short black hair was shielded from the rain by a silk scarf tied under her chin, and her large black sunglasses showed me what I looked like upside down. The driver, I had seen depicted on a Grecian urn. He bore the perpetual smile of a movie star, and his starched shirt collar looked formidable enough for me to stand on.

She handed me a thick parcel, in it a ticket aboard an eminently-departing freighter and a cash payment to a blackmailer. I was instructed to call her if I needed anything, but the tuned exhaust of the idling engine let me know she wouldn't be waiting by the phone. She wished me *"Bon Voyage"* in a language I didn't recognize, and the car pulling away from the curb splashed water on my shoes.

# Two

Les Halles is the cheap, student area of Paris where eye-glassed bohemians in breathable clothes dress the windows and darken the doorways of boutiques and noisy cafes. Lately, it had become the kind of place you didn't want to find yourself after dark. It's also home to the busiest subway station in all of Paris, and where I was to *rendezvous* with *Mademoiselle* Savard, her letter and a bundle of bills burning a hole in my pocket.

The metro station had the same white-tiled bathroom look as stations in the States. I found the gate the letter described and took up what I thought was a strategic position, settling against the wall near a dark man French-frying a James Taylor tune on, what in his hands, looked like a ukulele. He stood at least six-foot-six in an itchy-looking sweater the color of a blood orange, and jeans from a decade he could only have read about. I nestled my face between the thick lapels of my pea coat and tried to think invisible.

The letter instructed Dile to wait at this metro stop, at a given hour, for three days in a row. The payment would be collected one of those three days, he was not to know which. I assumed I would be meeting *Mlle.* Savard herself; in the post-script she had promised to wear red flowers in her hair. Dile had given me a description of her that fit just under a quarter of the women on the planet. If he had somehow provided her my stats, we'd be as good as blindfolded.

Trains came into the station from both directions, spilled passengers over the platforms, and vacuumed up as many. I watched dozens come and go before an older man arranging his grandchildren on either side of him, stepped off the train trailed by a young woman in a purple dress, with small red flowers in her hair. She stood, shoulders back, with posture you didn't find outside of a government typing pool. She looked nervous waiting alone on the platform. Maybe it was the way any young woman would look waiting in a train station for the man she was blackmailing.

Her hair was long, straight, and only slightly darker than her olive skin. The sleeves of her fitted sweater ended just above her elbow and matched the lilac color of her flowing skirt. She stood on top of tall red heels tied to her ankles. The shoes looked racy enough for the strap to be necessary and shared the same heavy gloss as her bright red lips.

"*Mlle.* Savard," I spoke while I was still some distance from her. I was the one who felt like a pigeon, but I didn't want her to flit away by making a lot of racket behind her. When she turned around, it took me a second to make words. "I believe I have your letter."

She was younger than I imagined. She had large gray eyes that made her look serious, and a small pointed chin that didn't. Maybe in Paris she was the girl next door, but I didn't live in Paris. She was alarmingly pretty, and a lot of ugly snares were baited as beautifully.

"I suppose Sam sent you?" she said in a French-roasted kitten purr.

I nodded. "You are *Mlle.* Savard?"

She asked me to call her Adrienne. It was a name you heard a lot around the Adriatic, it referred to the sea. Many French names evoke nobility. A Parisian would have to try hard to name a child something that didn't.

She looked me up and down as if our Halloween costumes didn't match and giggled. "Where did he find you?"

"What's wrong with me?" I said and shrugged my pea coat onto my shoulders.

"Not a thing. There are a lot of sailors roaming *Parie*." She moved close, touched the bill of my Homburg, then the side of my face. "It used to be a look. It isn't anymore."

You couldn't take your eyes off her, and I wasn't about to for a few thousand reasons.

"Do you have the money?" she asked. It was enough to break the spell. Here I was writing in my diary, while she was cutting to the chase. She squeezed the lapel of my jacket in her fist, then smoothed it again.

On its way out, the ungainly envelope tore my coat pocket. By its heft, I felt sure she was making out better on this deal than I was. I tucked the money under my arm and cocked my head, like I was waiting for pool water to drain out of my ear. *Mlle.* Savard did not view my tough-guy act with any level of menace. Instead, she smiled gleefully as if I had produced a bouquet of puppies from inside my jacket.

"I have been instructed to tell you, *Mademoiselle*, that your business with my client is over. You are not to contact him or any member of his family. Understand that this is the only payment you will ever receive."

She laughed out loud. "You really have no idea what's going on," she managed through tears.

This beautiful woman made me hate the way beautiful women laughed; one hand on the opposite hip to keep her from falling to pieces, the other lazily draped over her heart as if it were in danger of arresting at any moment. By the time she regained herself, the back of my neck was on fire, and my teeth had ground to dust in my mouth. Whatever their dealings had been, it was obvious that Dile was a joke to her, and that I was a joke by proxy. Beautiful as she was, I considered punching her in the face.

The hard slap of the heavy envelope against her chest nearly knocked her off her feet and did what my speech had failed to do. Her eyes grew wide and she looked at me for the first time with the level of seriousness I thought the occasion deserved.

"Listen sister," I tried to keep my voice low, "my client is willing to pay sucker money provided you go away. But, if you think you can bleed him beyond this, the next guy he hires to deal with you ain't gonna hand you no envelope." She clutched the money with both hands over her heart. "This was a successful little score, congrats. Go buy yourself a closet full of new dresses and move on."

The girl began digging around in her purse. I half expected her to produce a gun from a balled-up tissue. She was visibly upset. She didn't take being threatened as cavalierly as blackmail. She started to turn away and I grabbed her arm. I couldn't tell you why I did it. She looked back at me through wild, trembling eyes.

"Take your hands off me," she snarled.

I didn't.

"I'll scream," she threatened.

I let her go. Extortion aside, I was in an empty subway station manhandling a woman I didn't know from Adam, or whatever French for Adam is. She said she hoped I would enjoy Paris and called me an asshole.

I let her go. My job was done, I'd delivered the money. But, I intended to follow her. As far as I was concerned I was on my own dime, and I was curious. She didn't seem like your typical blackmailer, I didn't believe for a minute I'd really scared her. To top it off, she was American. Her accent was pretty good, she had obviously lived in France for some time, but it's never long enough.

She stormed off toward the stairs that led to the surface. I waited until she was at the top before I followed. I kept my distance as we crossed the plaza outside. But, before she reached the street, a large man in dark suit nearly snatched her off her feet. She tried to pull free, but in his grasp, her thin arm looked like it had dried in a block of cement. He steered her toward a long, black Mercedes idling at the curb.

I had to run. He opened the car door and began to push Adrienne inside. She tried to resist, straightening her arms against the roof of the car, and digging

11

her shiny red heels into the concrete until they buckled beneath her. Her body began to bend like a willow branch under the giant's heavy hand.

I had built up a head of steam and lowered my shoulder into the middle of the big man's back. It was like tackling a side of beef, or a laundry truck. I felt my spine compress and imagined I'd bounced off him like a rubber ball. But, I had driven him into the open door, bending it backward on its hinges and sent us both sprawling onto the pavement. As I picked myself up, I caught a glimpse of a sizable handgun in a holster under the big man's jacket. Adrienne was standing with her shoes in her hands, and her mouth open. I grabbed her by the wrist and ran pulling her behind.

When I looked back, no one was giving chase. A second man had gotten out of the long, black car to help the first man to his feet. They were both dark, Middle Eastern or North African. The second wore a fez like the dervishes I had seen in Tangiers. They stood training their eyeballs on us from a hundred yards or more.

We pushed our way through the busy plaza and ran the wrong way down the first one-way street we came to, in case they were turning the car around. I don't know how far we had gone when she pointed down an alley that took us through a park as thick with people as with poplars. It was starting to get dark and I thought if I didn't trip over a couple lovebirds, I'd hit my head on a dogwood. We put our backs against the statue of someone famous and dead, and tried to catch our breath.

"We need to call the Police," I said, taking her by the shoulders.

"No! No cops," she repeated, pleading in an American accent as plain as my own.

# Three

We needed to get off the street, and she led me to a small hotel. I used my real name to sign the registry, a long thin tome more supplely upholstered than the lobby furniture. It was a touch of old-world style I felt sure I was paying for, the kind of thing that caused tourists to nudge each other in the ribs. I could have written Jacques Cousteau, the hotel clerk looked at my ID about as long as it took to hand it back to me.

She waited on the stairs while I counted out francs. I followed her again, this time up a couple of flights that made the handrail seem sturdy. Before I could hang the Do Not Disturb on the knob, she was in the washroom, locking the door noisily behind her. The water came on with a whistle like shift-change at a steel-mill and rattled the floorboards. I expected answers when that door opened.

This girl was in trouble, and she most likely had it coming to her. It was hard to say what that trouble was exactly, but the way she looked, it was fun to imagine. I've done my share of stupid things when it came to women, so I told myself to be smart when that bathroom door opened.

When the door did finally open, a hotel towel was shaking a stranger behind it. You couldn't have convinced me it was the same girl. The long, straight mane that had cascaded to the middle of Adrienne's back had been replaced by turbulent jaw-length waves of black vinyl. She had even managed to wash the warm, bronze complexion from her face. Gone was the cinnamon and lilac. In a Dead Kennedys t-shirt and black capri's, she was as colorful as newsprint. It was some trick, like ripping a tablecloth out from under spinning flatware. All that remained of the girl I had met at the metro were those starkly red fiberglass lips.

"Am I going to find the skin you shed hanging over the shower rod?"

"Save it," she said. The honey had gone out of her voice as well. She sat on the stiff couch by the window and emptied the contents of her over-sized purse onto it. She folded the purse in half twice and shoved it into a small pink backpack that had been among its contents. The rest she crammed in after it.

"You want to tell me who those men were?"

"You think I know?" she said with unconcealed exasperation.

I asked her just how many people she was blackmailing.

She ignored me and looked among her belongings for something that would make me go away. I sat down on one of the two metal chairs belonging to the impractically small café table on the opposite wall.

"How about we start with why you're blackmailing Dile?"

"He didn't tell you?" She seemed amused.

"No, he didn't. But, I look at you, I look at him, I get ideas."

"Well don't get any ideas."

I gave her a second. Maybe after she collected herself, she'd have something to say. She didn't.

"Look, sister, I think you owe me--"

"I don't owe you anything," she spit back. Then she called me something I didn't care for.

"Have you forgotten about the little ride you would have taken if not for me?" I pointed to myself obligatorily. I didn't want to be, but I was shouting. "You owe me something, and I'm willing to settle for an explanation."

"I'm getting out of here," she said throwing her backpack over her shoulder.

"You can't go out there!" I stood blocking the door. "There are men out there trying to push you into their cars!"

I tried to take her arms, but she drew back and held her hands like claws in front of her face, fitting me for cat scratches.

"Where do you think that ride was going to end?" I said remembering the holstered cannon. "The gun under that guy's arm would have freed up a lot of the time you spend breathing."

"I can't stay here – with you! You could be one of them."

"Sister, if I was one of them, I would have made you pay for the room."

She stood looking at me out of the side of her face. At least we weren't yelling. If we had neighbors, they were awake.

I held out my hand. I don't know exactly what I wanted to shake on, but I thought it a good sign when she took it. I asked if she was hungry. She said she was.

I was too and looked around the room for the fridge I knew wasn't there. "So," I said, "is there any place to eat in this city?"

Before I could enjoy my joke, I needed to hit my head on the floorboards and take a little nap. When I woke up I saw that I was going to owe the hotel a telephone. Adrienne had broken theirs over my skull and left me to bleed on the knotted rug.

# Four

The metal bell inside the broken phone chimed faintly as I plunked it down in front of the desk man.

"*Monsieur* has decided against having a telephone?" he mused.

"You'll have to add it to my bill." It was an old rotary job I hoped hadn't been appraised as an antique. The clerk didn't seem concerned and made it disappear behind the desk.

"*Baguette*," he motioned to the same basket of complimentary bread torpedoes I had refused at check-in. I wasn't up for a scavenger hunt to find which hotel lobby had complimentary prosciutto, or gratis Gruyere. I had a goose egg on the side of my ham face, and an empty belly.

The peal of a different bell, this one over the lobby door, rang and admitted three Parisian policemen to the small room.

I looked at the hotel clerk. "I said I'd pay for the phone."

The first *gendarme* stood in the center of the lobby, taking a mental inventory of the room. The black and white tiled floor reflected in the luster of his motorcycle boots. The other two wore baggy nylon rain parkas and stood shapeless and one-legged, leaning on either side of the door like ferns.

Shiny Boots goose-stepped across the checkered floor with his helmet under his arm and showed the desk man the under-side of his chin. He produced a picture the size of a Polaroid from his chest pocket and held it out for the clerk's inspection. But, when the desk man reached for it, the *gendarme* snatched the picture back like it was the family credit card. He spoke in French so forceful it could have been German. I understood *American, jeune femme,* and *metro.* When he was done, the clerk swallowed hard, and tilted his head reluctantly towards the American, fresh from *le metro*, standing next to them both.

Shiny Boots, pivoted ninety degrees with military precision, studied the picture in his thick, black-gloved hand, then examined me to determine if I were one, or several people. *"Monsieur,"* was the first word out of his mouth, and the last thing I understood. The desk man jumped in to translate. His name was Sergeant Something of the Paris police, and I was to allow these officers to escort me to the local prefecture for questioning.

"Will there be someone there who speaks the King's, or are you coming along?" I asked the clerk.

He mumbled apologetically to Sergeant Something's elbow. *Saltier* was the name embroidered in goldenrod on the left breast pocket of the man's motorcycle jacket. The *gendarme* cleared his throat, so I could better understand him, and continued in French. The clerk assured me that Sergeant Saltier's captain would be able to conduct the interview in English. As he said this, the two amoeba-like officers materialized at my sides and led me to the backseat of their Renault prowl car.

The Prefecture de Police is on the Ile de la Cite, an island in the middle of the Seine. The building itself is five-stories of ramparts with an open courtyard, that spans an entire city block. The building had been the scene of intense battles during WWII, so I kept my eyes peeled for German planes. The street outside the Prefecture was wet and my feet turned to fat mice on the tile floor of a long, wide hallway, in a very formal-looking wing. We came to a door with the number twenty-six stenciled on frosted glass. One of the amoeba produced a human fist, knocked lightly on the glass, and waited for *"Entre."*

Inspector Brun's name plate sat at the edge of a large metal desk like the caption of a photograph. Brun's office was ubiquitously paramilitary: four white walls, beige filing cabinets, and a light green tile floor. It was unclear whether Brun was moving in or out. Boxes lay open on the ground, and pictures of the

Inspector with assorted dignitaries leaned against each wall.

The inspector himself was framed by a window that looked out onto the courtyard. Brun was shy of average height, but a dignified man who made his polyester uniform look like it could stop a bullet. His once black hair was now silver with white infiltrates, and his unfinished mustache, judging from the pictures, was one that he was re-growing. Brun's age had infiltrated there as well.

When we were alone in his office, Inspector Brun produced a small tape recorder from the top drawer of his desk, connected to it a silver microphone which he laid on the blotter between us. He made eye contact, making certain my observance of his pushing *Record* with an exaggerated motion of his index finger. His arms moved with the deftness of routine. He tapped loose a cigarette from a soft pack and lit it with a heavy desk lighter. He offered me the pack, and just in case it was the last thing I would ever be offered, I took one. He pushed the lighter across his desk, leaning so far to do so, I could see the top of his head.

Once we were back smoking in our chairs, he introduced himself as if it were necessary and asked me to state my name for the record, which I did.

"How do you like *Parie?*"

"*C'est magnifique,*" I drawled through a plume of white smoke.

"*C'est magnifique, bon.*" He asked if I had had dinner. I said I hadn't. He assured me there was a very good bistro across from my hotel. "Perhaps you have found it already." He waited for a response. I had none.

Two debts all civilization owe to the French are table manners and police procedure. I knew the tape recorder belonged on Brun's left, juxtaposed with the salad fork, and I was familiar with this mode of questioning. The idea was to get me talking about anything, the subject didn't matter; sooner or later, almost involuntarily, I'd spill my guts, telling him everything he'd ever wanted to know. But I didn't know what he wanted to know, and I didn't feel like talking until I did.

"*Monsieur* Fairfax, you were seen having an argument with a young woman in *le metro* earlier today." He placed a grainy picture from a security camera in front of me, a picture of me with my hand clasped around the arm of *Mlle.* Savard. "What was the nature of this argument?"

"She wanted to raise the children Catholic, but I'm a devout Hindu," I said.

"What was the young woman's name?" he asked.

"If she told me her name, we'd still be talking." Brun wasn't laughing at my jokes. "Look," I explained, "I saw a pretty girl, I made the standard pitch, she didn't bite."

"And when she didn't bite, what did you do?" he asked.

"We went our separate ways."

"*Monsieur* Fairfax, did you murder this woman?"

I started to tell him how crazy he was, but he cut back in.

"*Monsieur* Fairfax a young woman, fitting the description of the girl you are arguing with in this picture, was found dead earlier today. The official autopsy is ongoing, but from her injuries, she appears to have been strangled. Her body was left in an alleyway outside of *le metro* station in Les Halles, not far from your hotel."

Brun produced two more photos from the file. The first was of a girl lying slack between an alley wall and a row of trashcans. Her bare legs glowed in the high contrast of the black and white snapshot, feet pointing in different directions, her body limp with the wilt of death. The second picture was of a face, washed clean, but very dead on an aluminum table.

It was going to be Adrienne lying behind those trashcans. I had crossed an ocean to threaten a beautiful blackmailer in broad daylight. The *gendarme* had canvassed the area for an American man caught on a surveillance camera. Now a police inspector was showing me pictures of a dead girl. She was young, and her body looked long and thin, made longer still by the perspective of the camera. She wore a sundress with flowers that buttoned up the front. When I had met Adrienne in the subway station, she had been wearing a skirt and sweater, not a dress, and that certainly wasn't what she had left the hotel in, though another costume change didn't seem out of the question.

The second photo, the morgue shot, didn't look like Adrienne. It didn't look like anyone. What I had seen of death had always looked unnatural. I couldn't imagine how anyone could identify even a loved one from a photo like this. The girl's face was void of warmth like wet clay. Her hair was dark where damp, lighter where it spread out over the table, long and straight. Where Adrienne had been warm and vital, this girl was gray and dead. The peace of death had failed to make her look serene. It was not the girl I'd met in the train station. I felt nothing, not even relief. Not until I saw the finger marks at the base of her neck, did I mourn this girl. Out of all this clay, someone had made a victim.

"It isn't her," I said. "This isn't the girl I talked to in the train station."

"We have reason to believe that it is," Brun said. His fingers were tented just under his nose. His elbows rested somewhere unseen. The case file sat in front of him like an empty dinner plate and he waited patiently to be served.

"The girl in *this* picture," I pointed to the security camera photo, "came back to my hotel room with me. You can ask the clerk."

Brun made a puzzled face. "I thought you had gone your separate ways," he said. "So, she must have bitten after all?"

Whatever the penalty for lying was, I was sure it was less than the one for murder. "Okay, she bit," I admitted. "I took her back to my room, she wasn't there ten minutes, changed clothes and left. Ask the clerk!" That refrain was already wearing thin. If Brun caught me in one more lie, I'd start to doubt my own story. The only thing I was sure of was that one of us had the wrong girl.

Brun let out a large breath I had not seen him take and switched off the recorder. "*Monsieur* Fairfax, I'm afraid I may have brought you here unnecessarily. Before you arrived, Sgt. Saltier relayed the hotel clerk's statement, which sounded very much like what you told me just now. Also, our medical examiner is placing this poor girl's time of death almost two hours before your little scene in the *le metro*. I hope you understand that a murder investigation is very serious, and that we must follow all leads to conclusion."

He clicked the tape recorder back on. "However, I am concerned why you chose to lie about leaving this woman in *le metro*. Also, the cut on the side of your head, I'm afraid, is bleeding again." Brun produced a folded handkerchief from his jacket pocket and held it toward me with a straight arm. "*Monsieur* Fairfax, what exactly is your business here in Paris?"

My blood soaked easily into the white linen handkerchief. I wanted to tell him I came to Paris to argue with pretty girls in train stations, I wanted to ask him why his little confession had been omitted from the tape, but seeing as I was still being questioned in connection with a murder, I decided against it.

"I'm working," I said.

"Working?" he asked.

I blew smoke through my nostrils. "Working."

Brun groaned and turned his attention to the manila envelope one of the amoeba had handed him. The envelope contained my wallet, passport, a key to the train station locker that held my duffle, and the remainder of the parcel that Grey's assistant, Shabin, had handed me at the port authority. He dumped the contents onto his desk blotter and read them like tea leaves.

"I'm an investigator," I offered.

"Like me!" Sarcasm flavored his skepticism.

"Private."

"I assume you have credentials," he said.

"If I did, would they do me any good? I'm kinda far from home."

Brun opened my wallet and frowned when he found no professional license there. "It would go a long way towards your credibility *Monsieur* Fairfax."

I was starting to hate this *Monsieur* business.

Brun opened the parcel that held my passport, my return ticket aboard a freighter leaving La Havre, and five hundred American dollars I'd yet to convert to francs, to cover any expenses. The bills, still bound by the bank band, caused Brun to study me from under the bush of a raised eyebrow. He perused article by article finding nothing to change the look on his face. He came to the last item, a little paper wallet, the kind banks give you when you open your first checking account.

"Loss prevention," Brun said.

"I'm sorry?"

"It says here that you work in the Loss Prevention division of AG Worldwide."

Thank God for Andrew Grey. "That's right, Loss Prevention," I repeated it as if trying to remember the name of someone I just met.

Brun clicked the recorder off again. "I hate thieves in my city *Monsieur* Fairfax. I wish I could crush each one under something heavy." He palmed the desk lighter. "Even ones that steal from Americans." He smiled and clicked the recorder back on. "I must warn you *Monsieur* Fairfax that any investigation of a French citizen must be done in conjunction with this office. If you have no questions for me at this time – "

"What was her name?" I asked. "The girl in the pictures."

Brun's pen stopped on whatever form he was filling out. "Of course, there are details we are not releasing to the public, such as the name of the victim, that is until her family can be notified."

I reached for the small silver mic and threw a tiny switch on its side. "You can turn it off from here, too. Doesn't make that nasty sound on the tape."

Brun made a noise in the back of his throat over the discovery of the tiny switch.

"The girl's name?" I asked again.

Brun somehow shrugged his face and waved his hand in deference, "Adrienne Savard."

Adrienne Savard, the name written at the bottom of the letter my gut had told me to conceal in the torn lining of my pea coat. The letter that, had it remained in the parcel, I would still be struggling to explain. My insides began a game of musical chairs. I was glad the cigarette was still burning in my face. I hoped the puckered, James Dean expression non-habituated smokers implore was sufficient to cover any reaction the name had produced. Luckily, the strong French cigarettes had created a veritable smog cloud between Brun and myself.

"Just a child, really. It is a senseless world sometimes, is it not?" Brun hoisted the tape recorder and microphone off the blotter like a wet cat and dropped it back into the drawer.

He put his hand into the air, not to shake, but to direct me toward the door. "The city of Paris appreciates your cooperation with this investigation. You are free to leave." Before I reached the knob, he added, "I must insist, however, that until notified by this office, you are not to leave Paris."

# Five

The shapeless parkas were waiting on the other side of the door. One shoved a three-ply ticket into my hand and aimed me back down the long corridor. I could see a door to the outside at the end of the hall and began to move my limbs mechanically toward it. The officers followed closely behind me, one telling the other a story I couldn't begin to decipher. His voice bounded one minute, mumbled the next. It was a joke or an anecdote, at the end of it they both laughed. By that time, we were outside. The officer who handed me the ticket took me by the arm and let out a whistle I'm surprised didn't stop traffic. One car did stop, a cabbie in an old Citroen. The officer gave me a jovial pat on the back and turned toward his squad car parked further down the street without so much as a glance back at me.

I looked down at the ticket, recognized the word *taxi*, guessed at the word for *voucher*, and managed to fit the lump in my throat into the idling car. My first thought was to re-route the cabbie to the coast, get on the next boat going anywhere, or swim the channel if it came to that. The very young girl I was sent to pay off was dead, and I had no idea who I had given the payoff to. I started tallying up all the things I didn't know. What did I know about the girl in the train station? I didn't exactly check her ID. What did I know about Dile, or even Grey for that matter? I needed answers. I needed a telephone. I needed a steak. My exodus could wait. My dinner couldn't.

The cab dropped me at the hotel and squealed away into the night. I saw the sign for the bistro Brun had suggested. It was so small I almost tripped over it.

I sat outside and ordered steak *au poive* and fancy potatoes squeezed out of a pastry bag. It was the best meal I had eaten in too long. I lifted my glass to a few *belle femmes* giving my third-rate skull a second look. I aimed the lump on my head away from the noise of the kitchen and toward the breeze coming off the boulevard. The night air was just cool enough to make it really throb. When I had drained my carafe of house wine, and sufficiently numbed my head, I returned to my hotel.

The same clerk was behind the desk in the lobby. I asked if he had replaced the phone in my room, he made a face and apologized that he hadn't. He pointed to a phone booth built into the lobby wall next to a kiosk with pamphlets on what to do while you're in Paris, and a cigarette vending machine at least as old as the phone I had broken. The booth was the size of an airplane restroom and I had to hang my elbow out the folding door just to dial. The line clicked for nearly three minutes before Grey's assistant, Shabin, in her school mistress voice was asking if I had any idea what time it was. I really didn't.

"I need to talk to Sam Dile, this thing's gone busto," I told her.

"You were to deliver a package. Has something happened to the package?" she asked.

I let her have it.

"Oh, I delivered the package, to a girl with flowers in her hair who knew all about it. Then someone tried to push her into a car. We hid out in a hotel, and while she's pulling a chameleon act, the girl who Miss Flowers is supposed to be, is across town getting herself strangled and dumped in an alley. Somehow, I managed not to tell the cops anything about the first part after they hauled me in for questioning about the second." I let her process that while I breathed at her. "I need to talk to Dile," I said after a minute.

"That's quite impossible. I'm to be your liaison in all matters."

"Of course, it's possible. He has a number, you call it, he answers, we talk. Look, the cops know I didn't murder anyone, but maybe they think I know something about it, and Sister, I just might."

She told me not to hang up; the line was silent for some time.

The clerk had disappeared when I first stepped into the booth. He re-emerged now with a new phone for my room. He held it up for me to see, gave a toothy grin, and a demonstrative thumbs-up. I smiled and waved, neither of which may have been visible from within the confines of the phone booth.

Dile finally came on the line in what sounded like the tail-end of a panic. I asked him if Shabin had filled him in, he said she had. I re-hashed it for him anyway. I said I had no clue as to the identity of the girl in the train station, besides her being American, and I didn't think it was a coincidence that she was a doppelganger for the Adrienne Savard who was strangled around the time of our meeting.

"But the girl from the train station is still alive?" he asked.

"She was alive enough to ring my bell with the hotel phone. But, that was hours ago. She could be at the bottom of the Seine, or the top of the Eiffel Tower." Gears were turning in Dile's head. It must be some machine because I could hear it shift, back up and go in every direction.

"You did what was asked, you delivered the money" he said resolutely.

"I don't know who I delivered the money to, and some poor girl is dead. I'm not supposed to leave Paris, and if the police call me in again – "

"You can't say anything! It would be a breach of confidentiality," he sniveled.

"Sure," I guessed. "And I'll ride it as far as I can." Sailing instructor-client confidentiality. Brun would punch holes in that like a Cuban middle-weight.

Dile was silent for a long moment. "What do you want, more money?"

This time I cut him off. "I'm not asking for more money, I'm asking for more information. I'm stuck in Paris for the duration. I can spend it taking in the sights, or I can spend it working. It's your dime. Maybe I can find out who the girl from the train station was. That might help you determine whether you're connected to a murder or not, whether we both are. But, you need to level with me. Who is blackmailing you, Sam?"

"This is what I want you to do," he spoke quickly now. "I want you to find that girl. Make sure she's alive. You work for me, and that's what I want you to do."

I told him I couldn't do it, that I didn't know where to start unless he told me who these people were, or if he didn't know, who he thought they could be.

"I'm not interested in opening myself up to any more extortion. You've been paid. You have all the information you need." With that the line went dead.

It wasn't all the information I needed, but it was all I was going to get from Dile.

I managed to extricate myself from the phone booth without taking the door off its hinges. I needed to think. Back home I'd take a walk on the docks. This time of night all there was to do was think, and sea air is brain tonic. I plugged a couple francs into the cigarette machine, hoping it wasn't ornamental, tugged on a glass knob, and prayed for something besides menthol.

The clerk was smiling and waving his hands around my new phone like a spokes-model as I crossed the lobby. Before he could thank me for something stupid, like my patience, I thanked him. I thanked him for straightening things out with the police. "I really owe you one," I read his name tag, "Jerome." I put my hand out, he shook it without getting too bashful on me. On the desk was a rocks glass filled with matchbooks, so I took one.

Jerome pointed sheepishly to my smokes. "May I?"

I tamped the pack against my palm, ripped it open, and tapped one loose.

"Something for later when the lobby's empty," he said, slipping the cigarette behind his ear.

I grabbed my new phone and took the stairs two at a time. I could retrieve my duffle from the train station later. It wouldn't be the first time I went to bed without flossing.

The new phone went back on the bedside table. I plugged it in, lifted the receiver, and listened for a dial tone. I replaced the receiver and finally lit the cigarette I had stuck in my face.

"That phone stays put this time, you hear me?" I said to the dark room.

"I'm sorry, I couldn't think where else to go." She was curled up on the couch, silhouetted by blue moonlight from the three cantilever windows that looked out onto the alley. "I went back to my place. The lock was broken. Everything was upside down. What if they had been there?"

"You wouldn't be here if they had," I said. "How do you know they didn't follow you?"

"They didn't." She retraced her steps. "I thought they might be watching, so I went to the roof," her voice was a conspiratorial whisper. "There's a landing there, once you shoo the pigeons away, you can jump to the next rooftop." She was panting as if having just made the leap. "I crossed the roof and went down the fire escape on the other side."

"You remember who these men are yet? Or am I a fool to think you'd tell me if you did?" I felt like a fool. She had gotten the better of me, and here she was asleep on the couch in my hotel room. I was mad at her. I was mad at her for thumping me in the head. I was mad at her for disappearing. I was mad at her for the fact that I wasn't mad at her.

"I don't know who they are," she insisted.

"Check the Rolodex, Doll, under B for Blackmailing."

"Shut up!" she growled, "I earned that money!"

The force of her words lifted her off the couch. I took a step across the room and stood in front of her. The light from the windows failed to illuminate anything but the floorboards. She was a void in front of me like something I couldn't remember. But, I recognized her perfume, just as it had been in the train station, sweet and sticky, like cotton candy.

"Who are you," I asked her.

"I'm Adrienne," she said feebly.

"Try again, Sister. Adrienne Savard was strangled earlier today and thrown in an alley. Saw the pictures myself at the police station."

"She's dead?" she sank back onto the couch.

"Yeah, she's dead, so you're going to have to find a new alias."

"Okay, I'm not Adrienne, but I knew her."

"I'm sure you did. This afternoon in the train station you looked just like her. The police thought so, too." Mention of the cops got her attention. "Our little exchange was captured on a security camera, and they traced me to this hotel."

"You have to help me!" She was breathing hard.

"Help you! How can I help you when I don't even know who you are? How do I know you're not a murderer?"

I struck a match and held it in front of her. Tears streamed down her face. Her hair caught in the tracks on her cheek. She was terrified, or she was acting. And if she was acting, she was fantastic. I was willing to believe either.

"She was my friend," she sobbed.

I turned her face up toward mine. "Your name, what is it?"

"They know where I live," she pleaded.

"Sweetheart, if the cops could find me here, what makes you think your boys couldn't do the same? Did you come up another fire escape, or did you walk right through the front door?"

The match blew out as she shot past me. I heard the door slam behind her before I could find the wall the door was in. I made the stairs in time to see her disappear from the lobby. Once outside I looked right then left. I didn't see her. No time. I had to guess. I went left. This wasn't the first woman I'd chased through the streets. They always went left. I didn't know if a man would always run right, I'd never chased one.

After a block of swimming through Parisians, I saw her. She wasn't looking back, but she was pulling away from me. She was running, and she was fast. She ducked down a side street, and by the time I made the alley, she was gone.

I started back toward the hotel. My heart was pumping, hard. Twenty minutes ago, I was exhausted, now I knew I wouldn't sleep. I felt for the pack of smokes that had been in my shirt pocket. They were gone, must have fallen out while I was running. I looked for them as I walked and found them in a puddle. I vowed not to buy another pack. I hadn't smoked in years. I blamed Inspector Brun. When I got back to the hotel I decided to take a cab to get my duffle. Jerome arranged one for me.

The cabbie took me north to Gare du Nord where the train from the Channel had dropped me, and where my duffle sat under lock and key. It looked like I would be in Paris for a couple days at least. On the way back, I told Jean, my cabbie to take me to the Prefecture de Police. After we crossed the bridge onto the Ile de la Cite, Jean asked if I wanted to swing by Notre Dame; he said they were lighting the west window and this time of night there would be "no jerks."

He was right about both. Jean leaned against the cab fender and lit a cigarette. He offered me one. What was with this city? I took it. He was an older man, white haired with a low paunch belly. He tucked the pack in his shirt pocket and kissed a rosary he wore around his neck. His eyes were large and watery. "The Virgin," he pointed up at the West Rose window.

I let the cigarette burn too long in my hand, and what was left of it fell onto my shoes. When I looked down, I realized I was standing at Point Zero. It was a trivia question for any navigator, pretty far inland for me, but I knew it. Point Zero is an octagonal brass marker laid in the stone walk outside of Notre Dame. A spiny sun figure had been cut from the brass, and the center re-filled by a circular piece, leaving the rays of the sun as dark crevices. Passers-by filled the crevices with one, two, and five cent copper coins, for good luck. The distance from this spot to other significant spots in Paris had been measured, recorded somewhere, for what purpose I couldn't fathom. Maybe you just collected information even if you weren't sure what you were going to do with it. Maybe relating all these places to this single point made them somehow relevant to each other; it tied them together however superficially.

Across the square I could see the Prefecture de Police. I would save my confession for another night. It bothered me that I didn't know the lay, didn't know how the pieces fit. I couldn't talk to Adrienne, no one ever would again. Dile seemed to know Adrienne, but not who the girl from the train station could be. She knew him enough to know where and when to collect the blackmail, and Adrienne enough to pretend to be her. Adrienne was my Point Zero, everything connected back to her: my client, a murder, and a mystery woman.

# Six

I wouldn't call the hallucinations that visited me that night dreams, because I wouldn't call what I got that night sleep. All of the sudden, I was in the Paris morgue with Brun. He rolled a stiff out of one of the lockers and pulled back the sheet. It was Adrienne. She wasn't sleeping either; she hopped off the table and looped her arm through mine. Brun pulled the sheet back again, and it was the girl from the train station, the girl I knew as Adrienne. She took my other arm. I was a kid with too many dates to the worst prom ever. Brun kept pulling back the sheet and dead girls of all shapes and sizes got off the table. All the girls wanted their arms around me, and their arms were cold as deli ham. I sat up in my hotel bed fighting to keep my heart in my mouth.

I showered with the curtain open. It got water all over the floor, but I was only pulling that curtain back once. At breakfast I made short work of eggs with tarragon and fresh-squeezed juice. The hair on the glass must have belonged to a gorilla in the back with a grudge against a bag of oranges.

I kept looking at the letter. It was the only thing I had to go on. I read it over and over looking for anything that might tell me where I could find the girl from the train station. I turned it over in my hands, it smelled faintly of perfume. A delivery truck sped by and the tail wind almost blew the envelope into the street. I pinned it under my empty glass. Through the thick bottom of the tumbler I saw the postage stamp like I was seeing it for the first time. The postmark! There were plenty of numbers on it; maybe one of them meant something. Maybe they could tell me where it was mailed from.

I had seen a letter carrier walking on the other side of the street. I tucked a handful of bills under my plate and ran out into the road in front of a car that didn't come up to my waist. I took off down the street or tried to. During the day the sidewalks were filled with people, and they were a lot less forgiving than those of the night. There's something romantic about a man running through the streets of Paris at night, in and out of the glow of streetlamps. Chasing down a letter carrier in knee socks to ask about a postage stamp received little deference from the commuters and baguette mongers.

After three blocks I saw him duck into a little tobacco shop. Inside, the letter carrier was sniffing tiny brown cigars with the proprietor like they were cinnamon buns. He was a little man, bald and sunburned, with eyes like lighter flints, and a heinous laugh. The proprietor of the smoke shop was three times his size and looked as if his lower extremities were wedged between the counter and the shelves behind. I held out the envelope and asked the little man if he could tell me where the letter had been mailed from. He said he could, turned away from me, and dragged one of the stubby smokes under his red nose.

"Two of those," I said to the meatloaf behind the counter.

The postman couldn't get the envelope out of my hands fast enough. He looked down the point of his nose and declared, "*Montmartre, voila.*"

I dropped a few francs on the counter, and the little man slid the smokes into his breast pocket. He asked if I needed a lift. I told him I wouldn't fit in his mail bag, went outside and hailed a cab.

I told the cabbie Montmartre, and he jerked the car north. He was about my age, with an unshaven face and a deep cleft chin. He drove too fast and the song he was humming was different than the one on the radio. I asked him where the young people lived in Montmartre. I knew he had misunderstood when he stopped the car in front of a couple of strip clubs near the Moulin Rouge.

The Rouge wasn't open yet, but the music spilling out of a cabaret across the street was tugging at the buttons of my pea coat. My only clue had led me to Montmartre, and my cab driver had led me here, so I decided it was as good a place as any to start. I didn't believe in fate as much as good luck. It was a good thing I was trying to do, I thought, and deserving of a little luck, so I went in.

There was no one guarding the door or taking tickets; I wandered through a small parquet lobby, pushed through shabby double doors that couldn't stop an insult, into a sizable ballroom. There was a long bar on either side of a sunken main floor filled with small tables. In front of a full orchestra were a pair of leggy tomatoes dressed like feather-dusters. Behind the plumage and sequins, the girls wore tank tops and cut-off sweat pants. The strings and brass weren't decked out either; this was obviously not a dress rehearsal.

Even at this early hour, there were a dozen or more butts in seats, and almost twice as many eyes on the stage. The audience was made up of gray old men, alone at their tables, with coffee steaming from their cups, and a twinkle in their eyes. By the posters in the lobby, this would be a nude review. I guess there was enough hooch in the toddies to make up for what wasn't on stage.

I bellied up to one of the bars and ordered a *café au lait* from a young woman in a tuxedo t-shirt and tactical pants. Her dark eyelids and boyish slicked-back hair, made her look like a trout. She was older than the murdered girl, but still young. I was about to ask her where she lived, but the coffee she was pouring looked hot and I didn't want it in my face. I showed her my ID from Grey Worldwide like it would mean something to her.

"I'm looking for someone," I said. "A girl; could be you."

"Well, you found me. But, I'm not looking for you." Her accent was thicker than the threadbare towel she was using to dry a highball, but her English was good.

"People your age that work around here, maybe go to school here," I sipped my coffee, "where do they tend to live?" She looked at me like I invited myself into her apartment and put my feet up on her cat. I gave her my least lascivious look and asked for a compass direction.

She said she lived on the north side.

I smiled and took out my wallet. "Any popular hang-outs?" I could see it didn't translate. "Where would you go to have a drink?"

"Try *Le Renard*," she said.

She offered it so quickly there wasn't time enough to insert guile; I took her at her word. I thanked her and over-tipped.

*Le Renard Rapide* was on the trifold map I had pinched from the lobby kiosk. It was a bit of a tourist haunt, but not entirely surrendered by the locals. It was a few blocks northeast; no need for a cab, or my cabbie, whose misinterpretation of my next request might land me in a brothel, or a cabbage patch.

The *Renard Rapide* was a kitsch, two-story adobe-pink *maison* with bright green shutters. The second half of the place is a one-story afterthought that wrapped around the street corner. The sign read *Cabaret*, but I imagined the only skirt-hiking or high-kicking came from middle-aged tourists who'd reached the bottom of their Boujealois.

I was afraid I'd rattle a floorboard loose with another cup of coffee, so I checked my watch and ordered a sherry. The old man behind the counter lit up, as if I had asked to see his baseball cards and produced two delicate rose-colored glasses he filled with imprecise drams. He drank the first one with me like we were war buddies then poured me another. The old man liked his sherry, and had doubled my tab without thinking twice, or me objecting. I raised the second glass to him and retreated before he sold me the bottle. I took a seat at a straight-backed pew behind a heavy wooden table with the same smooth, oiled age that had settled on the dark walls. As soon as my pew creaked, the old man scurried out from behind the counter and pounced on an upright piano on the opposite wall. He leaned against the edge of the bench more than sitting on it, to allow his short straight legs to work the pedals.

On cue, a woman that could have been his wife emerged from swinging doors to add vibrato-filled supplications to the plink and jangle of the piano. The stained-glass front door began hurling Parisians in from the street. The woman's wide arms were playing to an audience ten times that of the *Renard*, and the old man's torso swayed, caught in the eddy of the *chanson*. It was at once un-translated, yet completely understood. French blues music, older than any remembered sadness.

I had a tepid glass of sherry and an equally cool lead. I decided plugging the bar matron would be easier than poling the clientele; the waitress had to talk to you. A nod of the head was enough to flag down a bright-eyed blonde who would have looked more at home at a stein-hoist.

"You speak English?"

"Well I should hope so," she answered in an unaffected British accent. "Would you like a larger glass, love?" She said tickled.

"Yeah, this one's empty."

"Can I get you a pint?"

"It's a little early."

"Cup of coffee?"

"No more coffee."

"Saucer of milk then!" she laughed, gave me a good-natured shove.

I told her I was looking for two young women who might frequent the bar, promised her I was on the up and up, and flashed my credentials. I was already fond of flashing my credentials.

"What have they done, these girls you're looking for?"

I told her one of them hadn't done anything, except get murdered; the other had stolen a great deal of money from my client. She seemed willing to help, so I asked her, "Do you know Adrienne Savard?"

"Sure, but Adrienne wouldn't steal – "

Horror contorted her face. Trembling, she put her tray down to keep from dropping it. She looked as if she wanted to turn and run, but I grabbed her wrist. She looked at my face, curiosity replaced the horror and she sat down. She told me what she knew of Adrienne, describing the quiet girl she took for a university student.

"You ever see her in here with anyone?" I asked.

"I dunno, maybe other students," she looked from wall to wall, looking back in time, trying to remember. I tried describing the girl from the train station, the girl I knew as Adrienne, but it was no use. I'd exhausted her. Her memory had already become a memorial, a slow procession of every time she had seen the now dead girl.

Her name was Imogene. I asked her not to tell anyone what I had told her, that Adrienne's parents had only just been told, and that the police wanted it quiet. She said she understood. I asked if she knew where Adrienne lived, she didn't.

"Her father runs a casino. He owns it, or her family does anyway. It's not one of the big ones," she added as if only poor people owned small casinos. She mumbled that she'd get the drink I hadn't ordered and disappeared behind the swinging doors, leaving me with an empty rose-colored glass, a sad French song, and a date with a casino.

# Seven

*Le Rouleau Chanceux.* Imogene was able to give me the name of the casino before she clammed up altogether. I managed to flag down the same cabbie who had dropped me off at the *Rouge*, maybe he was following me. He was very much on board with a trip to the *Chanceux*; between that and dropping me off at the *Rouge*, I was proving to be his kind of derelict. His hack license just read Remy, like Cher or Rasputin. I could see a French military tattoo on his forearm, and his English was plenty good for conversation, mostly about roulette.

Far from the *Palais de Festival* and the *Cote D'Azur*, the *Chanceux* was sandwiched between a travel agency and a neglected hotel turned flophouse. Above a garnet red awning were tall, iron-clad windows crowned by a hand of four-foot high playing cards, painted on the brick and splayed like false eyelashes.

What the outside of the *Chanceux* lacked in opulence, I was sure the inside would make up for with chinziness. Inside was a parlor of six empty poker tables and light cane chairs. There wasn't so much as a hat-check girl between the cornflower blue felt of the tables and the busy sidewalk outside. The barred windows threw bright, castigating shafts of light in steep diagonals that failed to reach the tables but illuminated the empty room. However spartanly adorned, it was clean; the felt on the tables was newly stretched, and the wainscoting on the oiled wood walls was freshly painted. I looked all over for the lever that made the floor turn over, and the real casino appear.

Remy explained this room was where the pit boss banished the serial losers, the turnips that the *Chanceux* knew had no more blood to let. We pushed through a second set of double doors into the real casino, a grand room, three or four times the size of the first. It was a long room with tables on either side of a tiled center aisle. The design on the floor mirrored an impressive deco skylight that ran the length of the casino. The flood of celestial light made it seem as if God might be watching and wouldn't let you lose too big. It wasn't Cesar's, but it was grand enough to make you feel you'd been bested by a superior foe and were forgiven for going home empty-handed.

It was still early, and there was no action aside from a skinny teenager pushing a twenty-year-old vacuum, and the autonomous rancor of unseen slots. At the end of the long room was a horseshoe shaped bar and a yeti putting a stool through hell. He spotted us and motioned with two fingers for us to approach. Wherever you went, there was this guy: the big guy. Not fat, not muscular, just big. He's at the front door of every club, and the back of every box truck. He never has hair, or a smile, or much to say. This one sported a plum polyester suit with a soft sheen, and a black turtleneck. His face was wan, in contrast to the back of his head, which had looked angry as hell.

I told him that I was hoping to speak to Mr. Savard. The palooka looked annoyed at my English and turned to Remy. They whispered dinner menus to each other, unsweet nothings in French I couldn't understand, but softly in case I could. "*Sa fille*," the lug croaked. *Daughter*, I understood. He reached behind the bar for a phone. The mouthpiece of the receiver disappeared in the deep folds of his hand, he felt for it with his lips, then moved the receiver to his ear to listen. He hung up and spoke again to Remy. My companion threw up his hands, turned and walked the long, tiled hall back to the turnip bin. I hadn't moved but was still met with "You. Stay." His English for the day.

The big guy was pawning me off. He pointed a fat finger into the adjacent room of slot machines and turned his attention back to a bowl of nuts. I could see another man strutting briskly toward us. He was buttoning the front of a tailored suit that fit him like a four-fingered glove. His name was Rico Mindy, though I learned that later. He came to a halt in front of me already looking unhappy. He was short and trim, a small man, and that seemed reason enough to be unhappy. His bald head looked as if he shaved it, and his stubbled mug as if he couldn't. His chin was square as a sanding block, and he stuck it up at me, every limb taut in his robin's egg blue suit.

"Who are you?"

"I was hoping to speak to Mr. Savard," I began. "I don't know if you know this, but his daughter died yesterday, and I have some information that might help."

"Help what, bring her back to life?" He didn't laugh, he didn't so much as smirk.

"Help catch whoever did it."

"How do you know anybody *did it*?"

"She was strangled." I wanted to say, "you don't do that yourself," but I didn't. Watching the masseters bulge in his jaw, I didn't want a dumb crack to be the bone the little bulldog would latch on to.

"How do you know she was strangled?"

"The police," I said.

"I'm sure whatever you told the police, they will relay to Mr. Savard, if it would *help*?"

"Well," I hesitated. "I may not have told them everything."

"Ah," his lips slid uncomfortably over an asymmetric smile that looked seldom-used. "You're American?"

I looked from Rico to the big guy and nodded. Rico seemed to relax a little. He unbuttoned his coat and put his hands on his hips. His belt was snake or lizard, something you'd step on; it was the color of bone with a gaudy gold clasp, not very fashionable, not very French.

"So, Mr. American, you want to sell this information to Mr. Savard?"

"No, that's not what this is." Rico had just turned our car down the wrong street. "I'm an investigator?" It was a reach. I regretted it as soon as I said it.

"An Investigator? Like on TV? Like Kojack?" This time he did laugh at his joke, and turned to the Grape Ape, who was watching from his stool.

"You think I'm joking?" I asked.

Rico stopped laughing. "I will tell you want I think, Mr. American Kojack. I think you are very far from home. I think it was a mistake for you to come here. What I can't think of," he poked his finger into my chest, it found its way between my ribs, "is why you did not tell the police this information you have that is so *help*ful." He left his finger where it was, and I began to like it less.

"Can I talk to Savard now?" I was calm, but I let my annoyance ask the question.

"No one talks to Savard without talking to me first," he said, and twisted his finger clockwise.

"That's great," I said, and composedly removed his hand from my ribcage. "But, I don't feel like we're talking."

We stared at each other. The bells and sirens of the slot machines grew louder in the void.

"Alright," he said and rubbed his square chin. "Let's go somewhere we can talk." Without a word or a glance to the big guy, Rico started back the way he came through the cacophony of the gaming machines. I followed him through the arcade, checking more than once to see if the yeti was coming with us. He was still on his stool when we hung a left through an empty kitchen, and out a steel door into the alley. There was shade and a cool breeze between the buildings which threatened to spoil the wet ground and garbage smell ubiquitous to all alleys. It was quieter without the clangor of electric gaming all around us.

I wondered what, or even if, Rico had known about Adrienne's death. Did Savard know? Inspector Brun had not informed the family at the time of our interview, surely, they would know by now. What did I really have to offer? That an American girl, posing as his murdered daughter, collected a blackmail payoff that she may or may not have helped extort from an American businessman, across an ocean.

Rico Mindy punched me hard in the pancreas. His fist felt like a crow bar smashing my ribs. It doubled me up, but I kept my feet. Rico stood sideways, taking great care with the placement of his feet. He held his hands in front of his face, his body disappearing behind his forearms. I was in trouble. His gold watch caught the sun just before his fist smashed into my face. I could feel the corner of his knuckle in the socket and was sure my eye had exploded. My face was instantly wet with what I knew was my own blood.

I'm no stranger to getting punched in the face, but we hadn't spoken in a while. A handful of barroom skirmishes are no introduction to the sweet science. Drunks throwing haymakers have none of the brutal efficacy of a learned pugilist. I was twice this man's size, but he was going to cut me to ribbons. Rico vanished for seconds at a time from my field of vision. When I did locate him, he dug two right hooks into my side, and I felt a rib snap. I finally got my arms up in front of me with all the deftness of holding an accordion for the first time. Rico had no trouble slipping punches through my guard and stamped all my vital organs by order of importance.

Had he hit me a little slower, I might have had time to collapse. I floated target-less punches his way. He alternated freely between slipping the punches and absorbing them into his guard with perfect technique. My blows fell as harmlessly as pats on the back, atta-boys for his fine work turning me into a Picasso. It was a textbook left counter to my jaw that sent me spinning. I felt the power to my legs dim but come back online in time to keep me upright. As I stumbled, my right hand grasped the padded shoulder of Rico's blazer. I dragged him toward me as I tried to regain my balance. I could hear the slick leather soles of his shoes skid on the grimy asphalt. My left hand found the corner of a dumpster and I righted myself in time to absorb an upper-cut that nearly finished me.

Things were going black. I saw Sister Bernice, maybe my first conscious memory, I saw Shabin in her Euro-Disney convertible. I saw the sun rise over the bow of a freighter in the Atlantic, and the moon in a cloudless sky over Boston Harbor. I saw Adrienne Savard dead on a table, and the silhouette of a mystery woman growing darker in an unlit hotel room.

I felt the fabric of Rico's jacket under both hands now. He had taken a deserved respite from destroying me to issue a half dozen threats I was sure to not remember. With my last shred of self-preservation, I heaved my carcass into the air, pulling Rico and his jacket toward me. I leapt into his arms like a child jumping from a tree, or into a swimming pool. My hands clasped behind his neck, my legs wrapped around his waist. He should have driven me into the ground, but years of conditioning had erased those instincts. The boxer's imperative was to maintain verticality. He widened his base, swung his hands under me, trying to support my weight, but it was too much. I yanked down hard on the back of his neck, heard a crack, and felt his body tense. Rico made a sound like a gelded horse, and we crashed to the ground.

The damp grime of the alley floor seeped through the back of my clothes. Rico's body lay rigid on top of mine. I kept his head pinned to my chest as he cursed at me.

"My back, you fat fuck. I'm gonna kill you." He lapsed into French as my cobwebs began to clear.

Looking down at the top of his bald head, I considered trying to reopen his childhood soft spots, but I didn't have the energy. It was Remy who appeared in the alley, and finally dragged me out from under the frozen thug. The palooka in the plum suit emerged from the casino door. He was too late to the strange scene and had reservations about entering it at all. Once I was clear, he tucked Rico under his arm like an ottoman and carried him back inside without a word. Remy got me to my feet, and into his cab. He let me know I looked like shit.

# Eight

Remy sat in a chair in the light of a tall window, his feet propped up on the foot of my hospital bed, shoes leaving dirty U's on the blanket as he ate a bag of potato chips flavored like roast chicken. The crinkling of cellophane and the phantom waft of poultry roused me from my twilight state. Light Sedation they called it. I thought conventional wisdom was to keep you awake if a concussion was suspected. Why was some poor orderly not charged with waltzing me up and down the hallway with an espresso drip?

I'm sure Montmartre had had a hospital, I'm sure it had been closer to the casino, and I'm sure I didn't care. I could have kissed that cabbie for getting me the hell out of Montmartre. Remy had brought me to a hospital on the Ile de la Cite, because his wife worked here. The Hotel Dieu is an enormous neo-classical fortress that straddles the Seine with columns and arches, arcades and pediments. Now a hospital, incredibly, it had once been an orphanage!

It was a far cry from the St. Agnes Home for Children in Charlestown, MA, which from the looks of it, had always been an orphanage. I didn't remember arriving at St. Agnes, that is to say, I didn't remember being born. I spent my entire childhood there, left at seventeen to join the merchant marine, saw a bit of the world, opened a modest business, met a rich guy, was knocked cold by a beautiful blackmailer, tangled with a bantam-weight wiseguy, and was right back in an orphanage, like I had never left.

My chart was in French. Remy read it to me. No broken bones. No suspected brain injury; hooray for that, but the night was young. Some bruises over my ribs I didn't need chart to tell me about. And butterfly bandage squeezing my left eyebrow together. The stitches itched like hell. I ran my tongue over two chipped teeth the chart had failed to mention; I guessed a dentist would need to be called in to make that diagnosis.

My eye, the one I thought had exploded, was solid red from the iris to the outside corner. They gave me some drops for it, which is exactly like instructing me to pour a thimble of water on my face three times a day. There was also a cream for the stitches, but no salve for the bruise to my ego.

When I was nine, a kid named Francisco, new to the home, pinned my shoulders under his knees, on the same tarry blacktop where we played red rover, and punched me in the face until I lost consciousness. We sat next to each other in Head Mother's office, perpetrator and perpetrated upon, reprimanded equally. She was mid-way through her lecture when she stopped due to the grotesque swelling of my face. Frank had broken my maxilla from beneath my left eye to my teeth.

I knew I hadn't done anything to warrant a beating that day. No one had to tell any of us at St. Agnes that life wasn't fair. Most of us couldn't even appreciate what we didn't have, we just knew we had already taken one lump that other kids hadn't. There was an unspoken pact that only new arrivals ever broke. No one needed any more stripes than life was going to dole out on its own.

All I could think about now, was finding the girl from the train station. Not because Dile wanted me to. Dile, who had begged me for help in Boston, and practically dismissed me in Paris. As far as he was concerned, his blackmailer was dead, and he hoped his secret with her. And not for Grey, a virtual stranger, who thought so little of my business, believed I would jump at the chance to earn some money on a wild goose chase.

What was Grey's interest in me anyway? The guy sailed in regattas, I worked on freighters. Did employing me help reassure him he hadn't lost touch with the common man? I could picture Grey smoking in an overstuffed chesterfield regaling the other idle rich with how he'd engaged a commoner for a ridiculous errand.

The truth was, I wasn't ready to go home. I know what a home is, and I know other people have them, like curling irons, or wooden legs. But, I don't. Rico could have stuck me and left me in that alley to die, like Adrienne. There was no one to place frantic phone calls when I didn't come home for dinner. Grey would go on running my business, until it was clear I wasn't coming back. And the neighborhood kids would put rocks through the shop windows before someone had the guts to brake in; like poking a drunk with a stick before you take his wallet.

I'd been a little lonely since leaving the merchant service. It wasn't running a one-man operation or eating alone in restaurants that bothered me. I appreciated the inane chit-chat that came with renting boats, until someone went on too long. Then it was, *okay buddy, let's not ruin what we have, just take the boat.* I thought that was enough for me. I told myself I was keeping my nut small. I didn't realize I was flirting with full-blown hermitage.

Something was different now. This thing had become more of an itch I couldn't scratch. Not exactly a *raison d'etre,* to borrow a phrase, but I knew I wanted to see it through. And it had been a long time since I'd wanted anything more than to be in one place, desired more from a woman than the uncomplicated smile of an obliging waitress or endeavored to angry my blood up beyond the level of ranting over traffic snarls.

It had been ages since I'd mixed it up with a bum like Rico. I'd hadn't gotten my ass kicked in over a decade and it hurt more now. But, it made me realize I had a life to lose. It's like I'd been underwater, and I hadn't realized how far until Rico had me fighting for air.

I stuffed my legs into my jeans and felt the letter wrinkle in the front pocket. This girl. All she had done to encourage me was laugh at me, run from me, and try to crack my skull with a telephone. She was in trouble. I didn't know if I had saved her from abduction, or from apprehension. She was my only link to a dead blackmailer. And she had taken the money! She was the trouble.

I tugged on and buttoned up the rest of my clothes that had been hung in a press-board cabinet. Everything was press-board and plastic, cheap and safe. The room was like any other hospital room, three white walls with a mint green accent wall behind the bed, the one wall the patient couldn't see. I guess the cool mint was meant to soothe the visitors. The floor was a discordant crayon-blue non-slip commercial surface that probably dated back to a previous color-scheme. As I paced the room, my shoes were silent as the grave, which in a hospital is especially unsettling. I stepped into the hall, a narrow corridor with cathedral ceilings, folded and contoured like paper lanterns. My room did not belong to this hallway; it too was silent, like a church or a library. I whispered *Bonjour* to an orderly guiding a somnambulist down the hall just to make sure I wasn't going deaf.

Across the hall was a window with a view of the garden. Down a long, wide flight of steps, surrounded by Roman architecture was an elaborate knee-high hedge maze. More like inverse crop circles; shrubs cut into triangles, spirals, and wavy lines quartered by perpendicular walkways. Each quarter looked haphazard, random. But the tessellation, the repetition of the mistake, over and over, gave the knowledge of intention, the plotting of the seemingly unconnected.

Remy returned me to my hotel. We shook hands for a long time, but I hoped never to see him again. He had pulled me out of that alley, but he was complicit too, in my mind, like blaming a maître de for food-poisoning. He laughed and said he was glad Rico hadn't killed me. Rico Mindy had been a boxing champion as a teenager, had come from Spain to Paris to train as a Junior Olympian, and competed in the French Boxing Federation, akin to Gold Gloves in the States. Always a tough guy, he'd fallen in with other tough guys, was incarcerated and had his back broken in a prison gang fight. Rico Mindy belonged to a world of criminality and violence that you read about in the newspaper and recoil. He wasn't a loser in a bar, with a hot temper, looking to fight after a couple of beers. He was an animal, without fear of the law, without fear of God. And Remy had left me with him, without a word.

# Nine

It wasn't Jerome behind the front desk at the hotel, but an older man, with a circle of fluffy clouds around his bald head, rubbing a pipe against a wool cardigan. He observed me over the pipe, as if he'd never seen me before either. I flashed him my key before I jogged the first couple stairs. I stopped halfway, loafed back down the steps, and with a labored *Merci*, took the complimentary baguette.

I let the shower spill over my head until the water running down the drain was clear. It took a while. The water only came in screaming hot or damn cold, and both made ghosts bang on the walls. The astringent soap was beginning to dissolve the oil and grime from the back of my neck and arms. French soap is the best. Even in a mom and pop joint like this, it's special. Lathers like crazy, lasts forever; just so long as it didn't make me smell like powder, roses, or whatever freesia is.

The cold shower woke me up and washed away a lot of self-pity. I was coming back to life, and I was hungry. The baguette had done nothing. There was a place I had wanted to go since I got off the train, a place I had heard other sailors talk about and just so happened was in the neighborhood. I wasn't about to get back into a cab, so I decided to walk. It was farther then I thought, and the walk did nothing for my head.

*Le Bistrot d'Estuche* was supposed to be a great spot for jazz and a steak, and I wanted both. The night had turned cool, and the restaurant hung clear plastic sheets around the outside tables, like an oxygen tent. Inside, the air was heady with wine and truffle oil. A long marble bar, curved like a treble clef through the heart of the joint, and the band was setting up right in front of it. I would be getting my drinks from a waitress, thanks. The hostess showed me to the kind of table they give you when you're alone, a single seat by the kitchen, with an obstructed view of the band. If there were someone joining me, they'd be ducking plates of *au poive* all night and go home wearing an *escargot* or *duex*.

My waitress was young and plain; bobbed straight hair, pale complexion, the kind of girl who is always cold. She was dressed in a sweater, a wool skirt, and tights. Her English sounded like it might be phonetic, so I holstered my charm and ordered the special; *Couer de Romsteck*, rump steak, a cut you didn't get in the States. She asked if I preferred *maître de butter* or bone marrow, I said *both*, and she smiled uncomfortably as if I had ordered a bowl of eels.

The place was filling up and I could hear the first tentative chords coming from the band. An upright bass and an electric piano were manned by two gents with the typical road-hardened gypsy-look of professional musicians. There was a singer somewhere behind a pillar, but the first number was a bouncy instrumental well suited to the swelling buzz in the room.

I thought the *romsteck* called for port, which the hostess brought along with an appetizer, a ravioli the size of a dime novel in cream sauce. The hostess was a warm, middle-aged woman, not dressed for work, directing traffic, welcoming diners, and delivering the occasional *amuser bouche*. My waitress was probably somewhere getting a blood transfusion. The ravioli was the cure for whatever was happening in my stomach, and the port went right to work numbing the rest of my senses.

I cased the restaurant for the usual suspects. Mostly couples, or a couple of couples on dates, a table of tourists too happy to be anywhere, snapping pictures crowded with their distorted smiling faces, and one teenager trying hard to pretend he wasn't there with his parents. There was one other table for one, in the corner opposite my own, where a fella in a light green sweater sat alone. He looked pensive, like he was waiting for his ex to arrive with divorce papers. The tilt of his head made the glare on his glasses look like silver coins over his eyes. I raised my drink to him, but he wasn't looking my way.

I had drained a couple glasses before my dinner arrived. The cross-hatched slab of beef was shiny with melted butter and threatened to push the potatoes and cut beans onto the floor. Someone had forgotten to take the marrow out of the bone before putting it on my plate. Lying threateningly across the steak was half a bovine tibia, sliced lengthwise with a band-saw, still full of golden jelly. It seemed like a subtle hint not to run out on the check.

As if waiting until everyone had their steak in front of them, the chanteuse who had been hiding behind a column, now drifted a couple feet out into the harsh blue-white of track lights as far as the microphone cord would allow. I was expecting *Fever* or *Summertime* and was sure an Edith Piaf impression was in the offing, but I was wrong. She sang a Blossom Dearie number, so simply and sweetly, that no one ate a bite until she was done.

The singer moved about, offering the rest of the patrons a better look at her. She was wearing a red velvet number with long sleeves and a short hem, over black tights. Her hair was bobbed and bottle-blonde. She was younger and incongruous to the scrubby pros backing her, as if she'd turned down a baby-sitting gig to answer an ad for a singer in the Village Voice. There was no playing to the crowd. She swayed in the lights as if she were alone in front of her bedroom mirror.

She was an attractive young woman, and I wondered if that made her sound better. I thought I possessed integrity enough to admit if she sounded like a screeching owl no matter what she looked like. It was possible, after all to be attractive and talented. But, I sat alone at my table, as I had at most tables, and tried to convince myself I was more impressed with her voice. I am not a connoisseur of music. I have some records, and like every person with ears, I think I know from good. It wasn't the scorching hot jazz I had hoped to find, but she was something. Any connoisseur would have agreed.

*Pretending that we'll meet*
*Each time I turn the corner,*
*I walk a little faster...*

That's when I saw her. She slid through the front door like it was a loose slat in a junk yard fence and sat immediately at the table for one with the man in the light green sweater. She hadn't scanned the restaurant for him, she knew where he was sitting. She had watched him come in from somewhere hidden, making sure to arrive second. Just like the metro. How long had she been watching? Had she seen me?

She sat with her back to me, across the small but crowded restaurant; if she hadn't already seen me, she wouldn't until she got up to leave. I watched them talk. She was leaning over the table but kept the edge of it in her hands. He had sat erect and tense, running his leg under the table until she arrived. Now he sat back, slack in his chair, listening. They were as far apart as two people could be at the small table.

Green Sweater suddenly leaned in and wagged a finger at her as he talked. The bulbous red candle lit his face like a camp fire and replaced the coins over his eyes with flickering flames. He pulled his hand back quickly and looked to see if anyone was watching them. No one was. Except me. I looked down at my steak and speared the last sanguine bite.

They stopped talking. Green Sweater had ordered *frites* but hadn't eaten any. She plucked a long fry from the basket and snapped her teeth shut like a trap, biting it playfully, or mockingly, in half. He moved the basket away with the back of his hand. I scraped the remaining marrow from the cut bone with my knife. We both hated her. Without taking his eyes off her, Green Sweater slid a long white envelope, across the table.

She snatched the envelope, slid it into a drawstring bag worn taut across her chest, and turned to leave in a single motion. She was out the door before he could produce his wallet. He left a couple bills on the table, and I hurried out behind her. I had had too much to drink, couldn't figure the bill and jammed more than I owed in crumpled francs under my up-ended plate, sending chalcedonic jewels of oil and blood spilling across the table for a tip.

By the time I made the street, she was gone, and Green Sweater was halfway down the next block. He was wading through the loose rabble of dinner-goers on the sidewalk. He still had her in sight! I rushed to keep up, running where the crowd was thin enough, passing restaurants in seconds, their changing music like a warped record, out of step with the staggering clop of my heavy boots.

He must have been twenty yards ahead of me when he hung a left. I had to run to make sure I didn't lose him. I kept him in sight as I caught my breath, clinging to the dirty steel of a three-story scaffold and leaning on a pile of new brick. Pedestrians were taking to the street, circumventing the scaffolding like a crumbling mine shaft, or wishing not to pass the gasping drunk inhabiting it like a bridge troll.

Green Sweater turned down another street, and it was time to run again. When I reached the intersection he'd turned down, he was gone. I staggered in the direction I'd lost him, looking for my lungs in the gutter. I'd only managed half a block when he was walking back in my direction. She must have lost him, I knew the look. Green Sweater didn't know me, hadn't seen me in the restaurant, and couldn't have suspected I was following him. But, the alcohol in my bloodstream sold me on the necessity of crossing the street to avoid suspicion, and pushed me into traffic, narrowly missing the business end of a pug-nosed delivery truck.

The flash of lights and blaring horn spun me around and across the hood of a parked coupe. I lowered myself onto the shiny chrome bumper and watched Green Sweater pass me on the sidewalk. I took a minute to determine whether I was alive or dead, which direction was up, and the proper foot to lead with to continue my pursuit.

I followed Green Sweater a half-dozen blocks to a metro station. He was walking slower now, but it was still an effort to keep up. The wine and marrow had made my blood thick, and running had turned my heart into a drum beating against my guts. The caustic lighting and white elliptical walls of the subway tunnel made me nauseous. I steadied myself on a trashcan whose ashtray contents threatened to make me retch. I boarded the car next to his, crashed into a hard, plastic seat near a window and kept my bleary eyes trained on the door to his car.

We rode for a while, making several stops, none of which were his. I thought if the train dumped us out in some commuter parking lot, and he hopped in a car, I was screwed. But, the metro terminal spat us out onto streets just like the ones we'd left, row after dizzying row of homes book-ended by corner shops.

I'd followed him for several blocks without a single thought of how to confront him. Was I going to wait until he made it home, and ring the doorbell? I needed to grab him, pull him into an alley and give his arm a good twisting. Did I? I wasn't the one blackmailing him. Why wouldn't he talk to me willingly? *Hey stranger, can we chat about the tomato who's blackmailing ya?* That was stupid, of course he wouldn't talk. I was still drunk.

By the time I had resolved to grab him, he was bounding up the steps of a Brownstone. There were too many people on the street to try to pull him off the well-lit stoop. I ducked into the alley between his building and the next, where trashcans and bicycles were padlocked to water pipes. Here, there were only small windows, frosted or curtained, maybe bathrooms windows, at least ten feet up, and the cone of light from the street lamps did not penetrate the darkness here.

I grew impatient waiting for him in the alley. I walked across the street and tried to observe what I could through the large bay window, lit from within by warm yellow light. I could see the green sweater through the sheer curtains like a wound through gauze. He was joined by another figure, who shrank by a few feet in front of him. He shrank too and bowed his head. I was a drunk, in the cold and dark, watching a man eat the dinner his wife had kept warm for him.

I walked back across the street, took up residence in the alley, and waited.

Maybe he would have to take out the trash or walk a yappie dog before bed. Dinner was still warm in my stomach, and my pea coat was plenty thick. I could wait until morning if I had to. The port was wearing off, which made my head feel worse, but I began to think clearer. If he came out, I could ask him for the time, or a light for a cigarette. With my accent, maybe he'd figure me for a tourist visiting someone in the neighborhood.

Maybe the girl from the Metro wasn't his acquaintance, but his accomplice. I hadn't considered that. I still didn't know what they had on Sam Dile. I assumed my client, a married man, was caught in a badger game. Was I too quick to assume the man in the green sweater was another victim? Partners could have disagreements. Co-conspirators could meet in restaurants. Maybe he's the sneaker, taking the incriminating photos from a closet, or a window. He didn't look like muscle, but how much muscle did you need to intimidate a gnome like Dile?

It was getting late, and cold. Even sunk into the pockets of my coat, my hands burned like they were on fire. Lights were starting to go out in the houses across the street. No one had passed on the sidewalk for a while, and few cars had motored by. The moon was high overhead, a crescent moon, like a broken streetlamp. All was quiet but for the wind in the trees, the fallen leaves scraping across the pavement, and the subtle sound of bird wings, flapping in their nests, righting themselves during the gales.

I heard the door open on the stoop, and the soft pad of rubber soled shoes on the stairs. The man from the restaurant turned into the alley, no sweater, carrying a bag of trash by the knot at the top. I stepped back, deeper into the dark, where I was invisible. There was no chance to meet him on the street. No asking him for the time. I was standing in the dark alley outside his house at midnight. There was only one way this was going to go.

He lifted the lid of the metal can and place the bag inside. I stepped to my right to stay behind him. Leaves cracked under my feet like broken glass. He replaced the lid on the can and stopped to listen. I was sure he could hear me breathe, smell the blood and the marrow on my breath. The wind blew again, and he shivered.

Jumping on his back, I wrapped my arm around his neck and felt his windpipe give under my forearm. I dragged him into the dark, against the wall of his neighbor's house. My cigarette lighter was pressed hard against the soft space under his ribs. I wanted him to think it was a gun, or a knife, or a tank.

"The girl at the restaurant tonight --," I hissed into his ear.

"*Comme*," he blurted, so I started again.

"You met a woman. At the restaurant. What was her name?"

He wasn't fighting, but he touched my arm. "*Detendre*," he said.

I lightened the choke hold so he could talk, but pressed the lighter harder, and higher against his ribs.

"I don't know her name," he said in a pronounced but educated accent.

"You working with her?"

"No."

"How do you know her?"

"I don't."

"Is she blackmailing you?"

"*Comme?*"

"You know, what. Is she blackmailing you?"

"*Calme*! Please," he managed as I tightened my arm across his throat.

"How do you know her?"

"The girl. Came to my work," he panted. "She wanted money. I thought it was a joke."

"What does she have on you," I growled.

"Please, no."

I sank my forearm into his throat just enough to make him gag. My head started to feel strange. My heart beat like it was crammed into my skull next to my throbbing brain. If I didn't wrap this up, I didn't know which one of us would pass out first.

"What does she have on you?" I asked again.

Again, he shook his head no. I stepped on the back of his leg until he was kneeling on the ground. The alley was damp, and the air was cold. He was shaking harder now, as much with cold as with fear. I coiled my arm around his neck and pressed the lighter against the side of his head. I needed this answer.

"What is her name?"

He just shook his head.

I left him kneeling by his trashcans and vanished deeper into the black alley. Materializing on the next street, I crossed one more block just to be safe, and headed back toward the metro. The adrenaline was well worn off by the time I reached the entrance. I was shaking all over and threw up behind a lamppost.

A young couple that had come out of a bar stopped to monitor me, watching to see if I collapsed. They were huddled for warmth, the girl tucked neatly under the arm of her much taller beau. They wore long matching scarves, belonging to a school or football club. The guy approached, motioning for his lady to stay back. He was tall and thin and spoke to me in French long enough to hand me a cigarette. I stuck it in my face with a *Merci* and held still while he lit it. He gave me a friendly slap on the shoulder and waved for his girlfriend to come along. She gave me a wide birth as she scooted past.

# Ten

The early morning sun pushed through the hotel room windows with little impediment. Jerome rang to ask if I intended to extend my stay. I told him to give me the rest of the week.

I felt lousy about roughing up the man in the Green Sweater but reminded myself he was never in any real danger. Still, he hadn't deserved what he got, some of which was probably meant for Rico Mindy. Green Sweater was a mark, no different than Dile, no different than I was at this point. I felt duped, even though I hadn't been party to the original act. And there had been an act, even if I didn't know what it was, or why it was worthy of blackmail. All things being equal, wasn't the simplest explanation likely the right one? If a beautiful woman is blackmailing a man, it's going to be over sex. Or was that just the extent of my imagination?

My interrogation skills needed work. I had to believe there was more to get from the man in the green sweater. He confirmed that the girl from the Metro was blackmailing him but said he didn't know her name. Assuming he could be believed, he'd given me nothing. I still had his address. I could try him again, maybe this round I would ask him for the time on the sidewalk. Although my accent would give me away. An American stopping him on the sidewalk outside his house the day after an American had roughed him up over his trashcans, seemed dubious. My next lead was going to have to come from somewhere else.

I was examining the underside of my pillow, debating whether to get up when Jerome rang again. He informed me that a Mrs. Catherine Savard requested I call her when I woke, concerning a matter which she had described as "urgent."

I calmly inquired why he chose to take a message instead of transferring the call to my room. Jerome explained that Mrs. Savard had not wanted to be transferred and had instructed him to deliver the message.

I rang the number that Mrs. Savard had left. A woman answered, stated in perfect English that she was Mrs. Savard's *domestic*. She placed me on hold for a long time with no music.

"This is Catherine," It was a practiced, affected voice, belonging to someone who talked for a living, maybe on the radio.

I introduced myself only as far as being the gentleman she left the message for.

"I understand that you're looking into the death of my daughter, Adrienne."

"No ma'am, not exactly. I believe her name was used in the perpetration of another crime, but right now I couldn't say the two are related."

"You're investigating a crime involving my daughter," she said, "my daughter who was just murdered. Isn't it reasonable to assume the two are related?"

It was a fair assumption. I apologized, and Mrs. Savard accepted my condolences. I was surprised at how together Mrs. Savard sounded. It was over the phone, but her voice had remained emotionless even at the word "murdered." I asked her who had given her my name.

"I have my sources. I'd really rather not discuss this over the phone, if that's alright with you."

I said it was. She gave me her address in Chaillot, and I said I would come straight away. Her source had to be Inspector Brun. He knew I was in Paris as something more than a tourist and knew where to find me. Rico hadn't so much as asked my name at the *Rouleau Chanceux*. Despite being cleared of any involvement with Adrienne's death, Brun too thought the crimes were related. Maybe this was his way to keep tabs on me. Or was it a test to see if I intended to steer clear of his investigation?

I showered and ran the electric over my face. Knocking some stubble off made me look a lot less haggard, and my eye a little less swollen. I grabbed a couple croissants and a cup of coffee near the mouth of the metro. I had heard that the Chaillot Quarter was fancy digs, with honest-to-goodness mansions, and some of the oldest money in all of France. Mrs. Savard instructed me to take the train to Passey or La Muette, but recommended Passey as I would pass Balzac's house. I wasn't in the right humor for sight-seeing, and I didn't know or care who Balzac was. Besides, there was a Maritime Museum in the middle of Chaillot. If I was venturing anywhere further afield, it would be there.

From the train, I walked along the Seine until I reached the park Mrs. Savard had described; her address was easy to find after that. The Savard home could only be described as a squat mansion. It shouldered its way between two larger, older estates, whose high hedges served to obscure the Savard home completely from their view. The house itself was a bright white neo-classical building with cornices and decorative pilasters between tall rectangular windows. A short lawn spaced the home back from the street and endeavored to convey great dignity within an abbreviated footprint. In contrast to the neighbors' hedge giants, the Savard lawn was dotted with manicured topiary the size of coffee cans. However diminutive, it was the Savard's private Parthenon.

I pushed the bell for the door and heard an elaborate chorus chime inside. A brass name plate beside the bell read *Brugnol* and caused me to double check the address I had scrawled on the hotel stationary. Ilsa, Mrs. Savard's domestic, a woman in her early fifties, opened the door looking very much like you would expect, in a black broadcloth dress and white collar. I pointed to the plaque, "Is this the Savard residence?"

"*Monsieur* Fairfax I presume. It would be good of you to mention the name plate to Madame. No one ever does."

She took my coat and directed me to a sitting room not far from where we stood. It was nearly as white as the outside of the house. White walls, white marble floors and a tall white fireplace, flanked by two teal vases filled with fresh flowers. The only other spot of color in the room belonged to a pair of rose-pink divans facing one another, and the flowing auburn hair of Catherine Savard smiling at me from a wheelchair.

"Mr. Fairfax, I'm so glad you could come." She spoke so softly I could barely see her lips move. She raised a slender finger to bid me enter the room then placed it next to the rest, neatly folded in her lap.

"I thought I might have the wrong house, it says Brugnol on your bell."

"Yes, that," she said. "Brugnol was the name Balzac posted on the front of his *maison* to hide from creditors. If only it were that easy these days."

Balzac again, I braced myself in case she would say they were related. I couldn't believe anyone who claimed relation to a historical figure, it was too easy. You could have George Washington's head in jar on your mantle and I wouldn't believe you.

My host was a very attractive woman. She was of indeterminate age, somewhere between thirty and fifty, but where? She looked to have had Adrienne young and carried her physical immaturity into adulthood. Her skin was smooth and shiny as gilded porcelain, with the same air of fragility. In the race for beauty, she had gotten there first, but showed the weariness of having been beautiful for so long.

"Mr. Fairfax," she began.

"Please, call me Mickey."

"Like the baseball player?"

I shrugged. I preferred him to the mouse.

"Look at me, I know sports," she said.

"I'm sure you know a lot of things. This is a lovely home."

Mrs. Savard gave a knowing glance. "The investigation begins." She motioned for me to sit and wheeled herself closer. "You want the whole story?"

she said, as if it were gossip.

I didn't know what I wanted, but I had a feeling the whole story was the only thing on the menu. "Ma'am, I can't help but notice you're American."

"Canadian actually," she tossed wavy auburn hair over her shoulder. It was beautiful, bouncy, shampoo commercial hair, and it made the room smell like lavender. "It doesn't make any difference once you're here does it? If you're not Parisian, you may as well be from the moon." She made a motion, dismissing some long-remembered slight.

"I wasn't always in this chair," she confessed with a smile.

The exact lines of her body were hidden beneath flowing satin and shoulder pads, but she didn't fill out the garments much more than the hangers had. She was petite and looked as though she always had been.

"I came to Paris to study ballet," she said with a gracefully lifted arm. "When I realized I couldn't dance, art. And when I realized I couldn't paint, I got married."

Mrs. Savard tittered at her joke. I didn't know if this was self-awareness or self-pity. It seemed a stretch to pity someone while sitting in their mansion, though that kind of humility comes from certain rearing. It was a playful line; I was sure I was not the first to hear it.

"Sounds expensive." I took a long look around the room; it was white, shiny and fancy, like heaven in the movies. "Have you always been wealthy?" I didn't know how else to ask it.

She colored to match the divans. "Yes, money is what I brought to the marriage."

"What about Mr. Savard," I asked. "What did he bring?"

She stared at me for a moment with narrowed eyes, I didn't know if she was formulating an answer, or if she was angry at me for getting off the topic of her so quickly. She took in a long breath and gazed about the room as if choosing an answer off the wall.

"He brought the only thing besides money that makes a person successful."

Having no idea what made a person successful, I blinked at her.

"Vigor," she said finally. "I never did much with my money besides spend it. He says it's because I never had to work for it. I suppose there is some truth to that. My husband has done a lot with my money. And he has worked very hard to get it."

"I understand you own a casino," I said.

"The casino, a playhouse, partners in several restaurants." She waved her hand as if to indicate more. "When I met Antoine, he was managing a night club. For a time, it was *the* place to be, maybe in all of Paris."

She was transported thinking about it. She wasn't looking at me anymore, and I could almost see the movie playing behind her eyes.

"It had the best music, the biggest dance floor, good food and strong drinks. I was there on a date, but he didn't care. He came to our table with a bottle of champagne, just as dark and shiny as obsidian. I don't even remember the name of the boy I was with. Antoine literally pulled me out of the booth, onto the dance floor, and that was that."

She was looking at me again. The movie was over.

"He is the only man who ever treated me like I wasn't made of glass. Ironically, it wasn't long after we started seeing each other that I had my accident." She moved her flat hands back and forth along the tops of her thighs consoling them. "On top of a horse is a bad place for an argument, Mr. Fairfax," she said gaily. "Oh shoot, Mickey." She pounded her small fists on the tops of her still legs.

Ilsa came into the room with a silver tray, set it down on the white marble coffee table between the divans, and handed Mrs. Savard a tumbler of bright red liquid buoying a lime wedge. I took my drink from the tray with a polite nod. My God, it was Campari.

"I've never ridden a horse." I offered.

"Filthy beasts." She had taken a long draught of her drink as if she needed it and began to speak before swallowing it completely. "Frankly, I'd trade the lot of them for lawn bowling."

Mrs. Savard blushed as she blotted a drop of Campari from her chin with the back of her hand. She said she hoped it wasn't too early for a drink. I lied and said it wasn't.

"How long after you married did Adrienne come along?"

"Ah, Adrienne. That is why you're here," she wagged an accusing finger.

I don't know the difference between a breath and a sigh, but she took one of them.

"Loyalty, Mickey. Loyalty and vigor. That's Antoine Savard. He married me, even after the accident. We didn't have a real wedding, not while I was in this chair. My vanity wouldn't allow it. Does that make me terrible?"

I said I understood.

"Adrienne came into the world not long after. Such an unloved child."

Taken aback, I waited for her to continue, but she didn't. She took another drink and looked away to another part of the house.

"Oh, I'm sorry," she said rejoining me. "That probably sounded terrible, too."

I wanted to agree.

"I'm a lot of things, Mr. Fairfax." She stopped, looked down at the glass in her hands, and started again. "I am not a lot of things. I am in fact very few things. Not one of those things, however, is maternal. I never imagined I would be a good mother. And I don't know that Mr. Savard ever imagined himself a father. We never discussed children before we had one. Still haven't," she erupted with another quickly stifled laugh. "So yes, I am afraid that Adrienne did not receive the love and attention that other children enjoyed."

"I've seen pictures of your daughter, she was very pretty." I could see

Mrs. Savard beginning to slouch in her chair, shrinking into the past. "I'm sure she had friends, and bet she got a lot of attention from young men."

"A beautiful girl can garner a lot of attention from men without receiving anything close to love." She spoke the words to her glass.

I replaced my drink on the tray and nudged the book on the coffee table; *Les Fleurs du Mal*, The Flowers of Evil. The cover depicted an auburn-haired woman baring her chest, tempted by a devil holding a rose to her lips, and a skull behind her back.

"Are you familiar with Baudelaire?" Mrs. Savard asked.

I picked up the book. I didn't know Balzac, and I didn't know Baudelaire. "I'm not an educated man, Mrs. Savard."

"It's poetry. Passionate, but bitter. Very Parisian. *Do not look for my heart anymore, the beasts have eaten it,*" she recited. "That copy was given to me by a professor from the university. He gave the most dramatic reading at one of our parties, and I insisted he bring me a copy." Catherine wilted a bit. "We used to throw a lot of parties. Unfortunately, you don't have to be absent from society long to be forgotten."

Catherine Savard was not your average shut-in. She was cultured and beautiful; it was easy to imagine her at the height of her powers. But her cloistering had allowed those gifts to become unnatural, like a colorful insect impaled in a display case. The lack of a proper audience had Mrs. Savard showing some rust at playing the old Catherine.

"Mickey," she said. "Tell me something about yourself. I've told you so much about me, I feel a bit silly. It's been a while since I've talked to anybody interesting. Tell me something, anything. Not about your job, something else." She leaned forward and rested her chin on the back of a thin bent wrist.

Mrs. Savard had not asked about my investigation, or whom I worked for; although Inspector Brun may have told her. She seemed unconcerned about the tape holding my eyebrow closed, which had not escaped the notice of her maid.

And she had not asked how her daughter was involved in something that would bring me across an ocean. Adrienne's murder seemed no more relevant to my business there than if I had been selling encyclopedias. She spoke glowingly of her husband but had been careful to insinuate that there had been problems. Married or not, I got the feeling that Catherine Savard looked at me as a man who had come to call on her.

"I've spent a lot of my life at sea." It was all I could think to tell her. I didn't talk about growing up in the orphanage, it elicited the wrong feelings in some people, especially women like Mrs. Savard.

"Well, that explains the coat at least." She allowed herself a snicker, before making a concerted study of me. "It must be very lonely at sea. I can see the loneliness of the sea in your face."

She wasn't wrong, but I felt like she was projecting. "Is that Baudelaire?"

"I'm sorry, was that rude?" She was jovial again. "There is something he writes about men who love the sea. That neither of you can truly be known. And that you fight each other, like brothers, for eternity." She held up her fists and the wide silky sleeves of her blouse made her slender arms look like a marionette's.

I never fought the ocean. And it wasn't my brother. The ocean was one world, and land another. I liked life on the freighter, it made orphans of all men. On ship no man had a family, a house; no man had more than could fit in his locker. All men ate at the same table and faced the same mortality. Land was where you leveraged and plied to have more than the next guy, to get in front of him, to climb over him, and pull a woman out of a booth away from him. I put the book back on the table, pressing my fingers on the cover, that it should remain closed.

"Mrs. Savard." She stopped me and insisted I call her Catherine. I consented. "Catherine, do you have a picture of your daughter?"

"Possibly in the girl's room," she said.

I looked around the sitting room, and sure enough there were no pictures anywhere. The room was tastefully appointed, but impersonal, as if no one lived there at all. There was a second floor toward the rear of the house. Mrs. Savard showed me to the stairs and said she would meet me at the top.

"I have a chair lift down the hall. It's only big enough for me and the chair, better that no one should have to see me in it."

She wheeled away as I took the stairs. At the top were a couple rooms, one whose door stood partially open. I kept my feet in the hall as not to intrude but pushed the door wider. It was Adrienne's room, but looked as if it belonged to a much younger girl. White metal bed frame, pink curtains, bare walls. A single stuffed animal watched me from the bed. It was as if the room had been frozen in time before Adrienne was a teenager or had been consciously restored to that time.

Mrs. Savard joined me in the hall, and I followed her into the room. She fumbled through a few framed pictures which were stacked on top of a white writing desk, then with the contents of a couple of drawers. She looked as unfamiliar with the room as I was, and except for the speed with which she was doing it, didn't seem to know what she was looking for.

As she leaned over the open drawer, her silken blouse, held closed by a single fabric-covered button at the nape of her neck, opened on her back. Her opalescent skin was interrupted by the smooth pink line of a surgical scar just above her pant-line. I stood admiring her longer than I should have.

"Ah ha," Mrs. Savard produced a photo of the girl, and held it high as if she had pulled it from the lake. Perspiration had begun to form under her powdered veneer.

The picture was a few years old but bore a resemblance to the ones from Brun's file. Only here, the girl's eyes were open; doe brown eyes, not her mother's verdant green. Adrienne was tall, standing shoulder to shoulder amid grown men. She wore a black and white gingham dress cut close to her body. Her unsmiling face seemed to wonder why her picture was being taken at all.

"Your daughter was lovely." And she was. "She looks like her mother."
I said too casually.

"Please, I'm an old woman," Catherine snapped. She rushed to compose
herself, carefully blotting her hairline with the side of an index finger. "It's warm
up here," she said fanning herself. "We should go back downstairs."

I agreed and followed her into the hall. "Catherine, do you know anyone
who would want to hurt your daughter?"

"Mr. Fairfax, I don't know anyone who knows my daughter." She asked
if I would take her to the lift and pointed down the hall. She didn't speak and
rested her forehead gently on tented fingers.

When we reached the lift, I turned her chair around, and taking the
armrests, backed her into the small elevator. Our heads were close, and she
whispered *merci* in my ear so softly I could have imagined it. I closed the iron
grate and waited until Mrs. Savard descended into the floor.

I considered ducking back into the girl's room in search of another clue
but didn't. That room was no more hers than anyone else's. The girl that had lived
there had been gone even longer than the girl in the photo. I closed the door to the
mausoleum of the most unloved girl in the world.

I met Mrs. Savard at the bottom of the stairs. She had regained herself
and asked if I would like to continue the interview on the veranda. I said I did
have some more questions. She asked if they were going to be unhappy questions.
I confessed unhappy questions were all I had.

"Well then, you must do something for me, so the conversation isn't
entirely dreary." She turned her chair back to me and motioned that I should push
her down the hall.

We passed through a kitchen fit for a magazine, copper pots, more white
marble, and elaborate millwork, to a sliding wood door that led to the garage. In
the garage sat a small buttercream Crosley roadster, its convertible top down.
Zipping through the narrow streets of Paris and circling the Arc du Triumphe in

this car would make for a hell of a journal entry.

The smile had returned to Catherine's face, not pride in showing off the neat little car, but joy in seeing it herself, as if they were girlfriends who had attended different finishing schools. I hoped aloud that it hadn't been a misguided gift from Mr. Savard, but Catherine said she had owned it long before she was married.

"She's been with me a long time. I used to come out here just to sit behind the wheel," she mused.

"Used to?" I asked.

"She's rather low to the ground. I'm not strong enough anymore to get in and out, and Ilsa is no help. I rather embarrassed myself last time I tried."

I opened the car door with the sharp heel turn of a valet. Standing next to Mrs. Savard's chair, I carefully scooped her into my arms. She clasped her hands around my neck. Her body was warm, and the smell of her skin inescapable. I held her, feeling her weight in my arms before lowering her into the driver's seat. She was blushing, and her hand caressed the side of my face as she withdrew her arms from my shoulders.

I opened the tiny square passenger door, and wedged myself into the small English auto, my knees pressed against the dash. Catherine's hands moved lightly over the leather wrap of the wooden steering wheel and came to rest on the gear shift.

"I feel like we're on a movie set," I joked.

She jerked the wheel comically side to side, squared her shoulders to me and said, "Don't tell me to look at the road, I'm the one driving," with a perfect Vaudevillian cadence.

We laughed. I knew our little drive to the country would be ruined the second I started asking about Adrienne again, so I didn't. Mrs. Savard was a charming woman so long as she was permitted to steer the conversation. She seemed determined to take us down a route that was twenty years in the past, to a time before her daughter was murdered, or even born; to a time when she, herself was still pristine. It wouldn't hurt to pretend for a little while.

She told me she'd attempted to drive the little car from Paris to Frankfurt but turned around in Luxembourg due to the cold. She confessed ballerinas smoked like chimneys, and that all art school kids slept with each other. She was impressed that I knew the Canadian delicacy of eating maple syrup on snow and couldn't believe I hadn't seen any of her favorite movies.

"Why Frankfurt?" I asked, returning to an earlier part of the conversation. I didn't care about ballerinas, or who anyone slept with.

Catherine leaned away with wide eyes, taken aback by the question. "Because it wasn't France. I thought you'd be the last person I'd have to explain that to." She exhaled and melted back in the seat. "I wasn't running away exactly. I was coming back. Is that why you became a sailor? To run away from home."

I was starting to like Catherine Savard. Though, I couldn't imagine having less in common with someone.

She talked more about growing up in Calgary, University in Montreal, and her parents moving with her to Paris to foster her evolving dreams. They were gone now, and except for her husband, she was without family.

"Did Adrienne live her whole life in this house?" The foot in my mouth was done pretending.

"I suppose so," she said without conviction. "Do you enjoy talking to me, Mr. Fairfax?" Her eyes were cast down into her lap.

"Mickey, remember," I corrected her. Her expression didn't change. "You're a beautiful, interesting woman, Catherine." Superlatives always sounded disingenuous to me, no matter if you meant them or not. "I guess this just wasn't a social call."

Our country drive was over.

"I think you should talk to my husband. He spent more time with Adrienne than I," she said, but her message was clear. *Get out of my car.*

I went to open her door, and she slammed it shut again. "I think I'll stay longer. Ilsa will help me, if you don't mind showing yourself out."

"Are you sure, I thought you said Ilsa..." I trailed off. I knew the answer.

"Ilsa probably knows where my husband is today. You should ask her on your way out," her voice was a recording without tone or inflection. "I do thank you for coming. It was gracious of you."

I left Catherine Savard in the roadster, hands slack in her lap, eyes forward, looking through the windshield, looking to what I couldn't pretend to know. Orphaned by time, and childless by murder. She seemed broken beyond her injuries, and her considerable beauty made as comparatively inadequate as her diminutive mansion. She was the unloved mother of the most unloved child in world.

# Eleven

Ilsa was carrying the tray with our glasses into the kitchen. "Would you care to polish off your drink, Mr. Fairfax?" Ilsa said in a casual, off-duty tone.

"This one and some others." I didn't drain the glass, but I tried.

"Is *Madame* upset?" she asked.

"I don't know what *Madame* is."

Ilsa looked at the garage door, willing it to stay closed. "They are not a normal family."

I said, "I wouldn't know," and handed her my newly empty glass. "I didn't get anything about Adrienne from Mrs. Savard, can you tell me about her?"

Ilsa's pursed lips huddled to one side of her face as if I'd asked the square root of Egypt. She had worked for the Savard's since Adrienne was in primary school. "Those two paid a fortune to keep that girl in activities as soon as she could walk. Mister would complain about the money, Misses would complain about being left alone, but neither wanted it any other way. That poor child was raised by language tutors, piano teachers, ballet coaches, and riding instructors until she was eighteen."

"What happened when she was eighteen?"

"She said no. Not angrily, not defiantly, just no. Whatever the season, she would inform them: *I don't see the need to continue with German*, or *I won't be spending much time at the stables this summer.* And it all stopped," Ilsa said, doing little to fight the grin growing across her face.

"So, what did she do instead," I asked.

"None of us knew," Ilsa said. "She didn't tell them anything, didn't even tell them when she moved out. She took a few things with her when she left each morning, slowly smuggling out her own belongings. Then one night she didn't come home for dinner, and that was that."

I asked Ilsa if she knew where Adrienne had been staying. She thought she had the address written down somewhere. It wasn't exactly clandestine, but close.

"Do you know if she had a roommate? Or a boyfriend." I covered my probing about the girl from the train station throwing in the line about the boyfriend.

"If she had, she never brought them here." Ilsa waved me over to a roll top desk -- her desk -- in a little room off the kitchen. It was about as organized as the lobster trap coffee table where I did my taxes, but she seemed to have a system. Finally, she came away with an address scrawled on a piece of pink stationary. Ilsa said the address was in Montparnasse, but that she'd never actually been there, only mailed something to the girl.

"What was it that you mailed?" I asked.

"It was a book." The older woman looked over her desk wistfully, as if it were full of artifacts from the dead girl's life. "I knew the book she meant, the pages were stuffed full of letters, pictures, things like that."

"You read any of those letters?" I asked.

"Why, that would have been an intrusion," Ilsa said. Knowing one of Adrienne's little secrets was a comfort to her now. The girl had obviously trusted her with the address. Even as little as the maid knew of the adult Adrienne, it was more than her mother confessed to know.

"Il-Sa," Mrs. Savard voice came as a sudden scream from the garage, and it didn't stop. "Il-Sa!" It was as if she'd awoken from a nightmare, angrily, desperately howling for her maid. I waited for the older woman to bat me on the arm and assure me it was nothing, but Ilsa looked spooked and rushed to the sliding wood door. "Ilsa," Catherine's voice was low and guttural. "Ilsa, I want that man out, Ilsa. I want that man out of my house." I heard a banging sound that, from the faint, short chirp of the horn, I knew was Catherine's arms smashing against the wooden steering wheel of the Crosley.

"You had better go now, Mr. Fairfax," she said as she pushed open the heavy wooden door.

I could hear the maid speaking softly, contritely to Mrs. Savard, but it failed to stop her screaming.

"Obsessed with my dead daughter, you pervert?" with the door to the garage open, her screams reverberated. "My dead legs not enough for you?"

Catherine was crying now. It was time for me to go. Mrs. Savard continued to yell at me from behind the wheel of her roadster. She called me bad names and accused me of necromancy. I would like to have asked where Mr. Savard was today, as Catherine had suggested during her lucidity, but my next lead was waiting in Montparnasse. I showed myself out.

I took the metro to Montparnasse. I didn't know where the address was exactly, so I decided to get off the train somewhere central like Edgar Quinet. I missed my stop listening to a couple argue on the train. It was probably over something stupid like a toilet seat or where to spend Bastille Day, but in French it sounded vital to the continuance of mankind. I got off at Vavin instead and decided I was hungry. I walked down the main boulevard looking for some sympathetic soul that could point me toward Adrienne's building.

I stopped outside a restaurant called *La Coupole* and read the menu. They had Sole Meniere, but the gold columns inside told me I was underdressed. Across the street was a guy manning what looked like a hotdog cart. Of course, it wasn't hotdogs, but *Andouille* and *Saucisson*. I bought a link of the latter, and the hairy forearm of a man wrapped them expertly in newspaper, with a handful of *frites*. I'm sure French newspaper ink is the tastiest. He seemed adequately jovial, so I showed him the scrap of paper. He pointed down the boulevard, held up two fingers, then shot his hand to the right.

"*Abres*," the little man said. "*Parc*."

I thanked him, he smiled and handed me a piece of hard candy from his apron pocket.

I strolled down Boulevarde Montparnasse and took the second right. When I didn't see a park, I thought the old guy had given me a bum steer. The block was a thin wedge, a pie-chart slice representing the number of lactose intolerant Parisians, with a dollop of arboretum in the middle. A narrow street between buildings led me to an inner ring of apartments with views of the park instead of the boulevard. Adrienne's building was the first I came to. The clear glass door to the outside had no lock or buzzer. Inside were mail boxes with apartment numbers, but no names; mis-delivered mail stuck out of the thin metal doors of their intended recipients, nothing with Adrienne's name, or hanging from her box.

I resented that Adrienne's apartment was on the fifth floor, resented that there was no elevator, and resented most that street-side *Saucisson* and fries is not what Alsacian backpackers took with them into the mountains. I sat on the steps of Adrienne's building and had a cigarette. The people coming in and out of the other buildings didn't seem to fit any specific demographic, most were young, but not all, and many seemed to have kids, but that might have been due to the time of day.

I loafed begrudgingly to the fifth floor where only Adrienne's and another door stood. I fished a card out of my wallet to jimmy the lock, but when I leaned into the door, it opened. The lock was broken. The bolt of the lock had been battened with paper, so it would stay closed.

I stood listening for someone inside. It occurred to me I had taken breaking into Adrienne's apartment rather cavalierly until this moment. After all, I didn't know if she lived alone, with a boyfriend, or a troupe of mimes. I heard nothing, I thought of the mimes. I pushed the door open and waited for something to move or speak, nothing did. There were voices on the stairs behind me. There was nowhere to conceal myself; just Adrienne's door, the door to the other apartment, and a fifth-floor window I could jump through, with a nice view of the park. I glanced over the rail in time to see a couple disappear into a flat two floors down. I stepped into the room and closed the door; the battened bolt worked as intended.

The flat was small, a living room with doors to a balcony, the kitchen, and down a small hallway to the left, the bath and one bedroom. The edge of a couch cushion lay over the other like tiny tectonic plates, as if hastily re-positioned. A few of the drawers in the kitchen stood open, same with some cabinet doors. The bedroom and bathroom had been tossed with more passion. The contents of the medicine cabinet were in the sink, and trash can. The cabinet beneath the sink had vomited its contents onto the rug. And the shower curtain had been torn from the rings, as if anyone hid valuables behind a shower curtain. A silver toothbrush holder affixed to the wall, looked like a pair of brass knuckles, and held one toothbrush loosely in its grip.

The mattress of the queen bed had been obliqued enough to allow a peek under each corner. The sheets lay puddled on the shag. Two small drawers from a whitewashed bedside table had been emptied onto the bare mattress, and the rear of the bedside table kicked in, to insure there were no false backs. There had not been. A print of Van Gogh's *Café Terrace at Night* had been removed from the thin gold-colored frame it had been purchased in and torn from the cheap black backing. The contents of the closet had been evicted. A couple of small hat boxes lay open and empty. Shoes lay piled like the small logs of a camp fire, or pyre.

I went back to the living room, fixed the sofa cushion and sat down. This was a crime scene. The ransacking had been bloodless, but knowing Adrienne was dead imbued the apartment with violence. The same hands that had opened her kitchen drawers, held her neck until she couldn't breathe. The same force that tore the shower curtain from its rings, crushed the girl's windpipe. Had there been a struggle? Had she been here when it happened, had anybody? Nothing had been broken, besides the nightstand, not so much as a chair tipped over. Whoever had been here, was looking for something. Pictures, tapes, documents? Money? Maybe they were looking for the same thing I was looking for, the girl from the metro.

To the right of the kitchen was a pedestal table, two heavy wooden chairs, and a piece of cabinetry that fit snuggly in the corner. All were more provincial pieces than I thought I would find in the downtown Paris apartment of a young girl of means. Everything should have been metal and glass, and the color of the room changing constantly with the use of laser light. The pedestal table would have been more at home in the countryside with a couple of pies cooling on it, and a couple of children waiting underneath for said pies. Maybe these were pieces that were readily available at an outdoor market. Or maybe Adrienne was trying to build something worlds away from her parents' gilded mansion.

The corner cabinet had three shelves and a base with a door. The top shelf was home to a company of porcelain ballet dancers. The tight, top-knotted hair and wan faces of ballerinas troubled me. How could anyone appreciate the delicate lines being painted by their limbs, when their faces held only restrained anguish. Happy, pretty girls become cheerleaders; sad, masochistic beauties, ballerinas.

The second shelf housed a photographic exhibition, mostly pictures of the city, taken in black and white, high contrast, art school stuff; no pics of family, none that looked like friends. The contents of the third shelf lay at my feet; cookbooks, several French, Italian and Indian. They had been swept from the shelf to the floor without care. The bottom cabinet contained her nicer dinnerware; white plates covered with French country scenes in blurry red glaze. Behind the stack of dishes was a lone cloth napkin, the rest of the table linens lay uncouthly wadded on the floor next to the books.

I sat on the ground beside the corner cabinet and picked up a book. It was James Beard's *American Cookery*. Adrienne's betrayal of her Parisian upbringing was complete. I turned the pages. She had scribbled messages to herself in the margins, in French, *too much salt*, or *next time buttermilk*. Then I found it. Between the recipes for Crab Meat Mornay, and Lobster Fra Diavolo was a four by four-inch piece of paper, a communiqué in Adrienne's deliberate hand.

The paper itself was delicate, like the superfluous paper in a wedding invitation. I'd received one in my life, and it was still stuck to the frig door six years later. I looked at it whenever I forgot I was terrible, or remembered I was lonely.

It looked at first like another recipe; it was directions, but not for lobster. I knew my rights and lefts in French, and each line began with a G for *gauche*, or D for *droite*. I thumbed through the rest of the book and found a dozen more. I kept them in order, in case it was relevant, and went through the other books page by page.

I sat at the pedestal table and compared the handwriting of the directions, to that in the cookbook, and the letter to Dile. They looked the same. They looked like every woman's handwriting I'd ever seen, every name and number on a bar napkin, and a few *Dear Mickey's* that had been slid under my door. Only, the lower-case g's from the cookbook, and the directions, looked like a perfect number "8," immune to the left to right slant of the rest of the letters. Dile's letter contained only one lower case G, in the word "waiting," an almost closed circle, with an elongated lower loop. Maybe Inspector Brun had someone who could look at them more closely. Was I ready for a show-and-tell with Brun?

Adrienne's balcony looked out over the park, central to the cluster of buildings. There was a produce crate, on its side, for all your sitting needs, a coffee can, collecting cigarette butts, and a reasonably healthy potted plant, with a few discarded butts of its own. To the right, a precariously small iron ladder led to the balcony below, and the roof above. I'm not afraid of heights, but I'm also not a circus performer. The dismount onto the roof was what worried me, and I wondered how your average civilian was supposed to navigate this in an emergency. Obviously, the fire escape was built in an era when people were smaller in stature, and enjoyed livelier pastimes, like going over waterfalls in a barrel.

A low wall surrounded the roof that couldn't keep your knee caps from falling to their death. It was lined with birds. They didn't seem perturbed by my presence and continued whatever discussion I had interrupted. I hoped it was about the smell. They preferred the shaded side of the roof, adjacent to the next building. I stood an inch from the wall and peered down to the alley below. Not a single pigeon batted an eye. I lunged at them, raising my fists for some reason. Not a single defector. Finally, with a *shoo, shoo, shoo, shoo*, and a waving of arms that brought me into contact with no less than four different birds, I was able to clear a space on the wall. Standing on the edge, I looked across to the neighboring rooftop, felt a sudden stiff breeze at my back, and convinced myself that whether one could make that jump was immaterial. I climbed back down the fire escape, and into the safety of the dead girl's apartment.

On the ground floor, in a locked glass case, was the number for the Super spelled out in white plastic letters stuck in a felt bulletin board. I wrote it on my hand, I'm bad at remembering numbers. A letter had fallen off his name, and one from the phone number; luckily only one. I could see the missing number lying in the bottom of the case. I walked to the park to find a pay phone. I called the police, told them who I was, and asked for Inspector Brun. I kept my eyes on the apartment stoop just in case anybody showed.

"This is Inspector Brun," he sounded as collected as he had the day of our interview, but also feigning a little surprise, as if taking this unsolicited call was highly irregular.

I knew he knew who it was, so I just started in on him. "You're gonna get a call pretty quick from a Super saying he's got a missing tenant. You've already got the body, but I bet you've been looking for the apartment. It's Adrienne Savard's."

I let him digest that. He took his time doing it. "*Monsieur* Fairfax, I hope you have not been working my murder case?" he warned.

"No inspector, I haven't. I've been working my case, it just keeps bumping into yours." I gave him the address but withheld the details of my preliminary snooping. "I'm guessing it's not in her name since it doesn't look like your boys have been there yet. But, somebody has, if you know what I mean. You've been looking for it haven't you?" I gloated.

"Yeeeeeeees," he droaned. "We've been following all routine procedures." His tight, clipped speech was meant to suggest his impending inability to provide me anything further.

"You think it has to do with Mr. Savard, don't you? He sounds like a real charmer, but I think his daughter had her own racket, enough like the old man's to get her killed." I knew he would try to cut me off, so I slid my question in before he could. "Have you looked at Adrienne's bank accounts? Anything fishy, like large cash deposits?"

"Fishy?" he repeated. Fishy didn't translate. "Mr. Fairfax, I do thank you for the information you've provided, but I'm afraid I'm not at liberty to discuss this case with you."

I wondered if he was recording the conversation. "Well someone gave my name to Catherine Savard, and I turned that into her daughter's apartment. I might have more for you later." I was sure he was about to tell me to stop my inquest, or even threaten me with obstruction, so I hung up. I looked at the number on my hand and called the Super. After several rings, he answered and said he spoke some English when I asked. "I need to know who rents apartment 5A," I demanded.

"Why should I tell you?"

"Cuz, I think it's my daughter, and if it is, I need to know." I was trying the pushy asshole approach.

"5A pays cash, always months in advance. I don't have a name," he croaked.

"Well you better come up with one, cuz she's dead." I hung up. There were already a couple of beat cops ascending the stoop of Adrienne's building.

# Twelve

There didn't seem to be a beginning or ending address to the directions, only rights, lefts and street names. There were a couple words at the top, and a few at the bottom of each, phrases I would have Jerome translate for me later. I didn't want to get back on the train, so I walked down the main boulevard to a taxi depot I had passed and hired myself a hack. Studying the notes in Adrienne's apartment, I'd noticed most began with either a right or left on *Rue*, and all of those that began with a left, were followed by the word *Pigalle*. Armed with that, I asked the cabbie to take me to the corner of Rue and Pigalle and showed myself to the back seat of the idling car.

We crossed the Seine and headed northwest toward the Champs Elysee. He was savvy enough to skip the Arc de Triomphe at that time of day, whipping the car through side streets narrow enough to be alleys. He didn't want to idle through that mob, even if the meter was running. The car came to a screeching halt in front of a metro station in a large square.

The driver threw up his hands with a laconic, "*Allez*."

I handed him the fare but didn't get out of the car. "This is the corner of Rue and Pigalle?" I asked.

"*Regard, Pigalle*," he made an exasperated motion toward the metro stop with his right hand. "*Et, Rue de Pigalle*," he said pointing to the street leading away from the station.

I realized my *faux pas* and got out of the cab. Several streets radiated from the Pigalle metro stop in all directions, and they were all called Rue de *Something*. I'd essentially asked to be taken to the corner of Main and Street.

I consulted the street map outside the Metro stop. I traced Rue de Pigalle on the map starting at the station. Two dozen streets turned off Rue de Pigalle in every direction, and every branch had several tributaries of its own. Except for one: Cite Pigalle. Cite Pigalle was a small, dead end road from which you could only turn right or left onto Rue Pigalle.

This area of the Champs Elysee was all night clubs and modern restaurants. It was late afternoon and open doors and windows framed scenes of hustling wait staff, flurries of white shirts, foul language, and cigarette smoke. Cite Pigalle was a hundred yards of four-story buildings, ground-floor restaurants and shops topped with walk-up apartments. I walked it twice finding nothing unusual, meaning no neon signs, no giant X's marking spots.

Each of the directions emanated from this street, I was sure of it. From what building or business, I didn't know, but it was early, and the Champs Elysee was sure to look a lot different when the sun went down.

I took the train from the Pigalle station back to my hotel. Jerome would be on shift in a few hours, so I had time to do a little homework. I pinched a trifold street map from the lobby; unfolded it was bigger than the café table in my room, so I spread it on the floor. I marked every spot where a set of directions ended. They appeared in every quarter of the city, but none further than just outside Paris proper. Most traced an efficient line to the end destination, but a few did not – their paths zig-zagged across the city, before terminating, like the others, on the outskirts.

I'd had the map pretty marked up by the time I presented it to Jerome. Two big red dots marked the Pigalle station, and Cite Pigalle, and looked like the thorax and abdomen of a spider. The legs of this headless constellation were splayed all over Paris. It was a monster movie, and I hoped plying Jerome with cigarettes would keep him from calling the white coats on me.

"Why do you want to go to these places, man?" Jerome had thankfully dropped the *Monsieur* business.

I asked him what was wrong with them.

"Nothing, really, just nothing to see."

We stood at his counter, filling the lobby with smoke, and studying the map like it was blue prints of a bank vault.

"Once you get past here," he traced a circle with his finger through the middle of the city, "it's just neighborhoods."

Not one of my destinations was inside the circle.

"What's the word in English," he blew a perfect smoke ring, "Suburbs."

I asked him to translate the little phrases at the top and bottom of each note. He grabbed a handful, and flipped through them like baseball cards, reading them to himself, laughing at a couple.

"They're people," he concluded. He read them aloud, flinging each one into the air as he discarded it. "Curly hair, ugly nose. Old, fat, toupee. Boring teacher-type, green sweater."

I snatched the last one out of air and clutched it in both hands. I found the corresponding dot on the map and couldn't believe I hadn't noticed it before. It was the man in the green sweater's street. Jerome said the few words at the bottom of each note were numbers, just spelled out. One twenty-nine. Forty-two A. Fifteen, second floor. Mystery solved.

I pictured Adrienne following these men, through the streets of Paris, to metro stations, watching them in their homes. Sounded like standard fare for a blackmailer. But I'd been in this girl's room with its pink curtains, childhood trophies, yellow and blue ribbons. I'd met her mother, and her maid, I'd thumbed through her cookbooks. Blackmail was supposed to come from seedy back allies, cooked up by pimps and thugs, lurking in the bushes or outside a window with a camera.

Where had she followed them from? There was a Point Zero, somewhere on Cite Pigalle, where all these paths began. These men had done something worthy of blackmail. The notes, found in her apartment, removed any doubt that she was party to it. What did Adrienne have on them? What was it that was so compromising, so threatening to the wrong person, that they hunted her down, and took her life to ensure her silence?

Jerome had answered the ringing phone and was doling out hotel facts in well-ordered French to an eager listener. A good hotel clerk is an oracle, a divining rod for their city. Any joint advertised on a flier or in a book was *passe* before the ink dried. But a good hotel clerk, kept a deft finger on the pulse of his or her own turf.

When Jerome rejoined me, I asked him if any of his guests ever sought less than legal entertainment for the night. I could tell by his flushing and a particularly hard swallow that he knew what I meant. I felt a like a heel when he said he didn't know any places like that and held his hands up like I'd demanded the till and his wallet. I apologized to him, said of course he didn't know any place like that, and settled him down with friendly slap on the shoulder. Then I asked him if he knew anybody who did.

* * *

The Hotel Lazarus was one of many places around Paris that touted its reputation as a flop house for every writer and artist of the gilded age. It was a mansion, and former home of Louis XIV's favorite general. Now it was hotel with frescoed lobby ceilings higher than you could comfortably crane your neck. The walls were gold and gilt without exception, and the deep echo from the lobby floor made every footfall sound like you were ascending the throne. The Lazarus had been a snooty place to get a high-falutin' room in Paris since the 17th century.

Having been a private home, there was only one way into the Hotel Lazarus, and once inside, there was no avoiding detection by the hotel manager. He was a thin giant behind a varnished oak counter. He leaned on long, splayed arms whose great span suggested he could easily defend the arched passages to his right or left if tested. This sentry watched my every step toward him, and I watched his concern and cordiality wane as I came into sharper focus.

"Can I help you, sir?" he labored with characteristic malaise.

"How did you know I spoke English?" I asked.

"I could only tell," he looked me up and down with a smirk, "that you are not French."

"Should I be offended?" I let the question hang in the air for a beat. The rangy manager was younger than me, he wore a sharp navy suit, and a yellow silk tie that matched the wall paper. His shellacked blonde hair looked like clay applied to his square head, then given texture with the tines of a dinner fork. His eyes were big and full of sea water, his nose a thin jag of bone, and his lips were missing entirely.

"A friend of mine asked me to meet him here. Mind if I wait for him?" I pointed to a bank of high-backed upholstered chairs in the lounge behind him. The manager turned and looked, his skepticism of me had him doubting that there was a lounge.

"Perhaps I could ring the room for you, sir." He said, lifting a gold phone receiver by its ivory handle. "What is your friend's name."

"Babby," I said. It was a name I made Jerome repeat for me several times, having no confidence that I had heard him correctly.

"Is that the first, or the last name?"

"I don't know," I said. "Maybe neither. Old Army buddy. Just know him as Babby."

The manager perused the register before reporting, "I have no one by that name, sir. Are you certain you have the correct hotel?"

"Hotel Lazarus, is there another location?" He didn't dignify that with a response. I drummed the fingers of both hands on the gold flecked marble top of the manager's counter; he stared at the right one, willing it to stop. "You have anyone working here named Babby?" I inquired with impunity.

"I'm sure we do not," he averred. "Do you not know if your friend is working here or staying here?" he chafed.

I held up my hands and shrugged, "That's Babby for ya." I'd humored myself enough; the manager's brow was already furrowed, and I didn't want it to cramp. "He said he'd meet me here. I'd prefer to sit and wait for him if you don't mind." I motioned again to the chairs.

I didn't wait for him to say no and made my way past him. If he was going to put his hands on me, it would have been then. Not doing it, told me a lot about how far I could push him, if I needed to. I took a seat and crossed my legs to show my contentment. He circled to the front of his desk with a tea towel and cleanser to erase all traces of our encounter and to show me he was watching. I stared back and rubbed the padded arms of the chairs, lending them my full endorsement.

Eventually Lurch was duty-bound to answer the phone, and away I went. The hallways between rooms were carpeted, red and plush like theater curtains. The padding under the carpet was so thick I thought I might get seasick if I didn't turn an ankle first. The walls were golden yellow with elaborate white molding and the door to every room was cased in black marble. I didn't find an elevator, but a narrow, spiral flight of stone steps took me to the second floor. It was the same as the last, gilded, but silent as the grave. Nothing short of a battering ram could breech the imperial wooden salon doors. Thankfully, *La Revolution* had had battering rams.

I didn't bother with the third floor, deciding instead to look for the kitchen. On the ground floor, I could hear the clank of dishes and a *melange* of voices behind a pair of swinging doors with porthole windows. The sun was still high in the sky, but the first dinner plates were already leaving the kitchen under golden domes. I tried in vain to read the name tags of the swift lads ferrying them past me. When the barrage of bellmen stopped I pushed through the doors and into the kitchen. There were sneers and raised eyebrows from half a dozen chefs, so I kept my back to the wall as a gesture of unobtrusiveness.

Some rudimentary French would have come in handy. Instead, I was forced to stop at the end of each row of stainless steel tables and sheepishly inquire, "*Excuse moi*, uh, Babby?" I was met with equal parts pity and annoyance. One wet-eyed lady chef, prepping long beans, in a hat like a fallen cream puff, looked at me like I was miming obscenities. Mercifully, at the last row, a stout, sweaty man with a neck beard, hacking at a mutton, buried his cleaver in the flesh-less animal's skull, held two fingers to his lips, and jerked his thumb at a door to my right.

The door led outside, where a bellhop stood leaning against a dumpster, the remains of a joint adhering to his protruding lower lip. His mop of hair was black and oily, his complexion ruddy and freckled. He was wiry, concave, with a hurt animal look that young girls were sure to gamble on, and regret later. He was a kid but looked anxious to move on from misdemeanors to more serious offenses. The name tag hanging from his open uniform lapel read *Sebastian*.

"Babby?" I asked.

"Who?" His breath smelled like heated metal, like pennies in an ashtray.

Terrific start. I didn't rush it. Instead I paused to light up. I offered Babby the pack, but he waived me off with an invisible gesture. "I'm looking for a fun place."

The kid looked at me but said nothing.

"Supposed to be somewhere on Cite Pigalle," I said.

He laughed. "No way, man." Babby pushed past me in a flash and stomped toward the kitchen door.

I ran to get in front of him. I put a hand against his empty chest which he swatted away immediately. His uniform jacket was lousy with the dank, herbaceous musk of weed. "Come on, man," I entreated. "I'm on three-day leave."

"Try the Rouge," he mocked and made a move to get around me.

"I ain't looking for no Cabaret," I snarled.

Babby stopped and gave me a hard study. "What do you know?"

"Couple other sailors were talking in a bar. Don't remember everything, it was late, and I was drunk."

"Were they Americans?"

"Yeah," I answered without thinking.

"I don't remember any Americans, sorry." He tried to move around my other side.

Most merchant sailors these days were German or Filipino, I should have played those odds. "Busy guy like you, you remember everyone you talk to?" I said indignantly with a little shove.

"Yes, I do." I could see Babby's arms stiffen in his uniform sleeves.

"Even when you're tight?" I held out the folded Francs I'd readied in my coat pocket.

"*Osssssstie*," he hissed. A smirk creased one side of the kid's ugly face.

Babby straightened his back and began buttoning his uniform. "You're a cop," he said.

I laughed. I opened my coat to show him the badge that wasn't there. "You have a lot of American cops in Paris?" I spit for effect, wiped my mouth on my sleeve and narrowed my eyes at the emboldened hoodlum. It was too much.

"You're a cop, *p'tit Chriss*. And if you're not, you're something." Babby tugged on a pair of white gloves like he was entering the ring.

"How's that?" I blew a cloud of smoke in his face.

"Because Cite Pigalle," he growled, "is not the place for you. *Degage!*" He shoved me hard with both hands and disappeared through the door, into a broiling hive of cooks and bellmen.

# Thirteen

I'd been made by a bellboy. Babby had gotten spooked, and clammed. But why? Was I less swarthy than I thought? Lurch had pegged me as a criminal, but Babby a cop. I needed to figure that out before I tried walking into Cite Pigalle, or I'd wind up in another alley.

I needed a walk. A street called Rue de Mouffetard was close, and the map I'd pinched advertised, among other things, a street market. Rue de Mouffetard was a trading route that had once run all the way to Rome. Now the boulevard was a mile of shops and street-side stalls. Vegetables of every color stacked like pyramids, clothing and handbags, paintings of all sizes, and broken bricks of marbled cheese. The street was closed to cars, but so coagulated with pedestrians I had to shorten my stride to keep from kicking the women in front of me in the ankles. Tall buildings gave the feeling of walking through a deep canyon and channeled enough of a breeze to combat the heat from the pavement and the collected mass of Parisians.

Eventually, I found a couple coin stands nestled between a man selling carved duck decoys, and a tobacconist. Two old men glowered at the infinitesimal, squinting their keen eyes like focusing microscopes, and pointing out pin-sized details with unsteady, gnarled fingers. One coin, completely green with oxidation, elicited a sound from the men like their first glimpse of a grandchild. Both hurried to produce jeweler's glasses and I heard their heads knock together as they jockeyed to view what, to them, was nothing short of treasure.

I kept coins and bills from every port-of-call my ship had seen. A sailor had to be economical about souvenirs. There is only so much room in a footlocker. All my trophies fit neatly in a Belgian cigar box. Nothing in my collection was rare, or valuable, never having money enough to secure anything rare, or valuable. I'm a sucker for a coin with a hole in it, or a bill with a pretty lady. I'd haggled with vendors in Arab and African ports selling drachmas and shekels supposedly from the time of Christ. Coins from 400 A.D. will look older than time itself to a tourist and are still common enough to be near worthless. Tiny mineral relics selling for tens to tens of thousands of dollars, that couldn't buy you a sandwich if you were starving. Like everything else in the world, it's only value is what someone else is willing to pay for it.

I bought a couple Vichy French coins from 1941, made of zinc and aluminum due to the war, and splurged on a bronze one Centime coin from 1848. That set me back eighteen francs. It was tarnished to an oily black. In the case next to it was another of the same year, shiny as a new penny, whose label bragged it had never been circulated. How could anyone know that? For fifty-five francs it was going to remain a mystery.

The antique jingle in my pocket didn't make up for striking out with Babby. I needed a pick-me-up and knew if I kept walking I'd stumble into a cup of coffee. I popped into the first *brasserie* I saw for a short and hot. There was a young woman ahead of me, very attractive, a lot like I had pictured the living Adrienne. She was tall, with long straight hair, carefully tanned skin, and athletic legs below the flounce of a short blue sundress. She seemed to know the lank *garcon* behind the register, who was playing it marvelously cool. But he didn't fool me. I could see in him the restraint of a circling wolf. His body was slack, but his eyes were trained on her. She turned to leave, and the wolf took my order.

"I'll have one of those," I said with a motion that was meant for the coffee, not the girl. It wasn't a flirtation; ordering coffee anywhere that didn't sell pancakes had become an ordeal. Still the girl looked back and smiled knowingly, familiar with the lasciviousness of men's minds where it concerned her. The wolf and I watched her leave with lupine eyes, then shared a grin like we'd finished building a go-cart.

The sun was setting behind the taller buildings, shading the still bustling street. Rue de Moffetard had become a sea of women. Like the *garcon* at the register, I had hungry eyes, and walking down the crowded boulevard was like looking in a butcher shop window. I'd grown up in a world of boys and nuns and come of age in one of sailors and barmaids. To me, all women possessed a certain sanctity, deserved or not, which was too often incongruous with my desire for them and a life at sea. The consequence was having the love life of a mayfly. I can't imagine my shore-leave romances enjoying the same arc as a life spent with your high school sweetheart, but I remembered women I'd known for three days as if we'd married and divorced in that time.

Femininity is powerful stuff. Some men do foolish things for a piece of it; in others it bred cruelty, resenting women for possessing something they coveted. I could imagine Adrienne, decked out like the girl from the *brasserie*, luring Dile into some entanglement he was too willing to believe. Her mother Catherine, despite alcoholism and mania, put herself together physically every day, even if mentally she was falling apart. Damaged as she was, she, like many women, knew that her beauty was a currency she could always trade on.

I watched as the women ahead of me turned into cafes, or shops, or stopped to model something. I lingered behind a young woman with eyes like black glass, and a dimpled smile; she bought macarons before crossing to the other side of the street. Another in a youthful linen romper, wrinkled by her cafe chair, carried an over-sized woven straw bag and her long neck balanced a matching hat. She stopped at every stall that might have offered a practical replacement for either.

I crossed the street and pretended to peruse the nondescript junk at a crowded stall. They sold more touristy things, postcards, cheap lithographs of famous paintings, Eiffel Tower pencil sharpeners, and small wooden boxes with

*Paris* carved ornately on the lid.

I was surveilling the building up the block I'd seen the girl with the dimples disappear into. It was a full five minutes before she emerged again. She walked toward me down the sidewalk, I turned my back as she passed, then stepped into the street behind her. My heart was beating fast, I told it to stop. Following her on purpose felt like looking in a bedroom window. The crowd thinned out between us and I felt sure she could hear the clop of my shoes and the beating of my heart. Dimples threw a glance over her shoulder, looked me right in the face, made no visible show of concern, and continued on her way.

Ten steps later, she took another peek. This time I was sure my face gave me away. She'd seen me, however briefly, when she bought the macarons, and I had to believe she recognized me now. She stopped at a newsstand and pretended to look at a bottle of brown shoe polish. I'd been made. I walked past four more businesses and ducked into a lunch spot, a cheap linoleum concern with plastic chairs, and two dozen chickens on huge rotating spits sweating over a pile of potatos. It only took another minute for her to pass by. I could have resumed tailing her but called an end to the little exercise before I alerted the *gendarme*.

I walked back the way I came behind a young woman whose bright magenta hat made her look like a match-stick. She wore a black and gray striped cardigan, beat-up jeans, and sneakers. The waves of black vinyl, today were frizzy curls under that wool Cloche hat, and the backpack *du jour* was canvas with leather straps. I wondered how many costume changes were inside.

I watched her buy a stamp at a news stand, then hand the letter back to the proprietor who put it with his outgoing mail. We passed rugs, lamps, sunglasses and scarves before hitting a vein of bookstalls. Tall wooden shelves, tables, and crates, all stuffed with books, mostly in French, but classics from Jane Austin to Hemmingway, brooded at me from English dust jackets.

I heard her voice chime over the murmur of Parisians, "Excuse me," in her excitement she had forgotten her French. "Do you have any more like these?"

She held three small books for the seller to see. The older woman answered her in French, touching her consolingly on the arm.

I followed as she plumbed deeper into the shop, dragging a finger across book spines like a stick against a picket fence. Stacks of cheap paperbacks ran the length of a narrow table. She was scanning the dime novels, tittering at titles like The Passion of Blackbeard, or Android Lolita. She hadn't noticed me, and even with the table between us, I could have reached out and touched her. It was as if I had conjured her myself, and any loud noise or sudden movement would cause her to dissolve back into the ether.

I didn't know what she would do when she saw me. I didn't know what I would do. There was an isthmus between the table and the shelves along the back wall of the shop, where I had unwittingly cornered her. She bumped into my chest trying to squeeze by.

"*Pardon*," she said.

I put my hands on her upper arms and guided her past. It was only then that she lifted her head enough to see my face.

"Don't run," I breathed. I took my hands from her arms.

She didn't run. Her eyes trembled like the day I'd grabbed her in the metro station. Those eyes. Light and gray as gull wings. I held my hands up, to show her they were empty. She moved to put the long table back between us. We studied one another silently, and the din of the sidewalk dwellers swelled.

"Did I do that to your eye?" she asked flatly.

"Nah, you gave me this." I showed her the goose egg that was still prominent on the side of my skull. "You disfigured me," I said. "I can't wear hats."

She didn't laugh. "You look like someone beat you up," she offered.

"Someone did." I told her how I'd found out what I could about Adrienne, and about my rum luck at the *Chanceux*. I told her about the pounding Rico had given me, bruising my ego, and suggested she swam in some dangerous circles.

"Why did you do that?" she scolded. The tendons on the backs of her hands were taut and raised as she gripped the edge of the table.

"A girl is dead," I said in my defense.

"What do you care?" Her eyes were big and wet. She was mad, or scared, or both. I watched her push whatever feeling it was down with a raising and lowering of her hands. "I'm sorry I hit you. I didn't know you." She corrected herself, "I don't know you."

"My name's Mickey, I rent sailboats out of the harbor back home. My hobbies include coin collecting and keeping ladies from being pushed into German cars."

She still didn't laugh. Tough crowd. She hadn't smiled at anything since I handed her a brick of cash. It was a sizeable brick. That would set a high bar.

"Are you going to turn me in?"

"I seem to have forgotten my handcuffs," I said.

There was no danger now. The sun was shining, we were in a well-populated area, there were baguettes -- I was just a guy talking to a blackmailer in a funny hat. I knew the right thing was to hand her over to Brun. That wasn't what Dile had wanted, nor was he the reason I wasn't going to do that.

Without the tall red pumps, she stood no more than five-two. Without her fiberglass lips, her skin was olive, and her face placid as a Madonna. She was neither bombshell, nor bad-ass. I'd caught her on laundry day. She stood there reading my face. I was afraid of what might be written on it.

"There's nothing to hit me with in here," I joked.

"I don't know," she said. "Some of those atlases look pretty heavy."

She paid for the books and started down the street. I did my best to walk beside her, and she did her best to flit through the crowd like a finch. At the end of the boulevard was a cluster of African merchants under primary-colored tarps. She stopped at a bright orange food stall with smoke emanating from all sides.

She spoke to the gent inside with familiarity and used some pigeon Somali like a knife and spoon. The dark man was too tall for the booth and had adopted a droopy chorea when slinking around inside it. He handed her a bundle of kebabs in exchange for a few folded Francs, and gave us each a friendly tug on the bill of his Rastafarian cap.

We walked a little farther, away from the fray of Rue de Mouffetard, and stood under a streetlight, wordlessly dissembling kebabs. The books she had purchased were children's readers, in German, with dust jackets stained the color of tobacco leaves. "Where does a nice public-school girl like you pick up Somali?" I inquired.

"Gus is Berber," she corrected.

"My apologies to Gus." It crossed my mind that once she cleaned her kebab, she might try to stab me with it. "English, French, and Berber. You adding German to that list?"

She made an ugly face like she didn't know what I was talking about. I motioned to the readers, and she pushed them farther into the bag. Even if she weren't *en guard*, she didn't seem the type that talked out of compulsion.

She neatly folded her trash and disposed of it without concern whether I had finished. She started off again, and I grabbed her by the arm for a third stupid time. She turned toward me, not with trembling eyes, not with dagger raised, but with a look of resignation unbefitting her age.

"You have to tell me your name." It felt like groveling.

"Why?" she asked.

I had no reason I was willing to offer.

She pushed my hand from her arm. "Can we go now?"

I didn't ask where we were going, I just followed. There were no crowds to lose me in, no dark alleyways to duck into. We walked like any two people down wide, well-lit sidewalks. At times she took my sleeve at the elbow to steer us through the streets, all the while saying nothing, nothing about the city, nothing about Adrienne.

She stopped in front of a poster advertising the return of a popular museum attraction. *La Joueuse de Tympanon* was a mechanical female figure that played the dulcimer, an instrument like a piano, striking sets of strings with hand-held mallets. She said the automaton needed repair after a lunatic had broken her arm, and a piece of the underlying mechanism. Reports varied as to whether he was trying to steal *La Joueuse*, or molest the baroque robot which was made for, and in the image of Marie Antoinette.

Alongside a description of the repairs was a picture of the figure, with her skirt removed, as well as her wig, and the back of her head. Marie sat at her instrument, overly-erect, a shaft of metal protruding from her skull as if she were a science experiment, and naked from the waist down, as if freshly violated. I was curious why the artist had sculpted her thighs so faithfully if he had planned, all along, to cover them with a dress.

"I wish they wouldn't call her a robot," she said. "People are disappointed when they see she isn't bigger."

"How big is she?" I asked, like a dope.

She held her hands apart, intimating a box one-foot wide by one foot tall. Marie sat on her piano bench over a corrugated drum; like a music box, the drum rotated, and its teeth would trip a strip of metal that moved the doll's arm to hit the appropriate notes in time.

"I guess people picture robots running around, on their own," I said, "like in the movies, building spaceships, or making your breakfast."

"That's no kind of life," she said. "Stuck on that fucking piano."

"Well then, it's a good thing she's not alive?" I said.

Her gaze remained on the *Joueuse*. If she heard me, she showed no sign of it.

"You're not the same, you know?" I said. "You and her. You know that, right? She's got a steel girder holding her in place, you don't."

She stared back at me blank-faced. My words were not a revelation. They hadn't inspired or comforted her. She didn't giggle and blush, feeling there was someone who understood her. Instead the words passed right through her, like they had been spoken to someone else.

If she thought she was in the same boat as the automaton, it was a cop out. The crimes we committed against each other were always rationalized with gems like, "it's all I know" and "I didn't have a choice." When the truth was always closer to "it was easier," and "I wanted to." The violent reasoned their victims were weak, the swindler, that theirs' were fools. Thieves were redistributing wealth, and cheaters were toppling the Pharaoh. All for the greater good, of course.

Maybe she didn't see herself, but someone else when she looked at the *Joueuse*. The beautiful doll impaled on her instrument, who went through each performance mechanically, perfectly, and without passion. Maybe she looked at her with pity, knowing she was not the one without a choice.

She took my sleeve, and after a minute, we were walking again. We took the train to Les Halles, to the station platform where we'd first met. I followed her up the station stairs, through the park, and down the street to the front steps of my own hotel. She'd outsmarted me again. I'd assumed she was leading me to her place; that I was being taken into her confidence. Instead, she'd returned me home like a child lost in the city.

She crossed the lobby to the stairs, and flashed Jerome a look that wiped the smile from his face. He watched me ascend the steps behind her, wearing a sheepish grin, in case I dropped a folded note, or mouthed the words "help me." She was leaning against the wall outside my room, waiting for me to open the door, too tired from the walk to jimmy it herself.

"Leave the light off," she said standing in the center of the otherwise empty room. It was neither an order, nor request.

The room was blue-black with moonlight, and she stood in what night poured in from the windows. She let her bag slip from her shoulder, and I heard her cardigan land softly on the couch. I watched her black figure cycle through the familiar silhouettes of disrobing. She was a shifting Rorschach blot of every fantasy I'd had since we met, but that desire seemed darker now. Here was a woman I knew ensnared men with sex, and I was dancing in the trap, believing myself an animal with neither fur nor meat at risk.

The Chimera finally settled on the slender shape of a woman. She was petite, with thin arms, but a swimmer's shoulders, broader than her narrow waist. Rectangular hips disrupted the tapering lines of the rest of her body. They were the wrong bones, a woman's hips bolted to a girl's body, added for function like a luggage rack on a sports car.

"You can have whatever you want," she spoke without seduction.

"And what do I want?"

"What all men want."

No man believes he is "all men." What she meant by "all men" was all that was low, animal, and abhorred by women. She was making it plain our encounter would be sordid. There would be no opportunity to earn her affection. My dessert was being thrown down in front of me like I'd refused to eat my dinner.

She grabbed my wrists and pulled my hands to her throat.

"You want to hurt me?" she whispered. "You want to get back at me?"

"I don't want to hurt you." Words I had never had to say.

She let go of my hands. One fell back to my side, the other lingered loosely around her throat. The edge of my thumb found the spaces between the rings of her windpipe.

"I don't want to hurt you," I repeated, convincing myself that it was true.

She was playing a hell of a game. If she wanted me off balance, I was. If she wanted me to want her, I did. I would have already left Paris if I hadn't. She was handing herself to me, but it was a concession. I'd finally outflanked her, and sex was just ground she was willing to cede in retreat.

I found her face in the dark and pressed my mouth against hers. The taste of cardamom and coriander mingled with the sticky sweetness of her perfume. Her hands groped and searched my back, as if she were looking for a switch or lever. What she hoped that lever would do, I didn't know. She held herself so close to me, I couldn't see her. It was a conditional acquiescence. She was handing me the keys to something with a combination lock.

Our limbs argued. I tried to take her to the bed, but she seemed rooted to the floor. I left her in the light of the window and sat at the foot of the bed. She wasn't going to make me someone I wasn't. Even off balance, I knew where the line was.

"If there isn't a part of you that wants me, then you should get dressed," I said.

She didn't get dressed. Instead, she came toward me, disappearing and reappearing through the shafts of light in the room, lowering herself onto me, closing her arms and legs around me. We faced each other like adversaries; rival spies working intently to diffuse a bomb, or to repair the machine that would save us both.

# Fourteen

She lay with her back to me, the sheets pulled under her chin. No longer back-lit, she became more than a silhouette. I was now certain she had a head, a shoulder, and at least one arm.

"Who do you think killed Adrienne?" I asked. I felt she had been formulating something to say as we lay there, and I didn't want to give her all night, lest she invent something short of the truth.

"You're here with me and you're asking about her," she said petulantly.

She sounded like Catherine. I wasted no time reneging on our unspoken deal. She'd given me something she believed I wanted more than answers. I wanted her, but I wanted the story, too. I didn't know which I wanted more; I had simply taken the first one offered.

"Anybody threaten you?" I asked.

"What do you think?"

It was a stupid question. The business of blackmail is a threat, a threat of exposure, of embarrassment and ruin. It wasn't hard to imagine the prospect being met with threats in return, even from those who paid. That's what I would have done. I would have paid. Let you think you had me. Then I'd find you.

Some threats had to be more credible than others. Clearly, Dile was no threat. Green Sweater, despite an angry pointed finger, was just a Joe from the burbs. Were they all boneless men like Dile, or had the girls found a tough customer?

"How did you and Adrienne meet?"

"University," she answered.

"School of Business?"

"Ha ha," she said laconically. Then, "Dance."

I thought of the figurines in Adrienne's apartment, and easily pictured the woman in my arms with an unhappy topknot. She didn't, however, have a dancer's body. She lacked the muscled legs, and exaggerated sway back of a ballerina. There was a chance she hadn't meant ballet, but it was Paris, and I doubted the Lindy Hop was offered at the University level.

"Whose idea was it?"

"Adrienne's. Of course," she offered too easily.

I asked how Adrienne picked the marks, but she said she didn't know. The mattress was old, and the springs of the bed-frame translated her every fidget. She held my hand between hers, one below my wrist, the other coiled around my extended forefinger. I could feel the wet of her mouth on the tip of the finger she could decide to snap off if the need presented itself.

"I didn't do the things she did, you know," her terse staccato, stamped the words out one at a time like license plates.

I wasn't sure I believed her, but with my arms wrapped around her, I didn't care. We were talking like normal people; if we kept talking she was bound to say something that was true. There would be time later to sift through it all, and pan for what was real. I pressed my lips against the blade of her shoulder. "Why do you do it?"

"What do you mean, why?" she said. "Money."

"There are plenty of ways to make money."

"Like making boats?" she goaded.

"I don't make boats, I rent boats," I told her. "And teach people to sail them."

The idea of building boats, even dinghies made what I did seem small. Shipbuilding had to be in your blood, handed down like a birthright. I didn't know what was in my blood. Find somebody named Cooper, Mason, Miller or Smith, ask them what's in their blood.

"Well, I don't know how to do that," she said dismissively.

*I didn't have a choice, it's all I know*, I thought.

"Did your father teach you to sail?" she asked.

Every bone in my body told me to say '*Yes.*' '*Yes,*' was what people expected. The truth was an opening, a door you allowed some in, a wound you kept covered. "No," I answered.

She continued like she hadn't heard me. "I can picture you as a little boy, out on the water with your parents, wind in your face, thinking it was just the best thing in the world."

"Yeah, that would be," I managed.

"I didn't know my parents," she said. She turned in my arms and spoke warm words into the hollow of my chest. "I was raised by a woman I called my grandmother, but I know she wasn't."

"Did she tell you she wasn't?" I asked.

"No. I just knew."

I waited for her to say more, but she didn't. I didn't have the guts to ask the next question. *Are your parents alive? Why did they leave you with that woman?* All the questions I'd been asked a hundred times. Some detective.

"She taught me to dance."

I felt I knew where she had invented the lie, and her doubling down on it made me angry.

The two middle fingers of her right hand walked purposefully down my arm, a tiny ballerina holding up a tutu. The figure came to an abrupt halt, and performed a little bow, one slender finger elegantly extending behind the other. She parroted a perfect pirouette, and couple of leaps, and nestled the small, loose fist on my shoulder like a swan.

The puppet show made me want to believe the dancer business. What did I know about ballerinas anyway? "Where was that?" I asked. "Where you lived with that woman?"

I could see enough of her face to watch her eyes darting, searching. She knew she couldn't pass herself off as French, that ruse hadn't survived our first encounter. The fact that she had to consider it meant the explanation she'd trained herself to offer wasn't going to hold water with me, and she knew it.

"Color-ado," she half-stammered.

That figured. If not Colorado exactly, the lack of a regional accent like my own meant she'd grown up somewhere west of Tornado alley.

"When I was in school, a friend's mother told me our name was French," She said. "It started kind of a fascination, I guess. Like Paris was someplace that had been taken from me." She laughed to herself and closed her eyes. "It's silly. My parents may never have traveled farther than the next town over. I'd never know."

My soulmate.

I knew Fairfax wasn't my parents' name, rather the city they were from. The nuns wove kernels of truth into the names they bestowed on those of us who were left nameless to try and root us to something. I went there once when I was eighteen. Didn't know where to start looking, and walked around aimlessly, thinking someone might recognize me. *"Aren't you so-and-so's boy? Spitting image."* Nothing like that happened. I ate a sandwich, applied for a job in a factory, and took the evening bus home to Boston.

"I feel like Paris is the only city in the world," she said.

Her gray eyes looked misty and fell from my eyes to my mouth. I took the hint and kissed her. She kissed me back, reaching with her arms to pull me over top of her.

She began laughing, begging me to stop. I've been told I like kissing too much and too fast, and it's probably true. She was smiling, it was hardly torture.

"You gotta stop doing what you're doing," I said. I wasn't trying to ruin the mood, I just couldn't get it out of my head.

"Don't you like what I'm doing?" she teased.

"You know what I mean. It's not right."

"If I get caught, I get caught. Then I sit out for a while. Those are the rules, everyone knows them. But, they're not going to catch me."

"I caught you," I said.

I must have said something adorable, because she playfully dabbed at the tip of my nose.

"I'm not talking about it being illegal." What she said about 'sitting out' made me wonder if she'd spent time inside. "Don't you think what you're doing is wrong?"

She looked at me sideways, like she knew the words, but had never heard them in that combination.

"It's not the same as stealing." Her fingers were walking again, this time over my chest. No dancing, just out for a stroll. "I trade in a very exclusive commodity," she explained. "My confidence. I offer it to those who desire it, and it is every bit as tangible as a meal, tickets to a show," her eyes danced across my face, "or an insurance policy."

"It would have to be a pretty bad meal to wanna kill the cook." She couldn't believe what she was saying. But, this bizarre rationale wasn't for my benefit. She was entertaining herself and looked pleased doing it.

"Why don't you stay here for few days. If I'm out there shaking the tree, people are gonna start falling out of it. It's no good to have you on the street."

"I can take care of myself." She hadn't considered my advice for a second.

"Are you listening? There are people out there looking for you," I said.

"They're looking for Adrienne," she said, turning her back to me again, and pulling my arm over her like it was part of the sheets, "not me."

"Adrienne's dead, and you're still collecting. How long do you think that's going to last?"

She turned sharply and looked over her shoulder at me. "How do you know that?"

"I saw you," I said. "The night at the restaurant. The stiff with the sweater and the glasses, he handed you an envelope just like I did."

Her eyes were angry and incredulous. She pushed my arm away. "What do you think you're doing?"

"At the time, I was eating a steak," I said.

"Were you following me?"

"Ha," I laughed. "I'd have to know where to find you to follow you."

"It won't bring her back, you know," she said, "finding who did it."

I said something naive about justice and holding people accountable. The bed-springs complained again as she shrank away from me. I edged closer, held her tighter, waiting for another thaw. It took longer this time.

"I guess they had it coming," I conceded. "What they were doing, these guys were no angels."

Her body coiled tighter. She bit down on my finger, not so hard that it hurt, but testing how far she could go before it did. "You underestimate the meanness in women."

We lay in the moon-lit room, listening to the street outside. Even at this hour there were murmurs, laughter, and stray shouts. I heard the distinct crash of a bottle of beer or champagne against the sidewalk, the whoosh of its contents, the dissolved crackle of carbonation, and the instant lamentations.

Her hair on the pillow was darker than the night sky. The moon shown its reflected light on her bare shoulder, giving her olive skin a pale-green, third-hand glow. Nothing was hers. The scheme had been Adrienne's, as well as the marks. Now Adrienne was gone, leaving her to reel in lines and hooks already cast. Who knew how many more there were? Maybe it would stop after she'd collected them all.

"There is a woman," she said suddenly. "Adrienne met with her a couple of times. I think she was warning Adrienne to stop."

"Why do you think that?"

"Adrienne never looked happy when they met," she explained. "She's an awful woman. Tacky and vulgar."

She said the woman's name was Marguerite, though it was something of a stage name. She was a local celebrity, an actress/singer/dancer, and a mainstay on smaller stages. She told me the places where Adrienne had met with her and gave me an editorialized physical description. I was looking for a middle-aged harlot, somewhere between the drag Queen of Spain, and a Pagliacci rodeo clown. Ethel Mirman in fishnets.

I asked if she knew anything more about her, what she could be involved in, who she might be connected to, but she said she didn't know. I told her I would track down Marguerite in the morning and find out what there was to find out. If this woman was involved in Adrienne's death, it would be like walking into a lion's den to ask if she'd had enough to eat.

She turned over to look at me. She touched the fading blue swallow stippled on my chest like she was noticing for the first time that I was more than a big mouth and a pair of grabby mitts. The bird meant I'd logged five thousand nautical miles. By the time I'd earned a second one, I'd stopped caring. I never looked at my ink anymore. I wasn't proud, nor ashamed; I just wasn't that guy anymore. She looked up at my face like I was someone she recognized. It has been a long time since a woman looked at me that way, the way I'd always wanted someone to look at me.

She closed her eyes and I studied her face. Her jaw deviated to the right just enough to make the two sides of her face look like different people. The right side was long and thin, and made her look solemn, even plain. The deviation gave her left a rounder cheek and a steep curve to her small chin. The effect was impish, younger and mischievous.

I didn't want to let her out of my sight. What were the odds of whole thing blowing over if we just waited it out under the covers?

Who was this woman who lay inches from me? Maybe she was right, and we didn't need names. In this room, I was the man and she was the woman, like it was in the garden of Eden. Only when there were three of you, did you need a name. Even then, if two of you were talking, you could just say, "the other guy." Maybe having names required a foursome.

At my confirmation, I asked Father McConnell, how a man on a desert island could be a good person, with no one to tell him about God, and no one around to be good to. His answer was an unsatisfying catch-all. It only made sense that being good required other people. So did being bad. And as soon as you had other people, you needed names. You needed a name to be able to say, "*this is mine*" and "*I did that*," and so that others could say "*what have you done, Mickey?*"

Other people meant someone was watching. Like God. The nuns were always worried about those of us who couldn't remember our parents, afraid we would equate that with there being no God. There always had to be someone watching who would care. If even God wasn't watching you, what would you be capable of? If these two young women, whom no one seemed to know, felt they had found themselves on islands of their own making, what were they capable of?

"Lynae," she said softly without opening her eyes. "My name is Lynae Cuvier."

# Fifteen

I awoke with a violent start. The room was still pitch black. I had dropped off for less than an hour, but she was long gone. What a dumb slab of chump steak I was. She'd loved me up, waited for me to nod off, and strolled out the door. I hadn't deemed it necessary to tie her to the nightstand, but I could have kept my eyes open. It would have served me right to wake up on the floor in an empty room. As it was, my wallet was still in my pants, and my duffle in the closet. Typical. Embarrassing. There are a lot of words for it, and I was all of them.

I had her in my room, in my arms, and yet, I was back to zero. I could forget finding her on the crowded streets of Paris again; especially now that she knew I was out there. There were women who had wanted to get away from me before, but this was starting to hurt my feelings. It wasn't a total loss; besides the more tangible spoils of the night, I'd gotten my next lead, and she'd told me her name. Lynae. I wasn't gonna scribble it on all my notebooks, but I repeated it aloud more than once.

I stumbled down the stairs, to the lobby. Good ole Jerome was behind the desk, asleep at the switch. We were a sorry lot. I woke him gently, not wanting him to fall out of the chair he'd leaned against the wall. He rubbed the sleep from his face and took a quick inventory of his desk. He hadn't seen Lynae leave either, but we gathered she'd taken the newspaper he'd folded to the crossword, the coffee he'd ordered from the cafe across the street, and the change from the coffee the delivery boy had left on the counter. Rolling the desk clerk instead of me was practically a love letter.

Jerome and I stood outside and smoked until the sky was light. He knew the places where Lynae had seen Marguerite and scratched out a few directions. I replaced his pinched Americano, and scored the first croissants of the day, which were hotter than the coffee. He was surprised I'd struck out with Babby. I asked if he knew anyone else with a line to the city's underbelly, he said he didn't. Babby had been the extent of his illicit network of hotel boys.

I went back to my room. Her ghost was still in the sheets, and there was a grin on my face that wouldn't wash off in the sink. Despite the coffee, I went back to sleep for several hours until the metallic clangor of the phone finally tore me from my reverie.

"Mickey, its Catherine."

That voice. The casual air she'd assumed wasn't lost on me. It was as if she'd only rang to let me know I'd left my umbrella.

"Mickey, I wanted to apologize for my poor showing the other day. I'm afraid I embarrassed myself, and I feel I was quite rude to you in doing so. I also couldn't have been very helpful with what I told you about Adrienne, and I do wish to help you."

I agreed to meet her for lunch. I insisted on someplace other than *Maison Savard*, I thought a change of venue would be good for us both. She agreed and asked where; I inquired if *La Coupole* had good *Meuniere*. She laughed and said it was a date. I tried not to read into her choice of words.

In the middle of *La Coupole* were ten tables arranged in a semi-circle around a large bronze sculpture. The sculpture was of two androgenous figures; one on the bottom frozen in a tortuous-looking back bend, head, arms, and legs raised toward the sky as if freshly crushed under some celestial wheel; supporting another figure, his mirror image, performing the same amazing back bend. The two were joined at the tops of their heads, and the tips of their heels, forming a complete circle. Hopefully Catherine and I would not have to be as dexterous to benefit one another.

Catherine had arrived first, as I thought she might. I imagine she'd made a habit of presenting herself and sparing her guest the imposition of watching waiters futz about where she would be most out of the way, the shameful dragging away of superfluous chairs, and the insincere apologies made to other diners for the inconvenience.

She sat alone, looking as put together as before, in a pair of camel-colored trousers, and a black silk dress shirt, with a large white collar and cuffs. The drink in front of her looked like coffee, and the smile she met me with was neither one of a starlet giving an interview, nor a socialite on a tour of homes.

"I ordered you coffee," was how she said hello. "Mickey, I want to thank you-"

"And you did," I cut her off, "on the phone, and it wasn't necessary then either."

She smiled, and her eyes looked soft, like they had during our better moments in the roadster.

"I scoped this place out earlier in the week," I said.

"And what did you think?" she asked.

"I thought it had nice windows."

She laughed a genuine, beautiful woman's laugh.

"Your daughter's apartment is just down the block from here." I slid her a piece of hotel stationary with the address.

She held it in both hands, stunned, as if the paper itself had belonged to the girl. "The police told us they found it; was that you?"

I nodded. I didn't mind taking some undue credit; Ilsa had kept Adrienne's confidence, and I meant to keep Ilsa's.

My coffee arrived, Catherine smiled and thanked the waitress. Her hands were unsteady, and her cup rattled against the saucer as she picked it up.

"It does hurt that she didn't want Antoine or I to know where she was living. We would have let her be, even if we had known. Maybe that's why she didn't bother." She turned the scribbled address over in her hands, then flicked a finger against it. "Fifth floor apartment?"

"No elevator," I added.

Catherine touched the wheels of her chair and drew her face into a bitter knot. "That's a bit of a *Fuck You* to Mommy Dearest, isn't it?" Her raised eyebrow let me know it was okay to laugh, and I did. It was good to see her in control of her bad feelings, with a firm grip on her sense of humor.

"Please don't think I'm being melodramatic, but it really is my fault the way Adrienne turned out. I've wasted years feeling sorry for myself because of my accident. I missed my daughter's whole life, not to mention twenty years of my own," she stretched the word *years*, until it had three syllables, to illustrate. "I just felt I had lost so much, so much of who I was. I can't pretend I could have been a perfect mother to Adrienne, but you're supposed to do the best you can for your child. If I'd found a way to be a happier woman, that would have been the best I could have done for her."

"I hate to break it to you, but you're not responsible for the person who killed her."

"That's why I wanted to speak with you again, Mickey. I'm not so sure."

Catherine scanned the restaurant, then leaned toward me. "My husband," she said in a hushed voice, "has not spoken since we learned of Adrienne's death. Not to me, not to Ilsa. He walks around the house as if neither of us are there."

I reminded her people grieved in different ways.

She sat up straight in her chair and wiped the lipstick from the rim of her coffee cup with her thumb. "Do you think he could have had something to do with it?"

Before I could answer, she continued, "I don't mean I think he did it. I just feel like he knows something he's not telling me. Me or the Police."

"If your husband were being blackmailed," I asked, "do you think he would tell you?"

She turned it over and over in her head. Her mouth popped open a few times during her deliberation, but she gave no answer.

"Are you aware of all of your husband's business dealings?"

"I'm aware of the ventures that we own and operate," she stressed the word *we*.

"Would any of those ventures bring him up against an unsavory element?" She gave me a look and allowed me to re-phrase. "Are they all legal?"

"Mickey," she laughed dismissively, "he's not a gangster."

"He does run with some pretty tough customers. He employs men who aren't the type that can hide what they are." I told her how I had been to the *Chanceux*, about Rico Mindy and what I knew about him, and how I'd wound up on my back in the alley.

She seemed to take notice of my eye for the first time and started to reach a hand to my face. I stopped her. What instinct was it in women to probe every wound?

"I'm sorry about your eye."

"And my ribs, and my spleen," I said. "I don't think I was supposed to leave that alley with my faculties, after no more provocation than the mention of Adrienne's name."

She fell back into her chair, her eyes cast down, but searching.

"Do you have any business interests on Cite Pigalle?

She gave a little start and shook her head. "No. We don't. Why?"

I let her have it. "I have good reason to believe your daughter was following men home from a place on Cite Pigalle."

Catherine looked horrified. "What do you mean following? Why would she do that?"

"I haven't figured that out yet," I lied. "But, I do think it had something to do with her death. Is it possible your husband and Adrienne were involved in something that wasn't on the up and up?"

"Is it my daughter or my husband that you suspect of being a criminal?" she said incredulously. "You're worse than the police."

I asked her what the police wanted to know. She said they asked Mr. Savard repeatedly if he'd received any threats, and if Adrienne's death could have been retaliation.

"*Retaliation*, they said. Retaliation for what?" Her eyes welled, and she busied herself drying them. It was the first show of emotion that I could contribute to the loss of her daughter. I asked her what Mr. Savard told the Police.

"Nothing. He didn't say a word to the police." She let her hands fall heavily on the table. "I know what you're thinking, Mr. Fairfax."

"Mickey," I said.

She smiled through tears. "My husband is not a criminal," she attested. "And neither was my daughter."

"What if I knew for a fact, that one of them was?"

Mercifully our lunch arrived before she could tell me to take a flying leap. Instead, she glowered at me over salmon pate. The extra lemon I had requested for my sole was cut in half and tied in two separate cloth sacks. I was getting the feeling I could find myself in a similar situation with Antoine Savard, should I have the pleasure.

"Do you know an actress, calls herself Marguerite?" I offered as an olive branch.

"Oh, are you going to see the show?" she replied.

I asked what show. Catherine said that Marguerite was the lead in a production of *Medea*, being performed in the *theatre space*, as she called it, that she and Antoine owned. I said I didn't have a ticket.

"It's actually sold out," she said with some surprise, but she had tickets in reserve and would leave one for me at will-call. She asked me if I knew the story. I held up my hands, and she remembered her company. "Medea's husband leaves her for a princess," she explained gleefully, "to get back at him, she kills the princess, then her own children."

"That would do it," I said. "I'm sure her husband takes it in stride. Does he tear his eyes out with his bare hands?" What I knew of Greek tragedies, people were always disfiguring themselves. Doubling-down on their grief.

I asked Catherine why she was surprised the play was sold out. She admitted they'd had a couple flops in a row, but they'd secured a new director, a young man who was putting on the kinds of performances people wanted to see.

"Can't go wrong with sex and violence," I added needlessly.

"Ugh, don't remind me," she said with a hand over her mouth still full of pate. She smiled and shrugged impishly at her impropriety. "She's twice his age, but I'm sure they're sleeping together."

"The director and Marguerite?" I asked.

"That old trollop is a survivor, I will say that for her. There is a saying in the theater about knowing when to exit. I don't think she's heard it."

"I take it she's been around a long time." I said. "She ever perform in your theater before?"

"Are you kidding," Catherine exclaimed. "She only plays our theater, I don't think anyone else would have her. She's a hack and a scandal." Catherine took a long drink of water, washing the taste of Marguerite from her mouth. "She is voluptuous, in a vulgar sort of way," she said in the way of explanation. "And that still sells seats in old Paris."

"Did Marguerite and Adrienne know each other?" I asked as nonchalantly as possible, keeping my eyes on my fish.

"No. Why should they?" she replied.

"I just imagined, since you owned the place," Another lie. It was getting easier. "How did your daughter support herself? Did she have a job?"

A grin developed across Catherine's face at the same rate as one arched eyebrow scaled her forehead. "Adrienne had no interest in starting at the bottom. She shared the naïve perspective, common to her generation, that having a superior was beneath one's dignity." Catherine said she wasn't sure, but she thought her husband had been giving Adrienne an allowance since she'd moved out.

The waitress brought our check and handed it to Catherine without hesitation.

"You said you didn't know any of Adrienne's friends, but did she ever mention an American girl named Lynae? I described Lynae with great restraint, in the least amorous terms I could muster.

Catherine smirked and stifled a guffaw. "Oh my, you really haven't gotten a picture of her at all. My daughter was an unrepentant snob, Mickey. She belonged to that class I spoke of, with no regard for anyone who, in her words, did not "belong to Paris." And, beautiful girl that she was, she possessed an unequivocally wounding glare, and the suggestion that she'd befriended an American would have gotten you the mother of them all."

# Sixteen

The Savards were majority owners of *La Comedie Montreal*, in the Tuileries. It was a small theater, but a prestigious location along the *Avenue De L'Opera*. Its original name was *La Comedie Marseilles*, made *the Montreal* by the imported Mrs. Savard, to the chagrin of those who "belonged to Paris." Catherine said the locals still referred to it as the Marseilles, and if asked directions to the Montreal, would feign ignorance.

The building was three stories of brick and windows that a plaque on the wall declared was in the Belle Epoch style. I'd have to take its word for that. It looked old and important in the way you want a building to look old and important. There was a foot of black grime at the base of the foundation that did not appear to be afflicting the neighbors on either side. Hopefully this production would be a success, and the Savard's could spring for a little elbow grease.

I collected my ticket from the young woman at the will-call window and she let me in to look around. She unlocked heavy brass double doors with etched glass inserts. The doors from the lobby to the theater were the same. The lobby floor was a green floral mosaic, and the ceiling, painted like the heavens. It gave you the weird feeling you were still outside, and with all the brass around, I worried about lightning.

The theater sat a couple hundred on the floor, with a second-story balcony on three sides. A great wooden arch held the curtain over the stage. It was painted dark bronze, and the curtain was not the typical red of other theaters, but a coral color, same as the curtains that lined the walls. It was a conscious choice, and the fabric new, but it gave the impression of having faded over time. The fixtures were brass as well and cast a tawny, filtered glow over the hall. It was light from a different time, a light that had left its source a century ago and was only now reaching the stage.

After my inspection of the Montreal, I decided to try my luck at one of the places Marguerite had met with Adrienne. The first was across the Seine in the St. Georges de Pres region, or what the stylish referred to simply as the *left bank*. The pulse of this neighborhood beat faster than the Tuileries, or anywhere else. There were more cars on the streets, more people in the café's, and the Parisians on the sidewalks moved with the haste and precision of New Yorkers. This was the neighborhood of the young and upwardly mobile, and I didn't like my chances of running into an aging stage performer.

*Les Deux Magots*, a name that wouldn't fly in the States, was written in glowing noble gases on the corner of a four-story apartment building, trimmed with ornate wrought iron, and balconies buttressed by stone corbels like the inside of a grand piano. A wide green awning wrapped the corner of the building and matching green umbrellas at each table made the guest's Ray-Bans unnecessary. Patrons were meshed together like gears and balanced stacks of gleaming white plates on precariously small tables. Every seat outside the café was spoken for, and every pair of eyes pointed at the street like a drive-in movie.

I sidled up to a young waiter at a server's station wishing his pen could do math. I folded a couple bills between my fingers and asked the kid if he knew the actress Marguerite. By the look on his face he knew exactly who I meant, and it gave our exchange the feeling of buying condoms at a supermarket. He happily took the bills and stuffed them into his shirt pocket. He said that *Madame* Marguerite was a regular for lunch, but that he hadn't seen her in several weeks.

"Has she died?" he posited.

"I have it on authority she's alive." I said. "Why do you say that?"

"She's old," he reasoned.

"You ever see her here with an American girl, young, your age?"

He hesitated. "Who wants to know?"

"Charles DeGaul," I said and handed him another bill.

He said he didn't remember an American girl and felt sure he would have. I said I'd like to have a look inside. He muttered something in French I interpreted as "knock yourself out."

The inside of the restaurant was a so sparsely populated, I wondered if the diners on the street knew it existed. Here, the cane chairs and frisbee-sized tables had been replaced with upholstered booths, and heavy wooden islands sealed with half an inch of shiny lacquer. The worst seats in the house belonged to the namesake *Magots*, two life-size statues of Chinese merchants in conical rice hats, with all the cultural sensitivity of a cigar-store Indian, affixed on a column in the center of the restaurant. By the insipid looks on their shiny bronze faces, they had both sent back the soup.

It was a slightly older set dining inside, but no one to be taken for the bawdy queen of the Paris stage. I got a coffee to go from the *brasserie* and retied my shoes for an encore of my walk across the Seine. The second meeting spot was beyond the Tuileries, in the Opera quarter at *Café de la Paix*. On route, I passed an opera house, a couple of theaters, and felt like I was on the right track.

I saw the marquee for *Café de la Paix* from a block away. There was no neon sign like *Deux Magots*, only dignified script letters on the painted marquee, over a curved glass awning that ran the length of the rather wide storefront. There were umbrellas here, as well, but too few to cover the nearly empty café tables. Nearly empty, save for one woman, undoubtedly the one I was looking for.

Marguerite sat angled on her hip, with ankles crossed, next to a small table, facing the street as if addressing a crowd. Her head was surrounded by a swirling cosmos of black bouffant, twice as wide as it was tall. Dark tortoise-shell glasses shielded her eyes from the smoke of a cigarette, in a long ebony holder, held next to her temple. The nicotine stains on her fingers told me the holder was a more recent affectation. Her full figure filled a sleeveless black jumpsuit, while a wide red belt pinched her in two. Her free hand fingered the fraying edge of a leopard print scarf tied in a knot around her neck. She had mastered the French pastime of looking simultaneously bored and preoccupied.

"*Madame* Marguerite?" I said as I approached.

"*Bonjour*," she returned without the slightest disturbance of her repose.

"I was hoping to have a word."

She had yet to look at me or move a muscle. The brush off in Paris looked a lot like it did in the States.

"Writer?" she croaked. "Critic?" Her words were miasmas escaping one at a time, disguised as thin wisps of smoke.

"No ma'am, I'm not a writer," I said, "and I've never seen a play."

She stirred for the first time to crush her cigarette in the ashtray and regard me from the ground up. The act of uncrossing her legs brought her body upright. She found nothing interesting about my shoes nor my belt, but nearly knocked my coffee into the street snatching my forearm from my side. Her skin was soft, but her grip strong. The hardness of a previous life lay beneath what could be buffed smooth or macerated by paraffin.

"A sailor," she exclaimed. Her voice was husky, and her accent thick. "Tell me you are a sailor."

I nodded. The day had been the warmest since I'd arrived in Paris. I'd left both my pea coat and Hamburg in the room, but Marguerite had spotted the tattoo on my left forearm. From her reaction, I felt sure she knew her way around a deckhand.

"Sit, sailor." she instructed. "Do not make me look like I am alone." She had been alone. "I should be seen with a mysterious younger man."

"Is someone watching us?" I asked.

"Always," she insisted. "They do not hound me as they used to, but I remain in the public eye."

"I have a ticket for the show tonight." Flattery seemed a promising tact with an actress.

"*Tres bon.* I am used to performing for sailors, but this is not a cabaret, *monsieur. C'est le theatre!* I cannot have you breaking chairs or smashing each other with bottles," she chided playfully.

I pictured Marguerite singing on top of an upright piano, in a sub-street bar in the Marais, or Montmartre, with a pack of sea-dogs making banquet-eyes at her.

"Why would anyone break a perfectly good chair?" I played along.

She smiled and touched my knee. "You've given it up, the life of the ruffian?"

I said I wasn't sure I'd ever lived it.

"I have always like sailors. They are an appreciative audience. All men should be lonely, as the sailor is lonely. The sailor's passion," she moved her fingers lightly over the skin of her arm, "is right there, on the surface."

"If it's on the surface, I'm not sure it's passion," I argued. "Passion comes from in here," I tapped my fingers against my chest. "And, I suppose we're as appreciative as any caged animal let loose on land. Though it fails to make better men of most."

She slid her glasses down on her nose and eyed me with orbs dark and exotic as oiled teak. "You did not spend the time in your cage baying at the moon like the others. Your time alone made you," she searched for the word, "*Contemplatif.*"

She took another cigarette from a slim gold case and waved off the offer of my lighter. She produced her own, gold as the case with an unruly flame three inches high. It danced about in the breeze, until the magus commanded it up the shaft of the cigarette, bending the flame in the air.

"You will escort me to the theater. We may continue our interview while I prepare." She disappeared with her purse into the restaurant.

I followed her as far as the door. The inside of the *Café de la Paix* was opulent. Every wall was covered in millwork and molding, as was the ceiling. Heavy iron fixtures held large milk-glass spheres of light like celestial planets over long formally set tables. The waiters, a gang of rogue concert pianists, wore waistcoats and bow ties and looked as if they hadn't eaten. They alerted like deer when the door to the restaurant opened. Marguerite showed herself to the powder room, and I returned to my seat.

A few minutes later one of the waiters placed on the table in front of me a small tray with the bill. I looked around and saw no other diners.

"You must be mistaken *Garcon*, I didn't order anything," I said.

"It is *Madame's* bill," he returned.

Veal sausages with onions, cheese, and several drinks.

"*Madame* just stepped inside." I said.

He rose up on his toes and cleared his throat. "*Qui, Monsieur. Madame is* inside," he confirmed.

I leaned my chair back to peer around him. I could see Marguerite through the window take a quick step to obscure herself a little more completely behind a column. I paid the check and the departing waiter held the door for my returning companion.

Marguerite put her arm through mine as we walked back to the Montreal in comfortable silence. As the star of the production she had her own dressing room which looked much lived in. There was the requisite dressing table whose mirror was outlined in yellowing bulbs, an ornate oriental screen for changing, and a couch for well-wishers, sycophants, and naps. The room smelled of food and cigarettes. Ventilation was limited to a window, fit for a pigeon, near the ceiling that had to be opened using a hook on a broom-handle.

"How many plays have you performed in this theater?" I asked, beginning my inquest.

"*Vingt-cinq*," she said counting. "Twenty-five."

"Do you know the Savards well?"

She had taken her place at the dressing table and looked pointedly at me in the mirror. "Do *you* know the Savards well?"

I explained that Catherine had given me the ticket.

She made a little noise in the back of her throat and returned to her lip-liner. "And Antoine?"

"I haven't had the pleasure."

"He gave me that screen." She nodded toward the dressing screen, three hand-painted scenes on gilt foil panels, framed in red mahogany. "He would sit right where you're sitting now. He liked to watch me get into costume."

"Did Catherine know?"

"What is there to know?"

"About you and her husband?"

"I'm sure she did. It was hardly a secret," she said with some resignation.

Marguerite was being candid. I felt she brought up Antoine before I did, not out of cheek, but because she knew I was headed there from the first mention of Catherine's name.

"What about the daughter?" I asked.

"What about her?"

"I dunno, her parents own the joint. She ever come around?"

"Only when she wanted money. Like any good French father, Antoine indulged her."

"Did you ever talk to Adrienne?"

She put down her eyebrow pencil and picked up another. "You must know that I have."

She had finished her eyes. They were thickly lined, with glittering gray lids. It was makeup meant for the stage, and from any other distance seemed garish. Turning sideways in the chair, she exaggerated the erectness of her posture, straightening her legs in front of her, and pointing her toes, an exercise to vouch for the litheness left in her sturdy limbs.

"She asked me about the affair. By then it was long over, and I told her so."

"And was it?" I asked.

She squared her shoulders to me. "Of course."

Marguerite kicked her legs in the air, then crossed them and looked at me like I was a duck dinner. I wondered if she ever turned it off, or if every man was a potential customer, every set of eyes belonged to an audience member, and everything under her feet was a stage. I felt she was being straight with me about her conversations with Adrienne. I didn't know what else she could tell me.

"Would you like to see my costume for the show?"

"I like a good sneak peek as much as the next guy."

My interest wasn't totally feigned. The prospect of the play didn't thrill me, but Marguerite was a show. She rose from the chair with a flourish and scurried behind the screen like a chorus girl exiting the stage.

"Do you know anything about Antoine's other businesses?" I raised my voice to call over the thin screen.

"I've made some changes," Marguerite announced without hearing my question. "The director doesn't know. He's going to love it."

I repeated my query and got the same response. It was showtime, and audience prattle was something the veteran actress was adept at tuning out.

Marguerite emerged from behind the screen one limb at a time; first a shapely leg, then an arm, the rest followed in long, deliberate, choreographed movements. She looked to the distance, waded through a jungle, was pulled violently in one direction then another. Her interpretive dance ended at my feet. The mystical journey had apparently been through the birth canal, because she stood in front of me as naked as the day she was born.

"What do you think?" she asked.

"My compliments to your tailor." I tried in vain to get hold of my eyelids.

Marguerite was handsomely built, though her more outrageous proportions had been the product of her undergarments. Weight had settled in her breasts and buttocks, and the curves of her hourglass figure had been blunted; but her bosom was ample, her legs firm and muscled, and her stomach hollow. It was a mature body, but statuesque. There was a lot to see, and I could understand the men of Paris lining up for a glimpse.

"And you're doing the whole play wearing this?"

"The whole play," she purred.

"You're going to sell a million tickets."

Marguerite straddled my legs. Her skin was hot and dewy with perspiration. Behind powder and *parfum*, were veal and onions; wine was heavy on her breath. She pulled my arms around her waist, and I sank my hands into her bare flanks. She pushed my rolled-up shirt sleeves over my elbows and inspected the tattoos on my forearms. She studied the shell-back turtle that signified I'd crossed the equator, then the anchor and serpent, that meant the Atlantic. The moto, *Hold Fast*, was printed on a banner around the anchor, and I watched her silently mouth the words.

"Was your relationship with Antoine over when it was over?"

"You are too curious." She kissed me like she was trying to extract a tooth.

Her fingers ran through my hair, then over my neck and shoulders. I don't know what it said about me that women thought I could be derailed in this way. I kept my eyes on hers, waiting for my answer; my hands were working hard enough.

"I sent some girls to work for Antoine, at a private club he'd started. Girls who had nothing for the stage. Pretty things, but shallow and common as plates. That was years ago."

Marguerite raised up on her knees and pressed her hips hard against my chest, the tip of my nose found its way into her navel for a second. She tugged on the back of my hair until I was staring at the ceiling. Hanging can-lights that lit the room shown behind her, lending her dark head a corona as she peered at me through the valley of her breasts.

"Do you know where this club is? What do you know about his partners, tough boys, a con named Rico Mindy?" I couldn't stop myself.

Marguerite sat back down on my knees. Her bust-first pinup posture wilted to a comfortable slouch. She covered her breasts with an arm, the other hand still in my hair.

"Your questions are starting to sound like an interrogation, *mon chere*. I have no interest in being interrogated." She patted the side of my face. "I do like you sailor, you're honest. *Quel dommage*."

Marguerite retreated to her dressing table and put her arms through a red silk robe but didn't tie it closed. She was waiting for me to block the rest of our scene.

"Did Adrienne ever tell you she was in trouble?" The question just came to me.

"No. I told you what we talked about. Why would she?"

"Because she's dead." The words were percussive in the small room, like I'd dropped a stack of newspapers. "Did you know that? Couple days ago, strangled and left in an alley."

Marguerite closed the front of the robe and sat at the dressing table. "That poor girl. It is a shame."

"Is it?" I probed.

"Of course, it is," she said without inflection. "It is a shame when any young person dies. When a young person dies, it means they should fear death. And if you fear death, what is the point of being young."

"Antoine's club, is it on Cite Pigalle?"

She said she didn't know, and I believed her. However bawdy and outrageous, Marguerite was a woman, and took the death of the younger woman as

125

a blow. Maybe it stirred some maternal instinct long ago and repeatedly buried. Or maybe the loss of any young person shone a light on the ignominy of a long-lived life, and the passing of days left to atone for time wasted. I felt it, too.

# Seventeen

It wasn't worth going back to my room for the couple hours before the show. There were plenty of places to loiter in Paris, it was and is a city of loiterers. So, when in Rome. After a minute's walk my shoes were crunching over the pulverized stone paths of the *Jardins de Tuileries*. Single trees cordoned off by chiseled white stone bricks were spaced like chess pieces between foot paths, none taller than twelve or fifteen feet, their bottom branches low enough for the park-goers to touch. The garden had probably been there for a hundred years, but looked like it was finished last month, an eternally adolescent forest to remind the public of Paris's eternal youth.

In front of me, the stone figure of a woman stood in a clearing. Her skin, a dark mottle of turquoise and black. Her hair crashed around her head like white caps against a craggy shoreline. She stood with hands held out; as I drew closer I could see they were filled with apples, two in her right hand, offered generously, and the one in her left seemed to promise more where that came from. The statue stood with her hips cocked, like she'd been standing there a long time. She was powerfully built, surviving on more than apples. Her body showed the endurance of orchards that had fed France for centuries.

The statue was of the Goddess Pomona, the symbol of fruit and abundance. She was ample, except where it came to clothing. The statue's likeness to Marguerite was uncanny, as if she'd posed for it, or been born from it. The exception, besides the classically bare runway, was the face. All the detail, the wrinkles and folds of a real body captured so faithfully in the torso and limbs, were absent in the face. If it was meant to be the face of every woman, it wasn't.

The mouth was an expressionless slit, the eyes, holes cut in paper. The featureless visage looked more like a hockey mask than the face of a god. Her soul was in her body, and like Marguerite, was what she offered to Paris.

Thinking of Marguerite made me blush. She was a night at the captain's table, a single seat at a sumptuous feast. You knew you would indulge too heavily, drink too deeply, celebrate too raucously, wake up too late, and grin too guiltily whenever you thought of it. What Catherine offered, by contrast, was the opportunity to flatter her, and be flattered by her. She was the popular girl, your father's boss's daughter. She was rich, cultured, and beautiful. You would change everything about yourself to sit on a couch next to her and nod at her parents. And women like Marguerite made you wonder why the hell you were willing to do any of it. Marguerite was a meal you couldn't finish, Catherine was a portion arranged so artfully on the plate you didn't know it was dinner.

Everywhere I turned, it seemed, women were on the menu. Paris was a city filled with food and art and history, the City of Lights; but under every light stood a woman whose beauty was as much for consumption as any pastry or painting. Painters of Paris's most recent heyday were probably drunks taking their meals in bars. The results were images of Lady Liberty and Mother Earth modeled after whatever barmaid they were in love with that week. When they mastered painting pretty girls, they deconstructed them to circles and triangles, like stick-figure pinups. Maybe a city could suffer from too much art. It became a lens that modern times turned into a pair of dirty x-ray specs bought off the back pages of a magazine.

Anyone can get their hands on a little beauty, if they are willing to pay for it. Cabarets and brothels offer troughs for overfed animals to gorge themselves. But they also fed guys so timid they needed a sure thing, and others so lonely they wanted nothing more than proximity to another beating heart, if only for the hour.

There's nothing wrong with wanting the milk of human kindness to come from a pretty pitcher now and again. But there's a difference between hoping for the cute waitress and paying a woman in chaps to step on your balls. Madison Avenue can unearth a Helen of Troy-a-minute to hock everything from sodas to sedans, making beautiful women seem likewise, consumable. If happiness itself lay on a store-shelf with a price tag, who wouldn't reach for their wallet? I imagine if a man like Dile had lived in a dry county all his life, he may never have taken a drink.

I dug in my pockets for my lighter and found a handful of Adrienne's notes. I called myself a bunch of things, none of them good. If I was trying to find a killer, what was I doing holding a list of suspects in my hand? Why hadn't I given these to Inspector Brun? I knew what they were, they confirmed what I believed, what use were they to me now?

I thought about Adrienne. She was a knockout, long hair, long legs, as seen in men's fantasies for as long as there have been men. Lynae, on the other hand was mousey, next to Adrienne, downright scrawny. She had a kisser, the kind that could launch a thousand ships, but the rough trade Adrienne was in called for a certain kind of physique.

Adrienne was beautiful, but made of tougher stuff, her mother's skin stretched over her father's bones. Catherine had been a ballerina, but Adrienne a jock. What was a girl to do with power and aggression no longer channeled into penalty kicks and horse jumping? I knew Antoine Savard was a hood even if his wife didn't. And Adrienne was shaping up to be a chip off the ole block. Maybe Cite Pigalle was a second apartment, the rocks onto which she lured foolish men, a Point Zero from which she could measure the distance from sin and guilt to a man's front door.

Whatever her role in all this, Lynae was adamant it was different from Adrienne's, and I believed her. When a slow song comes on, you know within four or five steps if your partner can dance. And our night together had proved to me that Lynae Cuvier was no dancer.

# Eighteen

The line outside *La Comodie de Montreal* was very long and very French. I had taken for granted the number of people I'd run into who spoke English. Standing in line, no one spoke to me, and had no reason to speak anything but French. I was having trouble ignoring it, and understanding a stray word here and there only heightened my anxiety. I was at a revival, everyone around me was speaking in tongues, and I wasn't even sure I believed.

My seat was at the far end of the first row, not the seat you wanted in a movie theater, but this wasn't a movie, so what did I know? The playbill was in French, I guess the Montreal didn't think they were vying for the tourist dollar. Seats were filling up, except for the one next to me. A woman down the row, looked at me, then the empty seat, and smiled politely. If I had a date, she'd stood me up.

The Orchestra started up to no one's surprise but my own. I peered over a short parapet into the orchestra pit, and sure enough there was one of every stringed instrument keeping a couple woodwinds company. Behind them, a guy was pressing his ear to the whispering skin of a kettle drum like he was listening for a train. The violist sat facing the rest and doubled as the conductor. Probably got two pay checks.

The program pictured a buxom brunette Medea, tapered like an Academy Award, not an exact likeness of Marguerite but she would have approved. The protagonist seemed to hover above a circle of colorless horrified faces. Medea was wearing a red toga belted by a golden rope, certainly more than Marguerite would be wearing, and was the only figure in color. Again, she would have approved.

The crowd was not what I had expected. I was prepared to be under-dressed, but as it turned out I wasn't. Not one man in top hat and tails, no dowagers in mink or fox, and not a single monocle in the bunch. There were a few men in suits, but they were hopelessly outnumbered. The decorum was not what I expected either. Here, in the birthplace of manners, this crowd had chosen to go on strike. It wasn't a library, but there was a lot of conversation, and even some laughter.

The theater lights dimmed and the kettle drum conjured thunder. The curtain was rushed open as if catching up to the action. Four men crept across a dimly lit stage. I assumed it was Jason leading the charge, he seemed sturdy enough, but the fellas behind him didn't look like much. Discordant horns blew, and streamers of red, yellow, and orange rained down on the men from offstage. Our heroes took refuge behind Jason's shield. They passed a sword to the front of the line, and Jason hurled it high into the air. Again, the horns turned loose a cacophonous blast. The head and neck of a large rubber dragon flopped onto the stage like a gelatin dessert.

Jason stood with hands on his hips as a barren tree was wheeled out before him on a creeper. What was hanging from it looked like a yellow bathmat. I knew this story after all, The Golden Fleece. I'd seen it in an illustrated children's book. That author had left out the part about his wife murdering the kids. I guess they wanted to end the story on a high note. Jason raised the bathmat over his head to a trumpeting of oboes.

The men filed out stage-left as the crew replaced the stalagmites of the dragon's lair with an idyllic hillside, spotted with trees and square white homes. A single spotlight shown on the stage and from behind the wooden arch stepped Marguerite, *in flagrante*, as promised. The stage was dark outside of the spotlight, and only the closest rows could make out her nakedness. As she stepped into the light, the crowd's reaction was a stir of applause, gasps, cat calls, and laughter. I knew the cruel remarks by their tone and caught words like *vache* and *chien*. Marguerite stood under that spot like it was the first rays of the arctic sun and accepted the audience's response as roses laid at her feet.

Her thickly lined eyes, scarlet cheeks, and skin two tones too dark had looked garish up-close, but on stage came into better proportion. Marguerite's impossible physique also came into better proportion. A less curvaceous actress would have looked as anatomically correct as a broomstick. I couldn't look away. Her headdress, her breasts and the dark hair between her legs were all bigger than life, everywhere you looked, there was just more and made the star look somehow extra-naked.

With a raised arm, Marguerite filled the theater with a voice that made my skin come alive and lifted me out of my seat. Everything after the shot seemed to happen in slow motion. It sounded like the felling of a tree, inside a tin can. I watched the dark hole open on her chest from nowhere, and the heavy stage lights lit a cloud of red mist at her back, that lingered in the air even after she collapsed. The crowd's reaction seemed muted; it was as if someone had turned their volume down. Through all of it, I swear I could still hear laughter.

People were out of their seats and rushing for the doors. Others remained, either frozen, or still believing it was part of the show. Several pointed to the fallen Medea, lying on the stage, others to a man in a silver and blue hooded windbreaker, standing in the center aisle, with a gun smoking in his hand.

There was only the length of the front row between us. He turned and looked at me, his face wild with fright. He looked down at the gun in his hand, and I thought he might point it at me. Instead he turned and ran.

I ran after him, passing the frightened front row shielding each other with anything they could, arms, coats, realized mortality and found religion. The shooter crashed into a side door and out into the alley, with me on his heels. He ran out onto the *Avenue de L'Opera* with abandon. I had to sidestep a taxi. He made it across the street and turned up the sidewalk. I crossed in time to see him duck down the next alley. A group of bus boys and dishwashers had tried to hold him up after he'd run through their dice game. A few still stood with their hands in the air as I ran by.

We crossed another street and down another alley. He ran with his shoulders shrugged, like a dribbling midfielder, and he was faster than me. He didn't look back, he knew he was being chased. He knocked over a couple trashcans which slowed him more than it did me. He turned again, up the next street, and forced us both to wade through a sidewalk crowded with dinner-goers. I closed a considerable distant by moving through the crowd in his wake, by the next intersection he was within arm's reach, and I laid out to tackle him.

We went to the ground along with a handful of bystanders. He turned on his side and went for his waistband, I knew he was reaching for the gun. I was laying on his legs and lunged for it. He reached it first, but I had two hands on the barrel. I got to my knees, which let loose his legs. He let go of the gun to shove me hard with both hands.

We both scrambled to our feet, and it was a chase again. People seemed aware of us now and parted like the Red Sea as we raced past. Their faces blurred together into a single fluid look of horror. The shooter ran into the busy street blindly, I heard a car screech and thought it hit him. But he was still on his feet and running, not across the street, but down it, in between the moving cars. I tried to follow, but he was pulling away.

All of Paris was laying on their horns. The street lights and head lamps were disorienting in the darkening night, cars roared around us like monsters, and unintelligible shouts and screams seemed to come from every direction. I couldn't keep up with him through the cars, but there was room to run on the opposite sidewalk.

I could taste blood in my mouth but didn't know from where. My legs wanted to cramp where he had kicked me. My head pounded. My field of vision was narrowing, tunneling. I was nauseous and running out of breath.

He had to have lost sight of me, because he veered to his left, to the side of the street where I had found room to run. He cut right in front of me.

We crashed into each other between an arcade and a newspaper stand. I found myself on top of him. His arms were pinned to his side, and I could feel him trying to pull them free. I constricted them tighter, trying to crush him between my knees. I laced my fingers together, and brought both hands down with all my strength, hammering his face. I felt the resistance of the pavement behind his head. I roared into the hole I wanted to leave in his skull, and expelled the fire burning my lungs onto him. Had I managed to keep hold of his gun, I would have jammed it in his mouth and pulled the trigger as many times as I could. I raised my hands again and brought them down hard as before. I slipped on the bloody mask of his face, and fell forward, arms splayed on the sidewalk.

I struggled to pick myself up, raising my head in time to see the leather sole of a shoe make everything go black and silent.

# Nineteen

"*Inspecteur,*" I heard someone call.

There was a light shining in my eyes, I couldn't see a thing. Whoever put my head in a vice, kept it there too long and cracked it. I'd never felt this badly. I rolled on my side and got sick. I could feel hands on my back, trying to help me, and the rough rounded shoulder of the curb under my palm. I was still on the sidewalk.

"*Obtenir de l'eau.*"

I recognized the voice.

"*Monsieur* Fairfax, can you hear me?"

"Brun," I mustered.

"Yes *Monsieur*, it is me," he spoke softly with deference to my condition, like you'd speak to your mother if she were hung-over.

They sat me up, and someone handed me a cup of water. The first drink tasted faintly of blood, but the second was terrific. I must have been laying there awhile because no one around me was standing, they had all joined me on the ground. There was a penitent paramedic on both knees, and a flat-foot sitting Indian style, like we'd been playing tiddly winks. The ever-dignified Inspector Brun was squatting in three-piece tweeds, not wishing to scuff his cognac colored Oxfords. Next to him, another cop, probably a Sargent, who outranked my playmate.

"He got away," I said. "I chased him, but he got away."

"Tell me what you remember, *Monsieur* Fairfax." Brun said.

"Stop calling me that, and I'll think about it."

"Please, Mickey," he conceded. "You did a foolish thing, chasing a man with a gun. Do you not see how serious?"

"I know it's serious, Marguerite is dead." The words made a bad sound in my ears and left a bad taste in my mouth.

"How do you know she's dead?" he asked perfunctorily.

"Because I saw that kid blow her heart out her back."

Brun murmured in French to the squatting Sargent who was taking notes.

And he was a kid, no more than twenty-two. I described him to the Sargent taking notes, close-cropped black hair, thick black eyebrows, and skin like baked earth, Arabian or Middle Eastern I thought. I said I saw him shoot Marguerite, that I'd chased him to this spot, and hit him hard in the face before someone shoved their foot mine.

"I think it was Rico Mindy that kicked me." I stated for the record. They all seemed to take notice.

"Are you sure?" asked Brun.

It made me sick to say I wasn't. I closed my eyes and tried to remember what I had seen. The still-frame in my mind was a square-toed dress shoe, maybe Italian, with a leather bottom, and a wooden heel. I tried to look around the shoe at the rest of my fuzzy memory.

"He was wearing a crayon-blue suit with white pinstripes," I said.

"*Crayone-Bleu?*" the Sargent questioned.

"Yeah, not blue like a blue suit is blue. Crayon-blue," I repeated futilely. "Blue-blue."

"*Royale?*" the paramedic offered.

We agreed on royal-blue.

I continued to flesh the picture out until I could roll it forward, and play it back, like frames from a movie. It was getting dark, he was back-lit by the street lamp. I saw his foot swing, saw the color of the suit from his jacket sleeve, and heard the short grunt of effort that brought the shoe up against my skull. No, I couldn't be sure it was Rico, and I told Brun.

"You got enough to catch the shooter?" I asked. "There was a whole theater full of eye-witnesses."

The inspector and officers looked at each other for a moment without speaking.

"We recovered the gun which several witnesses stated you wrestled away from the suspect," Brun said, "whom we also recovered. He was found two blocks from here, in a stairwell. With a clothesline wrapped around his neck."

Brun started to tell me his name, but I held up my hand. I didn't want to know his name. Paris had ghettos of its own filled with the young, angry, and disenfranchised; many were immigrants or refugees, desperately poor, and too easily recruited, no different than back home. The kid was dead the second he agreed to pull that trigger; I had only succeeded in making his last moments a little worse.

Bodies were piling up, and Lynae could be next. I needed to tell Brun everything. If I couldn't find Lynae, maybe he could. I leaned back, and the paramedic made a move for me with his latex hands. My playmate caught me in his lap, and held my head, like he was attending my dying words. Everyone relaxed when they saw I was digging in my front pants pocket.

I handed the Inspector Adrienne's crumpled notes. I told him how I had found them in her apartment, and my theory that she had been following men home from somewhere on Cite Pigalle and blackmailing them. I told him I witnessed her accomplice collecting a payment from a man in a restaurant, but left out that I'd stalked, accosted, and questioned him in the dark alley outside his home. I made no mention of Babby in my confession, even though he clearly knew about Cite Pigalle. I don't know what instinct compelled me to stick my neck out for the punk. The other notable omission in my gut-spilling was the name Sam Dile.

It was that moment I realized I hadn't removed Dile's note from the stack,

I never even thought to find it. Dile didn't live in Paris, Adrienne must have followed him back to his hotel. It was too late now. I wouldn't offer him up, but if the notes led the police to his doorstep... Maybe the Atlantic would prove too wide.

Brun was quiet as he waited for the Sargent's scribbling to catch up.

"Her accomplice," Brun asked, "what do you know about her?"

"Her name is Lynae Cuvier," I confessed. The guilt was needles in my belly. But, people were dying, and it was the best way I saw to protect her.

Brun stopped the Sargent from writing on his pad, and I could see the latter exchange a look with the other officer. Brun remained stoic.

"*Monsieur* Fairfax, Lynae Cuvier is not the accomplice's name," Brun said.

"What are you talking about?"

"*Monsieur* Fairfax," Brun mercifully cut in, "the intersection of *Rue Linne* and *Rue Cuvier*," he enunciated, "is a well-known one. It is an entrance to *Des Jardins*, a corner populated at all times with jugglers, clowns, and other street performers."

Clowns. Clowns! God damn this girl.

The *gendarmes* enjoyed a collective snicker. The two uniforms and the paramedic, squatting around me, having a good laugh, sounded like croaking frogs. Not Brun. The Inspector asked for the Sargent's notebook, stowed it in a side coat pocket, and dismissed the lot of them. He produced a pack of cigarettes, tucked one between his lips and offered me the pack.

"Same brand from your office?" I asked. "Couldn't handle one of those right now." I retrieved my own pack, and stuck one in my face. It was bent but it would light.

"*Gauloises*?" he asked as he lit my cigarette.

"I dunno. They're blue," I reported. I looked down at the pack, sure enough, *Gauloises* was written in tall gray letters above a picture of Hermes' helmet.

"It means Irish Girls. Makes no sense," he scoffed.

"Maybe they both slowly kill you." I reasoned.

"A man with your woman troubles should consider changing brands." He extended his pack for my inspection. *"De Troupe,"* he announced. "They were standard issue in the Foreign Legion."

The soft pack was made of unbleached cold press paper, stained at the corners by the oils of strong tobacco. The policeman's cap on the label more closely resembled a pith helmet, and the words *Manufactures De L'Etat,* were printed down the side. Made by the State.

Inspector Brun grew silent and I could see him churning his case's new developments into wrote computations. "Mickey, you may think what you did was brave, but it was very foolish."

"So, you said," I replied.

He took a long draft and turned it into fire from his nostrils. "What if this man would have stopped to shoot, eh? Even if he misses you, he hits someone else."

I hadn't thought about that, I hadn't thought about anything. I wasn't trying to save the day, running after him was just how I'd reacted. It was outrage, not heroism, like an old woman turning grizzly on a purse-snatcher, or a shop-keeper with a ball bat. Everyone in that theatre shared the same fear. We'd seen the same gun stop a life, and that selfsame fear caused some to run for the doors, and others to sit like plants. Only, my fear had been tinged with enough anger to lift me out of my seat and chase after the man who shot someone I knew.

"The criminal commits a crime. Runs away. We do not always chase," Brun explained. "We will find him, we are the police. You could have caused many more to die."

I did cause someone to die. Just as Adrienne's death had to be connected to the blackmail, I felt sure Marguerite's was connected as well. The web was widening. If she'd known anything about Adrienne's death, she didn't tell me. But, if someone was cleaning up, my going to see Marguerite could have been enough to put the finger on her.

"You will stop your investigation into this matter -- into all matters!" Brun's face was suddenly crimson with molten blood. His neck grew taut, and his collar seemed to tighten. His hands were balling into fists and looked like they might stop on their way to strangle me. "It is my investigation, and you will not interfere!" Brun's composure had been exhausted. The ferocity of his last order slowed every moving body on the sidewalk.

I raised my hand to signal I understood. I'd told Brun everything I knew. Almost everything. I didn't have any other leads. I was in bad shape and agreed that I should sit the rest of this one out.

He told the paramedic he was done with me. I refused to go to the hospital, not for an evaluation, not for anything. Brun looked to the medic for his opinion. The tech held his hands in front of his eyes like binoculars and stuck his tongue out like a dead dog. He thought I had another concussion. The Inspector shined a pen light in my face to investigate, and grimaced like I'd gotten a bad haircut. I signed a form refusing medical attention, and Brun arranged for an officer to take me back to my hotel.

If Brun had wanted me to stay out of his investigation, why he had given my name to Catherine Savard? If it was to cull information the police couldn't, I'd done it. I produced Adrienne's apartment, and handed it to him. How soon they forget! Maybe Brun had known Catherine before she married; they were close enough age, I thought. Brun sported a wedding ring and didn't seem like the torch-carrying type. Though Catherine was the kind of woman that was likely to have a few, burning somewhere. Maybe Brun had been the boy in the booth that Catherine couldn't remember. It was unlikely. I was certain there had been any number of boys, in any number of booths.

# Twenty

The nearest liquor store was three blocks from the hotel. I bought a bottle of Pimm's, and some club soda to try and settle my stomach and my mind. I mixed myself a couple of drinks, the way one mixes drinks alone in a hotel room. A plastic colostomy bag of ice melting on the café table. Two Dixie cups for a shaker. The paper-crowned glass tumbler, which can't hold enough ice to make a drink cold, nor enough liquor to make a dent in misery. The cocktail quickly became Pimm's neat, then Pimm's from the bottle. I didn't feel any better.

Jerome said something I couldn't make out as I passed through the lobby, perhaps a word of caution about carrying an open bottle and glass in one hand. Outside the night air made fog of my breath, and I'd left my coat lying somewhere on the hotel room floor. I would have to rely on my shirtsleeves and continue the cultivation of my inner warmth. Anyone left on the sidewalks was probably hurrying home, and the only cars on the streets were slowly moving taxis, prowling for fares. I was tired of taxis.

Ahead of me, a man stepped from a brownstone, tried the door behind him, making sure it was locked, and jogged the few steps down the stoop to the sidewalk. We were walking in the same direction. He looked about my age, my size, could have been me, just forty feet into the future. We walked like ducks for several blocks, ducks who needed their space.

He walked fast, so had the man in the green sweater. Maybe all Frenchmen walked fast. Maybe it was just the cold. He stopped at a traffic signal to cross the street which allowed me to catch up to him. I stood close enough to smell him, some spicy musk meant to mingle with the rank of cigarettes, make you smell like the Sultan of Bruni. He gave me a sideways glance, nothing more. Maybe he could smell me, too. All that time following Green Sweater, he never waited at a light to cross the street. *Who was this guy? The city is asleep, and he's worried about jaywalking.*

Maybe that's not what he's afraid of. Maybe he's headed somewhere, or leaving some place, he wouldn't want anyone to know about, and couldn't afford to be stopped for jaywalking, for anything else. *Where are you headed, you dog? What have you done?*

The light changed, and we started across the street. I let him walk ahead of me again. He was trying to walk faster now, I knew it. The little duck wanted his personal space back, thought the drunk next to him might want his wallet. *I don't want your wallet. I want to know where you're going.*

Did he know I was following him? How could he? I picked him up on a busy street and we crossed to another busy street. *You got nothing on me.* But, this time of night, he'd naturally be wary of any man following him.

We swayed like boxcars, me and him, our little two-man train, as we ambled down the walk.

How did Adrienne do it? Was it day or night? Would it matter? If this guy looked over his shoulder, what would he see? *A drunk who might get sick on him or ask him for a few francs.* But, what if it was Adrienne walking behind him this time of night? I doubt if he'd quicken his pace, or duck into a bar, and wait for her to pass. Hell, he might offer to walk with her. *Is that what you'd do, you old dog?*

What would she have to do to make him suspect she was following him? If he looked her in the eye, what would have to show on her face to arouse that kind of suspicion? Where would he have to be going to believe her, or anyone else might be following him? *Was it drugs? Gambling? Sex?* What else could it be?

"You going to rob a bank, is that it?" I said.

The man turned to look at me. Shit, I said that out loud. He kept walking. I let him go.

All this time, I'd been retracing Adrienne's steps. *Can't follow her now, not where she's gone.* And I still didn't know where Lynae fit. What was her role in all this?

When you're looking at your feet, the streets all look the same. The cafes, shops, and parks all disappear.

I imagined Adrienne, somewhere between me and the Sultan of Bruni. Adrienne following him, and me following her. Each of us unconcerned or unaware of the person walking behind them.

That thought made me sick. My stomach was sitting on top of my asshole, and I thought I might throw up. There was drumming in my ears. *Was someone following me? I'll turn around and smash this bottle in their face!* But, it was the glass I raised. I spun around to see who was there, who was following me, with my arm cocked, and the tumbler ready to fly.

A man and a woman were walking toward me, arm in arm. They looked startled when they saw me threatening to throw the glass. The man raised an arm in front of his face, the woman pulled him closer, her face buried in his jacket.

"*Psycho,*" the man said as they passed. *SEE-ko.* That's what it sounded like. *SEE-ko.*

I threw the tumbler anyway. It smashed against the side of a building. The couple didn't look back. Just kept walking. *Go home. Sleep it off.*

# Twenty-one

When I woke, I threw the empty bottle of Pimm's away. The makers would be getting a strongly worded letter. I welcomed the morning light, pouring through the windows. It was too painful to open my eyes to, but I sat in its beams, feeling them on my skin, until I was certain that I was going to live.

I had to step out of the shower to answer the ringing phone.

"Mr. Fairfax, this is Shabin, Mr. Grey's assistant," she said, not needing the introduction.

"Do you have any idea what time it is?" I needled.

"Hmph." It was as much of a laugh as I could expect. "I know exactly what time it is," she countered. She understood my joke, as she understood all things, and informed me that Mr. Dile was expecting a report.

"I thought you were to be my liaison in all matters," I reminded.

"Mr. Dile is worried, as is Mr. Grey. We understand there has been some trouble."

Some trouble. Like some earthquakes, or some gangrene.

"Yeah, I spilled mustard on my only clean shirt."

"Mickey," her voice stepped away from the typewriter. "We know that you were admitted to the hospital days ago. And we know about your involvement in the shooting yesterday," her voice was consoling, it was in the room with me, wrapped around my shoulders. She cleared her throat and continued. "Mr. Grey wanted me to tell you that he regrets that this errand has cost you personally."

"Is that what he said?" I asked laconically.

"I'm paraphrasing of course. His exact words were, *Tell him I'm sorry the thing's become such a damn mess.*"

The Thing. Like the prison sentence, or the goiter.

Shabin said that my hospital bill had been paid, along with the hotel bill, to the end of the week. The money I'd previously been given for expenses, I should consider my own. Danger Pay.

"I expect you shall require no additional funds for the remainder of your time in Paris," she parsed.

I promised not to spend too much on postcards.

"If you would like to return by air, you can fly directly into Boston. If you insist on another freighter," she groaned, "I'm afraid you'll have to, I believe the expression is, *go around the horn.*"

I told her I preferred the freighter. She gave me a date and time to depart from La Havre, or two days later from Fos Sur Mer, which I scribbled down, and some last-minute details I didn't. I hated to admit it, but I was glad about the money. Grey had fronted me an ample amount for a three-day job that I had stretched into a cool week. After settling the room bill, I'd have been in the red, and if I were on the hook for the saw-bones, I'd be swimming home.

I had a couple days left in one of the great cities of the world, and nothing to do. A doctor would probably have advised me to spend a day in bed, but good sleep had been hard to come by. Besides, I was ready to play tourist. My blood wasn't boiling any more.

I'd forgotten to ask Shabin about my shop, not that I missed the place. As a business man, I was taking it on the chin. I knew how to run the place; meaning I knew how to pay the light bill, and when a hull needed scraping. Here, I was getting knocked around and still didn't know the score. I was only guessing Dile had gotten caught chasing skirts. Guessing Adrienne had tried the same trick on the wrong guy. Guessing Lynae, a girl who couldn't tell you her name without lying, was in league with Adrienne, but Catherine had me doubting that. The whole thing was a handful of unmatched shoelaces, and I'd trade all of them to go back to losing my shirt at the docks.

And I had had enough of death. Adrienne was murdered before I'd stepped off the train in Paris, but the actress and her shooter had died on my watch, maybe even because of me. Marguerite's death especially, would haunt me. I hadn't been there that night as her bodyguard, but watching someone die in front of you, made you realize how powerless you were to protect anyone from the wolves of the world. It made me long for my life without anyone, or anything. *Losing* cost more than *having*.

Shabin gave me the number Dile had left for me to call. It took some time to connect. The phone ringing on my end sounded like corpulent doves. I anticipated some friendly banter with a secretary, but it was Dile himself who answered.

"Mr. Dile, Mickey Fairfax, your man in Paris."

"Yes," he said without animation. "I know. I'm glad you called." He struggled for what to say next. I didn't blame him.

I told him I'd done as he'd asked; that I'd found the girl from the metro, made sure she was alive, and admitted that she'd given me the slip twice. I told him the murdered girl's father owned a casino operated by a tough crowd, and that I'd been bounced out of there for asking questions. I said I'd found evidence of other men, like himself, who were being blackmailed. And I told him about Marguerite.

"Yes, I heard there had been another death," he managed. "Are you certain it's related to the first one?"

"I'm afraid so. The two knew each other, and they didn't just die, they were murdered, only days apart. It would be an amazing coincidence." I told him Marguerite was shot by a young man recruited from the neighborhood, who probably didn't know the who-or-why of what he was doing. "The cops found him garroted, cord still around his neck, a couple blocks from where I lost him."

"That's awful," Dile said, apologizing several times, not like a man lamenting the death of strangers on the evening news, more like a man who'd hit your sick dog with his luxury car.

"I'd seen her before, you know," he said. "The actress, I mean. I saw her in a production of *Trojan Women.* Must have been ten – no, fifteen years ago. She wasn't much of an actress," he said. Then, as if to avoid speaking ill of the dead added, "just a little one-dimensional. She played everything big and brassy. But, she was a presence! Even when she wasn't speaking -- it was like she was the only thing on the stage. She was full of life."

And now she was dead.

The line went silent. I hoped Dile was weighing the gravity of two more bodies. Reliving it for him made me angry. If you tell someone you were mugged in a seedy part of town, eventually the question will be asked, *what were you doing there in the first place?* No different than if you'd walked into a bear habitat, at the zoo, and were incredulous about being mauled. He had done something to put himself on the spot, something worthy of blackmail, which on its face, was a bloodless operation. Dile couldn't have anticipated this thing ending in violence, but now that it had, his shock and dismay felt recklessly naive. Sam Dile was a grown man and knew there were bad things in the world.

"What about the woman you met in the train station -- the one you gave the money to? Could she have killed the other girl, the one the police found?" he asked abruptly.

I told him I didn't think so.

"Why not?" he asked.

I didn't know why not. They were in cahoots, but it wouldn't have been the first criminal partnership dissolved in that way. Brun said Adrienne had been killed hours before I met Lynae in the train station, so there was time. The fact that Lynae was half her size, and that marks on Adrienne's neck suggested a man's hands, just meant she'd enlisted help.

I was protecting her. I'd been protecting her, right up to the second I gave the name Lynae Cuvier to Brun. She was right to haven given me a phony name. Despite my original intention, I'd flipped on her. I told Dile she didn't seem the type, and he dropped it.

"When she sat down at my table that day, in the café, I thought she was charming." Dile had tabled his despondency for the moment. "She was tall and beautiful," he spoke wistfully. "And her voice," he sighed, "I had to listen to it a while before I knew she was threatening me."

"When did you first meet her?" I asked.

"Right then and there. I'd never seen her before in my life."

I didn't believe him. Dile seemed to return to the present, and the agitation returned to his voice.

"She sat down at my table uninvited, helped herself to a thick slice of *foie gras* and demanded five hundred francs!"

Then it had been Lynae who'd baited the trap. I felt sick. Vessels strained as my calcified heart descended into the pit of my stomach. The short, stocky Dile would have stood eye to eye with her. There would have been no hiding from him, no disappearing under his chin. Had she asked Dile if he wanted to hurt her? Had he taken that bait too?

I was furious with Dile and felt betrayed by Lynae. I tried to tell myself this wasn't a case of your buddy kissing your best girl. I'd been sent to cover up for a man stepping out on his wife. Dile had been a con to Lynae, and there was very little evidence that I had been any different. I should have felt ashamed for falling into the same trap, looking into the pit, seeing Dile impaled there, and jumping in after him. But, that wasn't what I felt at all. I felt territorial jealousy. I felt the rawness of an exposed intimacy. I felt I was the one who had paid a hefty price, and it was Dile who'd received the same for nothing.

My leaden chest made it difficult to breathe. I wanted to yell at Dile, tell him to stay away from her, that she was mine! But that was all he wanted, and she wasn't mine. I wanted to tell him what a fool he was! But I was the fool. The blackmail had been perpetrated on Dile, but the joke was on me. I was not worthy of extortion. I could not be blackmailed. There was no one in my life to care if I slept with a beautiful girl in Paris, or anywhere else. I held no heart to leverage.

Shame, which I had kept in great supply since childhood, washed over me. I crushed my feelings of jealousy, betrayal, and righteous indignation under the heavy base of shame's unfailing obelisk.

"So, it was the other girl you had been with? Her partner?" I managed through my narrowing throat.

"What other girl? What partner?" he asked. Dile's voice snapped me out of my pitying stupor. "I met with one girl, one time. The amount she demanded wasn't much, so I paid. I thought that would be the end of it. Then I come home, and this letter is waiting! My God, if my wife had opened it," he didn't finish the thought, he couldn't. Dile exhaled a deep breath into the phone receiver. "I guess they were just feeling me out, seeing if I would pay."

Testing the waters made sense, especially for amateurs. He'd paid, so they knew they had something on him. He didn't kick at the small amount, so they asked for more. I guess he should have kicked, instead of hiring me to hand them a brick of cash.

"You being straight with me? You didn't sleep with either girl?" I asked. Dile didn't answer.

"Then what do they have on you, Sam?"

Sam Dile was quiet for a long time.

I had a hunch and I played it. "There's a private club here, on a street called Cite Pigalle," I said. "You know it, don't you, Sam?"

There was a long beat, then softly, "I know it."

"The first girl, Adrienne, her father owns it. She followed you from that club back to your hotel," I reasoned. "Does that figure with you?"

"I guess so," he said, barely audible. "I don't know."

"Tell me where it is, Sam. You don't have to tell me what, just tell me where."

Sam Dile gave me an address on Cite Pigalle. I could hear him weeping on the other end of the line.

"I'm going to take care of this, Sam." I spoke to Sam Dile like you would to a child too upset over upending a lamp. "You can trust me."

"That's my problem, Mr. Fairfax," he said. "I trust the wrong people."

# Twenty-two

It was still early. Waiting until dark to discover what Cite Pigalle was meant waiting all day. I knew this would be dangerous, and I'd had no luck at detecting danger in this city. Waltzing into a casino, put me in the hospital. Meeting a woman, I believed ordered a strangling, got me a burlesque show, and going to a play nearly got me shot. Not to mention the rotary phone smashed over my head by a blackmailing ingenue.

There was no way I was walking into Cite Pigalle unarmed. I didn't see any way of getting my hands on a gun, and I'd never used one that didn't shoot water into a clown's mouth. Besides, anything you brought to a fight, you were liable to have taken away from you. And the thought of staring down the wrong end of a stolen heater I'd overpaid for was wholly untenable. Knives seemed equally risky, as I was determined to leave Paris with all the skin I'd arrived with. I decided on something blunt. By the time I had dressed, Jerome's shift was over. I asked the pipe and sweater behind the counter for directions to a hardware store. His English wasn't as good as Jerome's, but he got me there.

*La Droguerie* wasn't far, and thankfully sold more than wine racks. A hardware store is a sadistic place when you want to hurt someone. If its heavy, hard, pointed, sharp, or serrated, they have it. Every aisle of this family-owned concern became the Tower of London, and I started to imagine the damage I could inflict with a post-hole digger.

I admired the heft of a blued-steel claw-hammer until the thought of it remodeling my basement had me replacing it on the shelf. Cast iron crescent wrenches seemed somehow safer than the hammer. They were long, black, and smooth as river stones, except where thin red lines of oxidation from being handled, outlined their beveled grips. The fellas in the engine rooms depended on wrenches like these, and I couldn't bring myself to make one my unwitting accomplice.

My foot found a cardboard box on the dusty floor filled with ten-inch lengths of steel rebar, cut for tent-stakes. I dragged one from the under the box flaps, its unnatural weight felt like solid evil in my hands. My fingers coiled around the ridges in the metal like the spine of a conquered animal. I had pulled from the earth something primordial, what the first man had used to kill the second. This bar had already committed atrocities and wouldn't mind committing others.

With my boot laced tight, the heavy bar held close enough to my leg to avoid detection. The store-owner manning the register watched me model my leg-iron and seemed reluctant to sell a stranger a single tent stake. I offered no explanation, only enough francs to cover the stake and a couple of carpenter's pencils, from a soup can next to the register. I thought the pencils looked like flattened thumbs. I think the man at the registers was bothered more by the size of the purchase; he knew full well this was not the first improvised weapon he had ever sold.

I spent the remaining daylight hours pacing. There were plenty of nights at sea when I had wanted to be alone, and the ocean had been too rough to be on deck. Nights like that, I spent confined to my quarters. Better just to lock the door and fight it out with myself. I could think of nothing but Cite Pigalle, and even in the City of Lights, there would be nothing outside that hotel room door for me until I knew it's secret.

When it was time, I rode the metro to the Pigalle stop. I found the address Dile had given me stenciled between two doors of a three-story building. One door belonged to the business on the ground floor, which looked to be an architectural firm. Behind the glass storefront were brilliant white drafting boards with stools like pieces of modern art. The walls were adorned with large canvas prints of the firm's finer work stretched over wood frames and bathed in track-lighting. In the empty office, they glowed in the dark like movie screens.

A sign outside the second door advertised the restaurant that consumed the third floor as well as the rooftop. Even from the street below I could hear the clink of dinnerware and bombilation of diners. There was no sign for what occupied the second floor. The door to the street had a large glass panel which a drawn curtain turned into a dim mirror. The lump in my throat swelled when the knob turned in my hand. Inside the door was a staircase to a landing on the second floor, the flight of steps to the restaurant above, and a man in a black suit standing by the only door.

I had seen him, and he had seen me. Turning back now was not an option. I took the first flight carefully, as the piece of rebar in my boot was not an orthopedic device and had already rubbed a hole in the skin of my ankle. The man by the door had a thick neck, and cheeks as pink as Virginia ham. He stood with his hands folded in front of him like the Secret Service, or an altar boy.

"*Bon Soir*," he said in a velvety baritone.

He hadn't been an altar boy after all, but a member of the choir. I returned a polite nod and continued toward the door. The Ham barred my way with a sturdy arm. He demurred an apology in soothing French, while balling his other hand discreetly into a fist. His size alone served as a warning. I picked out the word "*prive*" from his apology, it meant private. I had learned that word on the steps of a club in La Havre with a couple other equally drunken sailors.

"Vermouth," I said confidently. Dile told me there would be a code word and had given me "vermouth". It made sense to use a word that was pronounced the same in several languages, in deference to visiting perverts. The Ham looked confused, like I'd handed him a wet handkerchief instead of the money I owed him.

"Vermouth," I repeated without potency.

He waved over a second man who'd been sitting on a stool at the far end of the landing. I hadn't seen him until I'd reached the top of the stairs, and he hadn't moved until now. He was an older man with a smooth head and dark glasses. His body looked like a pile of large rocks, hastily stacked inside the same plum-colored suit the yeti at the casino had sported. The Ham whispered into his ear.

The second man gargled his orders. His voice did not belong in the choir and sounded like the lid of a tuna can in a garbage disposal. The Ham motioned for me to open my coat, which I did. He reached his balloon-animal hands around my back, under my arms, and tickled my waist. He stepped so close to me, I could feel his breath on my face. He gave a short grunt of annoyance, then cupped my ass with both hands like it was the last song at a middle school dance. I could feel his thick, rough fingers moving deftly down my legs toward the top of my boots.

Tuna Lid grumbled something dismissive on his way back to his stool, and the Ham gave up his search at the back of my knees. My clenched fists were ready to drive down the on the back of his porcine head when he looked up at me with a genuine smile. He straightened, opened the door and bid me enter with a delicate flourish of his giant hand.

The inside of the club was not what I expected. The carpet, walls, and ceiling were all deep red and lined with glossy black trim. The fixtures on the walls were gas; the burning oil thickened the air, and the diffused light made scanning the room like peering through Vaseline. A well-stocked bar ran the length of the wall to my left. Behind it was a curiously handsome fellow with butch-waxed hair and a mustache like a carnival strongman. He was tearing up herbs to mottle for a tray of Juleps.

Besides the bar, the gallery was a collection of upholstered chaise lounges arranged like diamond plate. There hung one grandiose oil painting on every wall, with a consistent theme. Each depicted a huntsman with a gun, a dog, or a boy. I don't know what I had anticipated, but it wasn't this. I thought it would be dark, seedy, with thumping music stifling screams. But, this place looked like a brothel from a spaghetti western and smelled like a Mississippi gin joint.

If I stood inside the doorway any longer I would start to suspect myself of something. I leaned on the end of the bar and waited for Handsome Dan to finish gardening. He looked like the template for a line of mannequins, and I really didn't want to order a drink from him, but I didn't see a waitress. In fact, I didn't see a woman.

Scanning the sea of settees, I found not one female face. There were men of all ages, younger men in fitted, modern clothes, and some older gents traipsing about in satin smoking jackets and leather slippers. This was a waiting room; the women were likely in apartments deeper in the club. Lurid little love-nests where they quenched men's blood-lust behind locked doors, willingly or not. Prostitution was legal here, but exploitation was not. A simple brothel could operate in the open, and every reason a place would need to remain clandestine made my skin crawl.

A group of men sat on the ground, around the campfire of a hookah pipe. There was a cloud of cardamom, of burnt apricot, and the whetstone smell of heated brass. One man blew a steady plume over his neighbor, diligently, medicinally bathing his outstretched limbs in perfumed smoke. A younger man had taken off his shirt. Another was getting a vigorous shoulder rub. Still another, naked to the waist, was being stroked like a house cat.

There were no apartments in the back, nor women being held against their wills.

I was being watched by a slender man from across the room. He slinked toward me, weaving through the maze of oak and upholstery. He looked like a matador, shirtless under his sister's bolero. I spun around and gestured for the bartender. He put down his pestle and wiped his hands. He was sinewy but tried to look broad, arms held wide, exaggerating the turning of his shoulders as he walked.

"A gimlet," I ordered before he could say anything in French.

The matador slithered between the stools next to me and said something to the barkeep. They exchanged a look, and I knew he had bought my damn drink.

"Hey, how ya doing?" I grumbled before he could speak.

His opening salvo contained the word *American* twice, so I'd succeeded in lowering his expectations for our conversation. He looked like a Bedouin prince standing there with his bare chest under that tiny jacket. His skin was dark, and his thick beard painted on. His head was a collection of black ringlets that looked wet and grew in number toward the back.

When our drinks arrived, I didn't wait to toast, and drained my glass. For all his machinations, Handsome Dan mixed a fine cocktail. The Prince thought so too and asked the bartender what it was called. *Gim-lay,* they repeated to each other. *Gim-lay.* The Prince rapped on the bar and ordered a round. He turned and waved to the group of men he'd left, and the bartender began filling another tray with coupe glasses.

I'd started something with the Gimlet, and in doing so, lost the element of anonymity. Among the group of men rising to join the Prince at the bar, was a familiar face. Babby stood staring at me with his jaw slack. His unbuttoned bellman's jacket opened on a concave chest and ribs like a hungry dog. Stripped and disheveled, he rose unsteadily like a boy soldier emerging from the smoldering crater of an English cannon blast. I watched his expression change from incredulity to menace. He leapt through the crowd toward the front door. There was no cutting him off. He would tell the two bruisers at the entrance the place had rats, and I was in for a rough time. I moved in the only direction I could, deeper into the club. There had to be another way out.

# Twenty-three

The fire escape of every building on the block, emptied into the alley. I pushed my way through the drink-seekers to a corridor I thought led in that direction. It was decorated like the first room, like twenty feet of intestines, at the end was a painting of a man in knee-highs, holding a musket, flanked by a Braque Pointer. Unfortunately, this was where the club stored their locked doors. Five golden door knobs and not one budged. The sixth door was the restroom and I ducked inside.

There were three sinks with mirrors on the adjacent wall and three small windows above them, that looked to be the only way out. I climbed onto the sink farthest from the door and pushed on the rusted window lever as hard as I could. It wasn't moving and felt like it might break in my hand. I pushed against the sill, but it was caked with paint and neglect. These windows hadn't opened in decades and weren't about to.

"Even if you got it open," a voice came from behind me, "there's no way down, just...," Rico made a low, descending whistle.

"No dumpsters to aim for?" I asked still standing on the sink.

"No dumpsters," he rasped. He shook a gold watch off his wrist and slid it into his pocket. "I owe you one, Kojack."

"I'm fine with you owing me." I didn't like Rico's math. Our first scuffle hadn't felt like a draw to me, and if it was his Italian loafer that had dimmed my lights on the sidewalk the day before, that put him well ahead.

"Thanks to you, I've been wearing this." Rico unbuttoned his sport coat, the lining was flashy stripes like ribbon candy, again, not very French. But, under the jacket was a hard, plastic orthopedic girdle, molded to the shape of his hips and waist, that rose to the middle of his chest, and cinched tight as a corset. He pounded his fist against the fastening like a Centurian against his shield.

"You wear it well," I said, climbing down from the sink.

Rico rushed me. He crossed the length of the tiled floor in an instant, stopped short, and retreated a couple steps to have his picture taken with his fists up. My clumsy, desperation move in the alley outside the casino had hurt him, and he stalked me more cautiously now. Rico darted in, throwing tentative, probing jabs, and ducked out again. Remembering my eye, I kept my left hand up like I was holding a phone receiver. He came in again, this time hammering the exposed left side of my ribcage. I absorbed the blow and felt the air rush out of my body; but, Rico had taken the bait. I stepped on his foot, pinning it to the ground, and Rico in place. Unable to retreat, the pugilist's eyes widened, by instinct, his arms snapped closed in front of his face like a clam-shell.

Grabbing him with both hands, I lifted the smaller man off the ground and slammed him on top of one of the sinks. His feet kicked, failing to find the floor. He hammered the side of my face and my eyebrow opened like a zipper. I tried to crush his square jaw in my hand. His stubbled chin wrinkled like burlap under my fingers and I slammed his head into the mirror behind, until it shattered. The shards still stuck in the frame were jeweled red with Rico's blood.

All of the sudden, my arm was wrenched to the wrong side of my body, and a python around my neck made it impossible to breathe.

"Get him in the office," I heard the disembodied order before the room went black.

When everything goes dark, a year can go by in a second, and a second seem like a year. The voices around me were becoming clearer, and the pinholes I'd been looking through were starting to widen. The first thing I could make out was a sickly white face above the ruffles of a tuxedo shirt.

"Are you back among the living, Mr. Fairfax?" the white face asked from behind a large oak desk.

"Savard?" My own voice sounded strange, like my head was packed with cotton.

"No, Mr. Fairfax," he said. He was an Englishman, with an affected accent common to Brits who have made their home somewhere off the island, in Africa, or India. "I am the Concierge. Welcome to my club."

"This isn't your club, it belongs to Antoine Savard," I argued.

"The club has many owners, and they see fit to entrust it to me. It's a responsibility I take very seriously."

The Concierge was a dapper, middle-aged man in a neatly cut tuxedo. His cheeks were hollow, and his eyes colorless. His hair, sallow as corn-silk, was slicked meticulously back on his head. The focal point of his bloodless face was a thin, black continental mustache.

"Rico here would like to break your back. Do you know why I don't let him?"

I said I didn't.

"Because I don't believe in holding grudges. Whatever has transpired in the past, belongs to the past. Grudges distract us from the present," he lectured. "And presently, we have a problem. It seems that some unscrupulous individual has been blackmailing members of our little club. And that, Mr. Fairfax, is bad for business."

"How do they know you're not behind it?" I accused. "Getting them coming and going. You think your clientele trusts a bunch of hoods?" Someone drove a truck into the back of my skull. Even sitting, it nearly knocked me to the ground.

The Concierge got up from his chair and stood in front of the large desk. "When organized crime in your country moved West from the streets of New York and Chicago, to the bright, beautiful playground of Las Vegas, it didn't take them long to realize they were making more money legally, with the casinos, than they had ever made with the old rackets. Success made it possible for them to go straight."

"Is that what you're running here, a reform school for tough boys?" That line got me an open-handed slap I thought ruptured my eardrum. I'd know that over-stuffed, throw-pillow hand anywhere. It was the Ham that had pulled me off Rico in the men's room, and stood behind my chair now, ensuring my behavior. I wondered if I could get to the club in my boot before he could pull my arms off.

"We may not have always been legitimate businessmen, Mr. Fairfax," he continued, "but I assure you we run a legitimate business here. We serve a niche clientele, and provide them with discretion, at a premium of course. In return they expect us to respond when someone is fucking with them."

Ire had brought color to the dapper man's face. He crossed the room and lifted the glass stopper from a crystal decanter. He poured himself a short drink that drained the color from his face again.

"We were very close to having this whole business put to rest, very close to catching our little rat." The Concierge looked down at the empty glass still in his hand. "Do you know what happened then?"

He didn't wait for me to say that I didn't.

"You happened, Mr. Fairfax. You knocked my man Aziz to the ground, and bent the door of my Mercedes," he said with a smirk. "You were supposed to deliver her, you were the worm on the hook. And instead, you managed to pull the fisherman into the water!"

Sam Dile had set me up. He had told this pack of vultures about being blackmailed, told them when and where the drop was. Best-case scenario, he used me to flush out his blackmailer. Worst-case, he'd supplied a fall-guy to take the rap when Lynae was the one found dead, strangled in an alley.

"Of course, you didn't know what you were doing," he continued. "You were coming to the aid of a damsel in distress. I might have done the same thing if I were in your shoes." The tuxedoed man stopped to imagine the scene. Knowing he would never have intervened, he smirked to himself, and the lids thickened over his downcast eyes.

"What do you know about her, Mr. Fairfax?" The dapper man selected a cigarette from a carved wooden box on his desk and lit it.

"I don't know anything more than you do," I answered.

"Oh, come now," he said, and snapped the lid of the little box closed like a trap. "You embarrass us both. You've met with her on a couple of occasions since that day." He pushed himself away from the desk and stood in front of me. He took the slim cigarette from his mouth and held it in front of his face, studying it. I watched the little red ember glow and fade like the beating of a tiny heart, listened to the faint crackle and hiss of the paper, and followed thin wisps of smoke raptured from the fire swirl toward the ceiling.

I was too slow.

With the slightest gesture, the Concierge had ordered the Ham to pin my left wrist to the chair with his enveloping mitt and wrench my right arm behind my back.

"Her name, sir?"

I shook my head.

He pressed the cigarette into the middle of my collar bone, where the skin is the thinnest, and the bone most prominent. He knew what he was doing, because it hurt like hell. Guys in the slammer who are part of an outfit are given specific duties. If you can read you're sent to the library to learn what can be learned about the law, financial institutions, and the human body. State-funded study-hall on what hurts, what maims, what kills; vital organs, pressure points, and nerve endings.

"Her name, sir?" He drew on the bent cigarette, trying to stoke the embers back to life.

Again, I shook my head.

Unwanted color was returning to the Concierge's face. A lock of hair fell in front of his eyes. He laid his manicured hand over mine. His palm was dry, and cold as marble. He stooped like he was lining up a billiards shot. I heard the flick of his lighter and watched the tuxedoed man place the end of my index finger in the middle of the tall yellow flame. I tried to pull my arm away, but the Ham's grip was like a vice. The pain was exquisite. I could hear the crackle of fire, see my flesh turning black, and smell my body burning.

"Her name, Mr. Fairfax! I want her name," enraged, he kicked at the armrest of the chair, smashing my burnt finger under the sole of his shoe.

I'd played it tough to that point, but the pain in my hand drew a howl I couldn't swallow. The end of my finger had plumped and split like a bratwurst.

My dapper confessor smoothed his truant locks into place and loosed his bow tie. The cigarette he had stubbed out against my collar bone was still between his fingers. It was bent and broken, but he ran his lighter back and forth until the length of it was ignited. His marble hand wrenched my head back, and I could see the mangled flames an inch from my face, dripping with fire.

The sickness of fear stirred in the pit of my stomach and spread to my unresponsive limbs. I tried in vain to wrestle free, but the lummox was too strong, and had too much leverage. I wanted that flame away from my face. I wanted out of that room. If it had been a man's name they wanted, I would have given it to them.

"Her name, or it goes in your eye," the Concierge yelled, and the trembling of his hand sent a drop of liquid fire onto my cheek. An errant ember floated into my eye, caught on my lashes and burned terrible and orange until I could blink it away.

"Lynae. Lynae Cuvier." I surrendered.

The dapper man backed away. He wiped the spent ember from my face with the flick of his thumb. "Is that what she told you?"

"That's her name," I said.

He crouched down and studied my face. "You are just the perfect fool, aren't you?" He laughed, as the police had laughed, and more laughter came from behind me. The dapper man's bay rum failed to cover the odor of pine tar, addressing a skin condition somewhere under his penguin suit. The Ham behind me smelled like a lunch counter, and I knew Rico Mindy was present as well, bathed in Fragonard that would give him away at twenty paces.

The Concierge returned to leaning against his desk. He was still grinning from my ignorance like he'd taken the biggest pot of the night with a bluffed hand. The Ham released me, and I felt the blood rushing back into my right arm. The feeling in the room seemed to have changed in an instant. When it came to Lynae, I really didn't know any more than they did.

"How did Savard take it when you told him you killed his daughter?" I asked.

He paused, "I'm afraid I don't follow."

"Adrienne Savard was the one blackmailing your members. She knew all about the club and tailed men she thought she could squeeze from the front steps. Told them she had pictures, maybe she did, maybe she didn't. Someone killed her and tossed her apartment like they knew what they were doing."

The look on the Concierge's face was one of confusion, like recounting the previous night's events to a fall-down drunk.

Rico appeared from behind me and stood next to the tuxedoed man, whispering in his ear. Except for Rico's athletic physique, he and the dapper man could have been Dickensian twins, separated at birth. All their collected genteelness had been poured into the Concierge, all barbarity into Rico. One polished like silver in English prep schools, the other steeped in grit and grime on the streets of Barcelona. Both born poisonous as apple seeds. Despite disparate upbringings, each had ended up a two-bit gangster, scraping enough off the luckless to afford a nice suit to be buried in.

"You were following her. The girl was meeting with Marguerite in the open; Marguerite who used to have your boss curled up in her lap like a house-cat. You figure she's in on it, so she had to go, too. Then you dump the kid that pulled the trigger for you. All this cleaning up is getting pretty messy." Fear and rage were fighting for control of my Adam's apple. My brain couldn't keep my lips from flapping. I went from out of the woods to talking myself into a pine box, and I couldn't stop.

No one breathed. We just looked at each other without blinking for several minutes.

"I'm not a murderer, Mr. Fairfax," the Concierge said, retying his bow tie. "I'm a good business man, and an excellent host, and right now I have a room full of guests to attend to." He stood up straight and buttoned his jacket. "I'm going to leave you to Rico now, I hope you won't hold any ill will against me for what he does to you."

The Ham grabbed the collar of my shirt, and the back of my pants, and slammed me prostrate across the big oak desk. Someone scurried around the side to grab my arms. It was the bartender. Handsome Dan had been in the room the whole time. The fear in his face and the trembling of his wide, apologetic eyes told me he had been consigned to this duty. As if it meant the difference between mine or his own, he held my arms like grim death.

When the Ham went for my legs, I kicked with both feet like a wild mule. I heard his big body crash into something behind. Dan let go of my hands, immediately holding up his own in surrender. I drew the piece of rebar from my pant leg, the Ham was charging me like a bull. I swung the iron as hard as I could at his head. I heard a crack and was convinced my club had broken in half. The Ham crashed into the desk, then onto the floor with an inhuman wail, cradling his shattered forearm.

The Concierge stood with his hand on the doorknob, watching the scene in disbelief. Rico waved a two-foot length of lead pipe over his head like he was fending off vampire bats. The pipe was the circumference of a grapefruit and would have turned my spine to confetti. He inched toward me. I had nowhere to go. There was a one-armed giant on the floor behind me, and the mustachioed bartender had petrified in the window that led to the fire escape.

It was just me and Rico. The Spaniard looked from my weapon to his, compared the two, and liked what he saw. He hefted the heavier club and beat it against his open hand with a smile. Rico inched toward me, practically salivating. His face was a twitching, perpetual snarl, and his tongue protruded from between his teeth anticipating the taste of blood.

He stood sideways, holding the length of pipe like a baseball bat, moving counterclockwise to his right, stalking me. I squared myself to him, holding my rebar like a fly swatter, slide-stepping to my right. I faked a lunge at him, and immediately reared back. My body bent like a crescent moon, the path of the pipe missing my mid-section by inches. Rico had swung with everything he had and connected with nothing. I struck at his face, but the iron stake only scraped his cheek. Had the rod been two inches longer it would have cracked the angle of his jaw.

The menacing smile disappeared from Rico's lips, but not the menace. He felt along his jaw line for missing stubble. Respect for any harm I could inflict on him melted under the heat of a murderous fever, a glint like fire behind his wild eyes. If his original intent was to work me over, even maim me, that was gone. I knew now, Rico Mindy was going to kill me.

My heart was racing. It was academic, if I didn't find a way out of this room, I would die in it. I would have to put Rico down long enough to escape.

I was almost glad he was holding that pipe. We'd done this bare-knuckled already, and we both knew the outcome. Though the size of my weapon put me at a distinct disadvantage, Rico seemed equally inexperienced when it came to a fight like this, and that gave me a chance.

We had danced in a circle, and I was in front of the big desk again. Rico came at me, this time swinging the pipe overhead like a sledgehammer. I spun away as the heavy pipe splintered the big wood desk. I put my right shoulder into his chest and wrapped my good arm around both of his at the elbow. I tried to smash at his hands with the rebar, but my burned left hand hurt too badly, and I heard the metal rod clank along the floorboards before I knew I had dropped it.

We wrestled for Rico's pipe. When I got both hands on it, his suddenly disappeared. I'd given him my back when I grabbed his arms, which made it too easy for him to slide them around my neck with a deadly proficiency honed, both in the ring and in the streets.

His bicep felt like an Idaho potato jammed against my right carotid, and his forearm, a piece of steel threatening to shear my head clean off. The hand on back of my skull pushed my throat deeper into the cleft of his arm, and the lights were starting to dim again. What blood was left in my brain banged in my ears. I tried to bend at the waist and flip him over my head, but he'd widened his base and his feet didn't budge from the floor.

I could hear him laughing in my ear between heavy breaths. I could feel the flat of his stubbled chin on the back of my head. I could smell the sweat on his face and the stink of his cologne. His arm was so deep under my chin it wouldn't budge. I tore the buttons from the sleeve of his blazer with my bloodied left hand.

I tried to take a breath, but no air entered my lungs. I could no longer hear the pulse of blood in my ears. I could no longer hear anything.

He was the smaller man, and I could move him. We'd made a half circle already. I could see the chair the Ham had pinned me to. I pushed as hard as I could with my legs and drove us backward into the edge of the big wooden desk. Rico took the brunt, and I hoped I'd cut him in half. His arms came away from my neck and I went spilling to the floor.

Or what I thought was the floor. I was sitting on something soft like couch or a beanbag chair, and it took shaking some cobwebs loose to realize it was howling at me to get off. I'd landed on the Ham, still lying on the floor cradling his broken arm like his first born.

Rico stood in front of the desk, his knees buckled. His eyes were wet, trembling with frustration like a wounded animal in a trap. The pipe was right where I had dropped it, on top of the big wooden desk. My trusty stake had rolled hopelessly far, to the other side of the room. Rico reached for the pipe. I pushed myself off the Ham and to my feet. Rico swung the bludgeon with a backhanded swing, too high, and I ducked it easily. I threw one right hand, catching him on the jaw, that I wouldn't trade for an RBI single in the World Series.

There was a commotion on the other side of the door, and the Concierge moved away just in time for it to swing open. Sargent Saltier and his chin stood in the doorway with his gun drawn. Rico dropped the pipe to the carpeted floor with a muted, impotent clank.

The room filled with *gendarmes*. Rico seeing his last opportunity, blasted me in the teeth, with a straight left that felled me like a redwood.

From my back I heard, "Don't give them anything, Gentlemen," the Concierge's voice ringing above the clamor. "It's our word against his."

Everyone got bracelets, I got smelling salts. Handsome Dan was relieved and would have looked as happy being led away in stocks. They cuffed the Ham's good wrist to the back of his pants, but all fight had already drained out his dangling, shattered arm. It took several officers piling on top of Rico Mindy to get him in cuffs. Dangerous as any three men in that room, he looked like a juvenile delinquent being led away with his coat sleeves bunched up around his shoulders.

That left only the dapper host, believed innocuous enough to be cuffed in front, presenting his interpretation of the events to Sargent Saltier in perfect French. The Sargent released him to the custody of two officers who escorted him from the room.

"No grudges, Mr. Fairfax," was the last thing he said before disappearing into the hall, and the absolute last thing he meant.

# Twenty-four

Police Inspector Brun's office looked the same as it had during our first meeting. The pictures with dignitaries were still on the floor, instead of the wall, and the inspector's mustache continued toward a full recovery. No tape recorder, just the pewter-haired lawman jotting facts beside bullet points in a thin manila case file.

"Did you have me followed?" I asked.

"No," he said without turning his attention from his work, "I thought you finally had had enough."

I looked like I'd had plenty. Rico had re-opened the gash over my eye and added a bruise in the shape of his fist to my jawline. I didn't have the nerve to look at my finger before the EMT wrapped it, but the Concierge lighting me up had reduced my urge to smoke.

"Officers located the residences from *Mlle*. Savard's notes, the notes you were good enough to hand over," Brun bristled a bit, and I could swear the lines on his forehead spelled the word *eventually*. He explained that upon questioning, several of the men admitted to being blackmailed and provided the location of the club.

As Libertine as the French seemed, there were still some very Puritanical laws on the books concerning the activities alleged to be going on at the club on Cite Pigalle, and a warrant for the raid was easily secured. Several arrests were made during the raid that had nothing to do with the blackmail, nor my capture. The cavalry had not arrived to rescue me, but to arrest the club's lounging clientele, whose only crime was a love life the government still considered illicit; a secret that allowed them to be blackmailed by the opportunistic, sociopathic daughter of a gangster.

As for the man who had introduced himself as the Concierge, Brun told me his name was Lavelle Nabors, though Interpol believed that to be an alias. Originally from South Africa, he'd fled prosecution there for everything from burglary to racketeering. As much as I like the idea of Lavelle and Rico sharing an eight by eight, there was a good chance Mr. Nabors would be boxed up and mailed to Johannesburg.

"I think Rico and the Concierge killed Adrienne and Marguerite," I told the inspector. "They knew someone was leaning on club members and admitted to trying to abduct Adrienne's accomplice from the metro station. Adrienne had met with Marguerite in public several times, they may have pegged her for an accomplice, and decided she needed silencing as well."

Brun, unphased by my accusations of attempted kidnapping and capital murder, pushed a photograph across his desk to me, like old friends resuming a card game. "Do you know this man?" he asked.

I looked at the picture, it was the man Lynae had met at the restaurant, the man in the green sweater. His mug shot had been taken with and without his glasses. Behind the strong lenses his eyes were beady, an insect's eyes, two pieces of gravel pushed into his face until they stuck. Without them, he had the divergent, far-away gaze of the blind. His nose and eyes were swollen like wounds, wet but bloodshot, as if he'd given up sleeping for sobbing.

"His name is Etienne Rimbaud. Married. Teaches music. No previous record. One of the men from the notes. When the officers asked to come inside, he confessed before they could sit down. He identified Adrienne Savard from pictures as the young woman who approached him on the street outside his home, threatening to reveal to his wife that he is a homosexual. She demanded five hundred francs." Brun looked up from the file.

"That's not a lot of money, is it?" I asked.

Brun shook his head, indicating it was not.

"Did he pay it?"

"He did," Brun said simply, "believing that would be the end of it. Two weeks later, mixed in with his usual bills, magazines and advertisements, was a letter. This time the demand was for thousands. On a music teacher's salary…" the inspector waved his hand in lieu of completing his sentence. "He said he had every intention of paying," Brun said and picked up a picture of the living Adrienne from the case file. "The letter instructed him to get a table at a restaurant in Les Halles, three nights in a row, and on one of those nights, someone would meet him to collect the money." Brun let go of the picture with both hands, letting it float the few inches back to the top of his desk. "But before their scheduled meeting, he sees her on the street, as he's walking home from work. Out of fear, anger, or just opportunity, he pulls her into the dark and strangles her."

"Is that your story, or his?" I asked.

The inspector said nothing and slid the dead girl's photo back into the file. "The very next day, there is another letter in his box, reminding him to keep his appointment, which must have been like seeing a ghost," Brun continued. "This letter, just as the first, is signed Adrienne Savard."

Next, Brun told me the part of the story I already knew. That the man in the green sweater met a young woman he'd never seen before in a crowded restaurant and gave her an envelope filled with cash.

"Then Rimbaud gave a strange account," Brun continued, "of an unidentified American putting him in a choke hold outside his home as he was taking out the trash. Seems this American, who was described as smelling strongly of alcohol, knew all about the blackmail." Brun left me an opening like a length of rope on his desk. "The manifestations of a guilty conscience I told him." The inspector gave me a long, knowing look that failed to stir my conscience.

"He admit to tossing her place?" I asked.

"He did not. Rimbaud said the first time he'd met the young woman was the day she threatened him. And the second, the day he killed her. He insists he did not know where she lived. He was by no means her only victim, and having admitted to everything else, I am inclined to believe him."

"Do you believe," Brun asked me, "that the girl Rimbaud met in the restaurant is the same girl from the metro station, the mysterious American accomplice, *Mlle.* Cuvier?" The inspector allowed himself, for the first time, to chuckle at the name that any Parisian would have known was bogus.

I vowed that when I made it back to the states I would introduce myself to the first French tourist I met as Somerset Boulevard, or Rudy Sixty-six, then fall down laughing.

"I know it was her," I said, without adding how I knew. "What do you have on her?"

"I am sad to say, we have nothing but a description from Mr. Rimbaud," the inspector said with an anachronistic grin. "That is where you come in, my friend."

We were friends again.

"I need to know everything this time, Mickey," Brun's smile had vanished as quickly as it had appeared.

I really had tried to tell Brun everything, sitting on the sidewalk, the day of the shooting. I wanted him to find Lynae, someone had to. I racked my brain for something else to say. I told Brun about her bathroom makeover, that I believed she had a penchant for changing her appearance. That she spoke fluent French, and possibly other languages. That she had been to Adrienne's apartment, after it was ransacked. I told Brun about Gus at the kebab stand; he might not know anything about her, but he was one more person that could, at very least, vouch for her existence. Lastly, I confessed it was Lynae who had put me onto Marguerite, telling me that she and Adrienne had met several times. If I was responsible for putting the finger on Marguerite, I wasn't alone.

"Is there anything else you would like to tell me? Anything you may have left out?" Brun asked knowing I had not divulged any information concerning my bogus Loss Prevention case, the reason I was supposedly in Paris to begin with.

I hadn't given him Samuel Dile, or even confirmed that he had been blackmailed. And I wouldn't. Not until I could talk to Dile again, gauge how angry I should be at him. If he had hired me strictly as a deliver boy, I could live with that. If he'd hired me as a fall-guy, I don't know how he could live with himself.

"How much do you think they made on this little venture?" I inquired.

"All of the men reported paying the initial five hundred francs. Few admitted to paying anything after that. Though more victims may continue to come to light," Brun added as a thinly veiled accusation.

As he was walking me out, the Inspector said they had yet to find a bank account for the young blackmailer beyond a savings account, started for her by her parents, unused since the girl was fourteen. If found, the money would be returned to the victims. Unfortunately, deposits of five hundred francs were not likely to raise any red flags. I told Brun I could vouch for the fact that it wasn't hidden under her mattress.

"There is something peculiar about the timing," Brun posited. "*Mlle.* Savard had been at this for some time. Of all the men questioned, the earliest was contacted over a year and a half ago, and considering the twenty or so known victims, that makes close to a victim a month."

"Seems more like an investment strategy than a crime spree," I added.

"Yet the men who admitted to paying the second sum, were only contacted in the last few months."

I asked the Inspector what he thought it meant and got a raised eyebrow for an answer. I brought the conversation back to Rico and the Concierge. If movies and dime novels had taught me anything, it's that even low-level street toughs were connected enough to have someone higher up the food chain spring them with a phone call. "When I hit the street, are those hooligans gonna be waiting on the sidewalk grinding axes?"

Brun laughed and tugged on his mustache. "This is *Pari, Monsieur* Fairfax, not Marseilles."

He held the door to the street open for me.

"It is funny," the inspector stopped me in the doorway. "My wife introduced me to a friend of hers the other day. The two have been friends for many years, I have even spoken to this woman on the phone several times, but for whatever reason, had never made her acquaintance until then. The very next morning, I see her on the train, and we realize we have ridden the same train for years. Days later, we meet again, this time during lunch at my favorite bistro, which she also frequents. We even swim laps Thursday mornings at the same gym. It is strange to think how many times we may have passed each other on the street, or even stood next to one other on the train, each believing we did not know the other."

# Twenty-five

The cab I caught outside the Prefecture de Police dropped me at my hotel just shy of four in the morning. My clothes bounced hard against the elastic spring of the hotel bed, with me in them. Dark, dreamless sleep came quickly.

I awoke sometime after nine a.m. without alarm clock, phone call, nightmare, or rooster. The Ham had stopped short of de-boning my shoulder, but it hurt like hell, and I had to rest my elbow on the sink just to brush my teeth. It still felt better than my head. Despite that, the guy in the mirror was almost smiling. Adrienne's killer was behind bars, Lynae was safe from him as well as from the crew that tried to snatch her at the subway station. I feared she was safe from me too.

I went for breakfast at the little café across the street. My waitress was particularly lovely, arriving at my table by clam-shell to pour coffee. Breakfast was perfect, the sun was shining, and the pigeons were keeping it under their hats. It couldn't last.

Jerome was jogging toward me, waving his arms. I doubted it was about croissants.

"Mickey, a man called for you, said it was important," he said.

"A police inspector?" I asked.

"No, an American." Jerome shook his head, remembering there were police inspectors outside of France. "I mean, he said he was calling from the U.S. I tried to tell him you were across the street having breakfast. He said to go and get you," Jerome looked perplexed, "that he would wait!"

I knew it was Andrew Grey on the other end of the line. Jerome transferred the call to a phone in the lobby, on a small table near the best window.

I took a seat in one of a pair of bow-legged Bergere chairs and picked up the receiver.

"Mickey, this is Grey, Andrew Grey." Grey sounded as if he were standing at his desk, though I imagined he would sound equally strident receiving a foot rub. "I'm afraid I have some bad news. Doesn't affect you directly, but I thought you'd want to know."

I braced for what it could be. I didn't own any shares of Standard Oil.

"I'm afraid that Sam Dile is dead. They found him this morning."

"What do you mean they found him? What happened?" I asked the obligatory questions.

"No foul play. By his own hand. Hung himself in a motel room. Note said so his wife wouldn't be the one to find him. He loved Birdie. That's Mrs. Dile."

"I know," I said, but I didn't know. Sam Dile never said anything to me about his wife, except that she was the reason he needed me to make the payoff. Maybe he loved her enough to keep her name out of his mouth when cleaning up his mess. I felt sorry for Sam, but whether it was to be with a man or a woman, he'd stepped out on his wife, and set everything in motion. He was a victim, but he wasn't blameless. And if he had set me up, he'd have that on his conscience, too. It was supposed to be one blackmailer he was feeding to the wolves, and now three people were dead. Maybe that was too many for Sam.

"Came as a real shock," Grey continued. "I hoped you taking care of this business for him would help. Give him some piece of mind. Didn't know it had shaken him this badly. Birdie said he was talking on the phone very late last night before he left and didn't come back. Was it to you? What did he say?"

I remembered he had said he was sorry. He said I'd know everything once I found the club on Cite Pigalle. I didn't know everything, but I knew why he was being blackmailed, and why he'd been so afraid. That's all he meant. He was afraid it would never stop. Maybe he'd regretted reaching out to gangsters.

They were going to murder someone for him and would eventually want something for their trouble. What would that cost him? Maybe he thought the next letter, the next call in the middle of the night would come from them. Or, Grey's endorsement aside, it would come from me.

"No," I said. "He didn't say anything to me." I didn't know what Grey knew about his friend, how secret he'd kept that part of his life, and I didn't see how it was my place to say anything.

"Damn shame. Good man. Feet of clay, like the rest of us, but a good man. I liked him." Grey's posthumous endorsement of his friend seemed more for his benefit than mine. "Did he ever tell you how he made is money?"

"I didn't know he had any money," I admitted. Grey knew Dile and I hadn't forged any friendships over two trans-Atlantic phone calls, he wanted to talk about his friend, and I let him.

"You wouldn't know it to look at him, but he was an oilman," Grey said proudly.

"Texas?" I asked. "Not much of an accent."

"North Dakota," Grey corrected. "No accent. Would have made a fine newsman. Didn't come from money, though," Grey said, resuming his eulogy. "His parents were working folks. Sam got a job in an ice cream parlor, soon as he was old enough."

As difficult as it was to accept the diminutive businessman as an oil tycoon, I was immediately comfortable picturing an adolescent Samuel Dile in an apron and paper cap.

"Saved every dime he ever earned, spent it all on an abandoned oil well. Bought it cheap, because it was thought to be dry. But, he drilled, until he could confirm it was dry. He went back to work, and when he had the money, bought another well, then another. They were all wells people had given up on. Don't remember how many he bought before he struck oil. But, just like that he was in the game."

Grey remembered his friend with a drink. Through the receiver, I could hear the ice cubes clink in the glass.

"Wildcatting they call it," Grey said. "Drilling wells that had already been drilled. Sam Dile was a wildcatter." Grey pitched a title for his friend's never to be written memoir.

Grey went on to tell me that Sam Dile had met his wife, Birdie, in California. She came from a well-to-do family, the middle of three daughters, and had never worked a day in her life, except volunteering for the Junior League. They met at a country club, during a charity golf event; neither played. Birdie was manning the League's refreshment table, attempting to sell lemonade and wilting pieces of cake, on a sweltering afternoon, to women who didn't eat. That day, Sam Dile made his wife's acquaintance over several sweating cups of lemonade. They married in their mid-thirties and had no children.

Grey had spoken to her that morning, she was understandably devastated. If Dile had died believing his secret was about to come to light, he died in vain. It seemed he had left his wife and friend as much in the dark about his life, as they had ever been.

"Are you sure he didn't say anything to you?" Grey asked again. "Anything at all that could tell us about his state of mind."

"He was troubled by the deaths," I said. It was true, and I didn't feel it betrayed any confidence to say so.

I knew I put Grey in a difficult position. He wanted me to tell him something he could relay to Mrs. Dile, something that might offer her some comfort. But, telling her that her husband was distraught over the death of his blackmailer would only raise the question of why he was being blackmailed. Grey and I, two people with no business to do so, decided then and there for Mrs. Dile, that it was better she not know why her husband took his own life, than to know he'd been unfaithful.

# Twenty-six

It was too early to drink. That's all you can think to do when someone dies, have a drink. You tell yourself it's to their memory, and not your sadness. I was mourning Sam Dile, not the man, but his death. He was the fourth person to die because of a perfumed letter written by a couple of greedy brats, the third I felt I could have prevented. If only I'd held onto Lynae that first day, turned her over to the police, it might have stopped at Adrienne.

I went back to my room to smoke. Never too early for a cigarette. It's a terrible habit I blamed Brun for reigniting. I resolved to leave the pack in the room when I finally bid *audieu* to Paris. After several failed attempts, I managed to open the cantilever window; the trick was to push the lower half forward until the top half hit you in the head, like a seesaw in a Three Stooges' gag. I rested my chin on the sill and dedicated myself to filling the alley with smoke rings.

I left the butt on the ledge and stood up straight in time for the phone to ring. I didn't know who it could be, but the arc of the morning had been in a certain direction. It was Catherine Savard, and she was frantic.

"Mickey, it's Catherine. I need you to come to the house, Antoine is out of control."

I couldn't cut in to tell her to slow down.

"I'm afraid, Mickey. He sent Ilsa away and he's turning everything upside down. Please," she said desperately, "I'm trapped here."

"Catherine, I'm calling the police."

"No," she shouted.

"Catherine, he's dangerous," I said.

"If you call the police, he'll leave, and I'll never see him again. Please! I just need someone to help me settle him down."

I'd precipitated the raid of this man's private club the night before, and the arrest of two of his lieutenants. We hadn't met, but I knew I was the last person that could settle Antoine Savard down.

"Please Mickey, you're the only one who can help me."

Before I could disagree, she hung up the phone.

Downstairs, Jerome had already finished his shift. I would like to have given him the Savard's address, with instructions to alert the police if I didn't contact the hotel within the hour. Trying to explain the request to Pipe and Sweater, his replacement, may set Franco-American relations back a decade with both of us drawing pictures in the dirt to no avail.

There wasn't time to take the train and make the long walk from the station along the Seine, so I flagged down a taxi. I was happy to see Jean, the cabbie who had driven me to Notre Dame. His rosary was right where he'd left it, under the exhausted crew-neck of his T-shirt. I wanted to believe then and there in God, and that my pot-bellied guardian angel was not driving me to my death.

Jean asked where I was from, and what brought me to Paris, which let me know he didn't remember me from my fare earlier in the week. My reply of *The States*, and *Just a stop-over*, failed to capture his imagination, and he returned his full attention to his polished, professional driving. The picture on Jean's hack license, despite being old and faded, looked like it was taken yesterday. His wincing eyes like cashews, their twinkle untranslated by the celluloid, his face lined like the sad clown at a circus.

He was singing again, under his breath at first, but louder when he needed to power his tremulous baritone. I imagined Jean in his youth as a gondola oarsman, singing old songs of lost love, to the percussive lap of canal waters. Age or injury would have forced him from that vocation to this one, but on a road that was smooth enough, he was transported in time and space back to that prior golden station.

He slowed the car to a stop in front of the Savard *maison*, and gave a nod of approval toward the gleaming white house.

"It's not mine," I said needlessly as I handed him the fare. He held up a hand in deference, and puttered cautiously away from the curb, back upstream.

I could hear Catherine screaming from inside the house. Yelling, more than screaming, and strained as if she'd be at it a while. I didn't want to ring the doorbell. If Ilsa had been sent home, I did not wish to meet Antoine Savard for the first time at the threshold, just to have a door slammed in my face. I tried the knob, it turned, and I entered cautiously as a cat burglar, which was one of several things I did not wish to be mistaken for.

Catherine was in her chair at the foot of the stairs. If Antoine had been turning everything upside down, he'd started at the other end of the house. Nothing was out of place. Catherine did not rush to my side when she saw me. She had stopped screaming, and the house was silent. She sat facing the divans, oblique to me and the foyer, and said nothing. Her head bobbed in front of her shoulders as if suspended by a reed. Her eyes were narrow, her mouth open slightly, tongue held for the moment between her teeth.

"Catherine, where is he?" I asked as I approached her like she was an unfamiliar animal.

The Savard home was not so large that Antoine could spring at me from any direction. There was only the kitchen to my left, the staircase, and two passages to the right of the divans; one likely to a study, the other the couple's master suite. I split my attention between the woman in the wheelchair and the passages to my right.

Catherine dangled a drink over the side of her chair. The heavy base of the octagonal tumbler had proven too unwieldy, and there was a small pool of scotch on the tile beside her, more spilled in her lap. She saw me look at the glass and rolled her eyes. She went to raise it demonstratively with an outstretched arm, and it fell to the floor with a single loud plink. The tumbler had fallen on its side, but the heavy base righted itself. A shard was missing from one of the octagonal facets. Still, the drink sat erect, broken, jagged, and still half full of booze.

"Oops," Catherine said flatly.

"Where is he?" I asked again.

She nodded toward the passage nearest the fireplace, the farthest corner of the house. "The bedroom," she slurred. "Not that he sleeps there… If he does sleep… It's not with me," she said suddenly raising her voice. Her words echoed off the vaulted ceiling and made the house sound cavernous and empty.

"He's leaving," she droned.

"Did he say that?"

"No. I told you he hasn't said anything to me in weeks." She looked for the drink her in her hand, then remembered she'd dropped it. "But he's packing."

"You said he'd stopped talking after Adrienne was killed."

She looked at me like I'd corrected her grammar. "How long is too long to not speak to your wife?" she asked.

"Have the police been by?" I asked. "They caught the man that killed your daughter."

"Who?"

I didn't know to whom Catherine's *who* referred, the police, her daughter, or the murderer, so I repeated the question.

"Is that all you're taking?" Catherine snapped, not looking at me. Her voice was shrill, not her practiced, throaty screen-test.

Antione Savard was standing in the passageway from the bedroom. His black turtleneck and dark blue suit, almost invisible in the unlit corridor. He looked exactly how I'd imagined; his eyes were round black onyx, his slicked hair patent leather, both polished to a mirror shine. His dark complexion and Roman nose suggested he was Sicilian or Greek. He had ten solid years on me but looked like he kept himself in shape crushing oil drums; I didn't want to find out how in-shape. He was already glaring at me like I was leaning against the fender of his car.

"Go ahead and leave, you've been waiting to leave since the day we were married," Catherine accused. "He thinks I trapped him," she turned her attention to me. *"No one is pregnant for eleven months.* What does he know? Women lose pregnancies all the time. I could have lost the first one without knowing." Catherine looked again for her missing drink. "Sure, I trapped you. It's what you do with apes. Should have cut your hands and feet off, sold you to a poacher."

It was a childish insult, but steeped in the poison of their personal history, she made it stick like tar.

"It took him ten years to have a real affair. The coward," she said, her voice trailing off. "Antoine, the great lover, turning his black light on waitresses, and understudies. Girls! Children really," she said accusingly. "Sure, he stopped. When he couldn't get it up anymore. What young woman wants an impotent old man, running a failing business, with his crippled wife's money?"

She was pushing all the buttons available to the long-suffering wife, without evoking, or desiring pity. Catherine wasn't holding her wounds up to evidence her husband's crimes, she was inserting them under his skin, opening old scars, and hoping to leave fresh ones.

I wondered how much Antoine was going to take. It occurred to me this was an old fight, unchanged for twenty years. He'd heard it all before, but I hadn't, and I didn't know how long he would suffer that. He had yet to say a word or move a muscle.

I broke the silence with the news Catherine had twice ignored. "The police have your daughter's killer in custody. He's confessed."

Catherine jumped in front of the statement like it was a speeding bus. "This is Mickey, we're lovers. He's half your age, and twice the man."

We weren't, and I wasn't.

"That's not true," I said. I could feel Catherine's roiling glare. "I'm in Paris investigating a case of blackmail," I continued. "A case that involved your daughter intimately." I wished instantly I'd chosen different words. "That investigation led me to a private club. A club for men that didn't want their sexual predilections known. Men your daughter thought were harmless. One of them wasn't. He confessed to killing her last night."

Neither Adrienne's mother or father spoke a word. Neither expressed anguish, or grief. There was no feeling of relief, of inching toward closure or healing. What hung in that room was blind rage. Antoine Savard had glanced at me long enough to know I was there before returning his dead-eyed gaze to his wife, whose teeth were bared, preparing to eat him alive.

"How much of that did you already know?" I asked Savard. "It was your club the men were leaving. Your men that were looking for the blackmailers. Your men that tried to cripple me with a lead pipe. And it was your men that killed Marguerite, believing she was in on it."

What followed was a beat of the loudest silence I have ever heard. No one spoke, and the quiet was an intolerable ringing in my ears. I had come to the Savard home for Catherine, but now I was there for Antoine. I held him responsible for Dile's suicide and Marguerite's murder, for Rico's existence, for the bruises on my body, and the deaths on my conscience. I was there to pick a fight.

Catherine broke the silence this time with uproarious laughter. "He doesn't own any club! He doesn't own the clothes on his back. It's all mine. The casino, the playhouse, everything. And his men," she chided, "they moonlight because he doesn't have the stones to reign them in. When my parents found him, he was just another grease-ball working in the kitchen. My mother thought he was handsome, told my father to put him out front. She was right, you would have thought he was born in that tux."

Antoine hadn't heard a word of his biography. He wore the same revelatory look as the Concierge when I told him that Adrienne was behind the blackmail. He was trying to fit these new pieces into the puzzle of his grief he thought complete. If Antoine didn't know his daughter was the culprit, and his men didn't know, then what motive could they have had for killing Marguerite? What motive did anyone have?

"Say something!" Catherine screamed at him. There were tracks in the powder on her cheeks, but they had long since dried. She gnashed her teeth and lunged against the tether of her powerless legs. Concealed among her flowing robes was a .32 caliber pistol she now balanced on top of her knees. It was a small gun, but she held it in both hands, like a dead bird, showing her husband what he'd done.

Antoine Savard let his coat slide off his shoulders and drop on top of his suitcase.

Catherine wrapped her hand around the pearl handle of the little gun and leveled the shiny nickel barrel at her husband.

It was Catherine who'd sent Ilsa away; Ilsa who knew the dynamic between the two and could provide the police with context and motive. She'd replaced her long-time servant with a strange man, a foreigner she could paint as a romantic rival, a burglar, or an assassin. Had I been summoned here as a witness, or a scapegoat?

Antoine stood motionless. Catherine's hatred crawling through his veins only quickened him now, like a hunter, euphoric over the closeness of death. Something had to die, and he would kill whatever he could to take his place. His nostrils flared, his lungs filled, and his hands held by his sides, were curled as if already wrapped around his wife's neck.

The fireplace poker came away from its rack with the low peal of a broken bell and sent the rest of the tools crashing to the tile floor with a terrible clangor. Antoine skulked forward, the point and hook of the poker dancing in the air as he firmed his grip on the handle. I lunged in front of Catherine instinctively, and as it turned out, needlessly. Antoine Savard had been coming for me.

I darted to my left, to get between him and Catherine. And Antoine, charging into the space I had voided, wound up almost behind me. He swung the poker like a baseball bat. I tried in vain to cover my head. But, his swing was lower, just below my shoulders, sure to make contact. The iron shaft cracked against my right elbow. The Ham's wrenching of my arm the night before had left it too weak to lift, too weak to cover my head. Had Savard swung for my head, he would have split my skull.

The pain in my elbow dropped me to my knees. Hacking blows fell across my back, the heavy wrought iron divining my unprotected spine. Antoine Savard kicked me in the ribs like a dog until he was sure I would stay down.

The house was quiet except for my railing cough, and the cries of pain I tried to stifle like a child at a library or a funeral. The length of my right arm was full of needles and wouldn't move, no matter how I begged it. It was hard to breathe. The pain in my ribs kept me from getting up. From the floor, I could see Antoine standing in front of Catherine, the poker held at his side.

"I never loved you," she said. "You were a dark, exotic thing that other women wanted, and that I could possess. And you never loved me. Whenever I heard someone praise you for your loyalty or make some pitying remark about how much you must love me, it made me sick. Feigning devotion with your hand up a waitress's skirt. You made me look like a fool – as if I cared what you did.

"You didn't stay out of love, or duty, or because I was pregnant. You stayed because I handed you the reigns." Catherine's voice sounded as if it had traveled a great distance. "I couldn't run the business, not in my condition. I needed your strength. You were strong enough to do the work, and dumb enough to control. You were a beast, and I your burden."

I pulled myself to my knees with the help of one of the divans. Antoine was less than six feet away, but it seemed like a mile. If I dove for the poker, I could miss. If I tried to take him to the ground, he could smash it over my head. Catherine was looking through me, reading my mind. There was a smirk on her face like her boyfriend had just pushed me in the mud for asking her to dance.

"We used to throw the best parties, Mickey," she said. In speaking to me, I think she expected her husband to turn around and finish me. But, I was no threat to him. She was the one with the gun in her hands.

"The house was always filled with interesting people," she said looking from wall to wall. There was a movie playing behind her eyes again. "And at the end of the night, we would pair off." She giggled. "I know what you're thinking, but we were all adults.

"Antoine was so obvious. I knew who he would spend the night sniffing around as soon as they walked through the door. Sloppy, easy women, falling out of cheap sequin dresses. Never anyone with any class. The little fools were so flattered that a refined gentleman like *Monsieur* Savard paid them such attention," she said mocking him. "If they had only known how recently removed he was from hairnets and aprons, how little the difference between him and the busboys they were used to fucking.

Don't think me jealous, Mickey," she laughed. "I played too. There were rich men, young men, artists, actors; they were not deterred by my condition," she said stroking the tops of her legs. "They liked the submissiveness more than they were likely to admit. Especially the rich ones," she hissed as if coiling herself around a suitor in front of us. "Some took more advantage than others. You felt what it was like, Mickey, holding me in your arms."

Antoine Savard looked back at me for the first time, but there was nothing registered on his stony face.

"It wasn't a traditional marriage, but it worked," she continued. "Until *Her*. After *Her*, the parties stopped. The house was no longer full of interesting people. Not once he had *Her*." The word *Her* crawled out of her mouth like an insect, it was something that required effort for her to expel.

At first, I thought *Her* was Adrienne. I'm sure key-parties go by the wayside when the kids are old enough to know how many uncles they should have. But, it was clear another woman had come between them, and I was sure I knew who.

"You stopped our parties, so you could be faithful to your mistress," she screamed at him. "That wasn't the deal." Her voice reached the incongruously low register of the day I'd left her sitting in her roadster.

"They ended it," I said.

"They ended nothing," Catherine shouted. "I ended it. I told *Her* it was over. And I said if it wasn't, that I would make the last hours of her life a nightmare."

"But that was years ago, why now," I asked. Again, Antoine looked back at me. His un-appointed advocate, the stranger he took for a gigolo, was pleading the case for his murdered mistress.

"Say you loved her, and I won't kill you where you stand." The ultimatum brought Antoine's attention back to his wife and the little nickel automatic.

"You said yourself, you didn't love each other," I pleaded. "What does it matter now?"

"Say it," she snarled.

Antoine Savard gave a shake of his black head I could hardly discern.

"You say it!" she screamed. "Give this to me. I want to know I killed the thing you loved."

Antoine closed his hand tighter around the heavy iron.

"After his whore died, I caught him crying. Can you believe that?"

I made a move for Antoine, but I was too late.

Savard leapt at his wife with a single ferocious swing of the poker. He let loose a monstrous roar; every unspoken word of the last twenty years smashed into one unintelligible syllable. A deafening clap of thunder seemed to come from the high ceiling, as if the roof itself had been torn in half above our heads. When I opened my eyes, Catherine's head was thrown over the back of her chair, hanging limp as a wet towel. A pool of blood was forming behind the wheels, spreading wider with every drop.

Antoine dropped the poker and clutched at his back. When he pulled his hand away, it was wet with black blood. He turned to face me, fingering a small hole in the front of his shirt. Blood, thick and dark as molasses, poured lugubriously into his hands. Savard steadied himself on the arm of one of the divans before sinking onto it. He left a maroon hand-print on the dusty rose upholstery like a doily.

There was no urgency to call an ambulance; she was dead, and he was dying. Antoine Savard sat in his living room, with his hand over his belly as if he'd finished his favorite meal. He sat with his back to the wife who had pursued him their entire married life. I sat on the edge of the white marble coffee table in front of him. If he was going to break his silence in these final moments, I would be there as his confessor. He was a social-climber, a gangster, and a philanderer. He might say he regretted it all, or insist he'd do it all again. He might try to convince me that he and Catherine had truly cared for one another or swear he had never loved her.

"Your daughter," I told him, "was murdered by a man she had been blackmailing. He saw her on the street, by chance, and killed her with his bare hands."

Savard refused to meet my eyes. Instead he regarded the stain on his shirt with annoyance at the thought of having to replace it.

"But, it was someone else who found her accomplice and tried to take her for a ride. That, I know, was your men. Someone also found your daughter's apartment and searched it. I'm betting that was your men, too. And I think somebody told them where to look, somebody who knew."

Savard lifted his chin from his chest, and his black eyes from the hole in his belly.

"If it was your men," I said, "then you either knew about a hit on your own daughter, or it was your wife who ordered it."

Antoine Savard said nothing. He sat in the bright white room, bleeding into the furniture like an ink spot. He would outlive his wife by a few minutes.

In her recounting of their life together, no mention was made by Catherine Savard of their only child, their murdered daughter, their most unloved Adrienne.

# Twenty-seven

"My wife thinks I am making you up," Brun said entering the room. Neither of us laughed at the joke, because it wasn't funny. I think we were both tired of people dying, even if it was people like the Savards.

As the only live body found in the company of two recently deceased ones, I was shown to an interrogation room instead of the now familiar confines of Inspector Brun's office. I had given my statement to a detective, a young constipated go-getter, and I imagined Brun had already read it. No longer having reason to, I spared no detail. I hadn't been stupid enough to pick up the fireplace poker or the gun, or to slip in Catherine's blood on my way to the telephone, so I was only under slightly more suspicion than any poor slob who had been present during a double murder.

My elbow looked like an eggplant and I couldn't bend it enough to put it in a sling. The ice bag it was resting on was the size of a condor nest and bled all over the aluminum table. Having no dry place to lay a case file, Brun had gone for a towel. He dried the table as dutifully as any busboy, in a Paris bistro, wearing a three-piece suit.

"So, you met Antoine," said Brun.

"He thought I was a fireplace," I said.

"Over the years, the Savards have been the subject of numerous investigations, so questioning them even about the murder of their own daughter was," Brun searched for the right word.

"Sensative?" I offered.

The inspector shook his head. His pursed lips pushed his mustache up his nose. "Shit," was the word he settled on. "They refused all interviews, always referring us to their attorney. *Sacre!* What would a lawyer know about a little girl?"

"About as much as her parents," I said.

I thought it was strange how young Adrienne was in Brun's mind. He was older than me, and maybe that was old enough to think of a twenty-year old as a child. I imagined he was a father, or even a grandfather. Maybe he had a daughter Adrienne's age, whom he remembered as a child, and would always remember her that way.

I didn't know anything about fathers, or how being one made you different from other men. All I knew about men was that they had jobs. The men who came and went at St. Agnes were there to fix the plumbing, patch the roof, or curse the boiler. At sea, the men, if they had families, didn't talk about them. Families were pictures in wallets or dog-eared photos taped to the wall beside your bunk. I knew more than a few Portuguese sailors who kept lockets, but most kept nothing. No one talked about family, it was considered bad luck, which suited me.

"Mickey," the inspector began without looking up from his case file, "what led you believe that the club on Cite Pigalle was owned by Antoine Savard?"

"Wasn't it?" I asked.

For my benefit, Brun ran his finger over a couple sheets of paper shaking his head, feigning an exhaustive second search for information he knew wasn't there. "We are still investigating of course, but as of yet, we have found no connection."

I'd just followed my nose. The waitress at the *Lapine* had told me about the casino, where I found Rico, and Rico was an asshole. I followed Adrienne's notes backward to Cite Pigalle, Sam Dile confirmed my hunch, and gave me the location of the club. The name Adrienne Savard had meant nothing to Dile, and he hadn't let on that Antoine's did either. When I found the club, Rico was there. I could tie Antoine's daughter and his henchman to both places. Was that not enough?

"I guess I just assumed one and one equaled two," I offered.

"That is the difference between the police and the vigilante, we do not have the luxury of assumptions," Brun lectured.

I didn't care for his use of the word *vigilante*. It made me sound volatile. I wasn't trolling the streets with a baseball bat, looking for jay-walkers and vandals, or busting up bodegas selling cigarettes to minors.

"How would Adrienne know about a club like that, unless her father was involved?" I posed.

"It is a good question," Brun replied somewhat patronizingly. "Perhaps she knew someone who *was* involved with the club," he proffered. "Like your friend, Rico Mindy, whom she could have met through the family's casino."

"Sure, I suppose." Catherine had mentioned the moonlighting of Antoine's men. "It didn't matter to my investigation whether he owned it or not," I reasoned. "I wasn't trying to bring down a syndicate, I was trying to find a girl's killer!"

"And did you find him?" Brun asked. "That night in the club, did you find the girl's killer?"

I went to open my mouth, but nothing came out. I could feel my face flush. I was twelve years old again, trying to conceal a baseball mitt and explaining to the sisters why my chores weren't done. Only this was immeasurably worse. No one had ever died before, no matter how unmade my bed was.

"We arrested Adrienne's killer, with evidence you obtained, I presume several days earlier, from the girl's apartment," Brun said with stale resentment. "You had her killer in your hands days ago. But you were drunk and found it more important to rough him up in the alley outside his home than to inform the police."

"I didn't know he was the killer," I said in my defense.

"And, how could you? Did you question him about the murder of Adrienne Savard?"

Brun knew the answer, but I shook my head anyway.

"I have *Monsieur* Rimbaud's statement, his version of your conversation, and indeed, you did not ask him about the murdered girl, only about the very live one from the restaurant," Brun said, eyebrow raised. "You did not ask the right questions. You did not conduct a proper investigation, and that was certainly not a proper interrogation of a suspect."

The inspector was showing me the proper interrogation of a suspect. Brun took a break from kicking my head in to light a *De Troupe*. The interrogation room was frigid, and the rich tobacco oil seemed to congeal in the air. It was the distorted lens that Brun now viewed me through.

"One could argue you did not conduct a proper investigation, because you are not a police investigator. But, the leads you chose not to follow, and the evidence you chose not to turn over, lead me to believe that you are not an investigator at all. Which begs the question, *Monsieur* Fairfax, what is the nature of your business here in Paris?"

I didn't answer. I didn't hang my head or look away. I watched Brun as he watched me.

"It does not appear that you were trying to find *Mlle*. Savard's killer, as you stated before, so what were you doing?" the inspector asked again.

"I was investigating the blackmail of an American citizen," I stated clearly. "It became clear to me that *Mlle. Savard*," I said peevishly, "was not working alone, and after her death I tried to discover the identity of her accomplice."

"Yes, her accomplice, the attractive young American woman who twice escaped your *custody*," Brun said incredulously. "And you believed this woman would be found at the club on Cite Pigalle, and that is why you went there?"

I didn't know if this was a question, or if Brun was feeding me my story, like the one he had concocted about Rimbaud's state of mind the day he killed Adrienne.

"No," I said. "I didn't think she would be there."

"Why then," Brun asked with voice raised, "did you go to a private club, with a concealed weapon? What purpose did it serve in your investigation of blackmail?"

Why did I go to the club? It wasn't because I thought Lynae would be there. It was because I had to find out what Cite Pigalle was for myself. I had to know why these men were being blackmailed. I had to know if Lynae was still in danger. I had to know what Lynae and Adrienne had on these men. And I had to know if I could live with what she had done. I wasn't trying to find a blackmailer, I was trying to keep one safe.

"I followed the wrong lead," I relented. I told Brun how I had thwarted Lynae's attempted abduction, about the Mercedes with the bent door, and how the Concierge had admitted it was his men who made the attempt.

"Whatever your motives, Mickey, you seem far more concerned with this young woman," Brun posited. "You may have failed to discover a killer, but you must be very certain you are not protecting a criminal."

Then the inspector really threw me for a loop.

"Can you provide evidence that you were not working with this young woman, that you were not party to the extortion?"

The pink pulpy letter sat in a duffle bag in my hotel room. I could give him the name Samuel Dile. The guy was dead, what did it matter? Grey or Shabin could tell him exactly what my business was in Paris. I could give him plenty. But, I wasn't going to. After all I'd done, if Brun suspected me of anything, he could take a flying leap. I wore the wounds of this case more than anyone. Anyone living. Maybe I worked it wrong, I couldn't argue that. I'm not an investigator. Adrienne's notes had proven a better angle than me poking a hornet's nest full of gangsters. And five more people had died. There was that. If

Inspector Brun thought he had me on something, then he should charge me. Maybe I deserved it.

"The *Ministere Public* is still determining whether they have sufficient evidence to charge you with interfering with a police investigation."

I felt the bight of the rope around my ankle.

Brun stepped out, leaving me alone with the prospect of jail-time in a foreign country. For the first time in a long time, I felt like I had a home, and I felt very far away from it. The inspector returned with a can of Coke, a Hyper candy bar, a bag of potato chips, and the promise of the worst meal I would have while in France.

"You should try to eat something," Brun said, as if the situation was entirely within my control. He was a one-man good-cop, bad-cop.

"Can I ask you something?" I wanted to get back to sitting on the same side of the table. "Could Catherine Savard have killed Marguerite? Not herself I mean, but ordered it without Antoine knowing? Did she have those kinds of connections?"

Brun seemed to consider it. His mouth curled into something that was neither a smile nor a frown. "I think you might be mistaken about who the big wheel was."

The silver haired inspector sat back in his chair and stirred a cup of coffee. He asked me what I knew of Catherine's side of the family. I relayed what she had told me; that they had moved, with her, from Canada to France so that she could pursue her many interests and had been people of considerable means.

Brun held his coffee cup over his heart as if taking an oath. He began to tell me the story of Joseph Klimer, a Quebecois and son of German immigrants. He grew up poor and cold on his parents' farm, mostly tending to goats, making money on the side selling bottles of homemade grain alcohol. He began selling his hooch to secluded taverns, then speakeasies in the bigger cities, where he met a girl name Anna Turnay, herself the child of immigrants, and a dancer. They married and soon turned Joseph's single still into the second largest bootlegging operation in Canada.

Of course, to be the second largest bootlegging operation means that you will inevitably run afoul of the largest. As Klimer spread his tentacles from his base in Quebec City to Montreal, he came up against an outfit with ties to an Italian crime family. The two factions came to an unspoken agreement on turf, and there was a period of ten years or more where they coexisted, during which time the Klimer's welcomed their daughter, Catherine into the world. Waiting until later in life to start their family, Catherine would be their only child.

Tensions between bootleggers flared as new leadership took control of the Italian racket, and Joseph Klimer, as witnessed by several on the street that day, shot and killed a man in broad daylight. The man was thought to be an assassin sent to kill Klimer, his wife and child, but fear of prosecution and retaliation was enough to force the Klimer's to flee Canada for France.

Klimer opened a nightclub and appeared to have gone straight, before rumors began to circulate that the club was the source of illegal grain alcohol, making its way to the streets of Paris. Joseph and Anna Klimer were shot and killed, sitting in their car, outside a theater in the Opera Quarter. Though the killing had all the earmarks of a gangland slaying, the Klimer's were without any known rivals in the distribution racket.

In the wake of her parent's death, Catherine Klimer, now Catherine Savard moved quickly to sell her parent's nightclub, and the family home, purchasing a casino among several other concerns, completely reconstituting the family holdings within a matter of days. The inspector on the case had been a good friend of Brun's and noted during his investigation the lack of cooperation from the Klimer's daugher. Several others within the department began to suspect the girl and her new husband of orchestrating the hit. Brun didn't know what he believed. But, if it were true, it told you all you needed to know about the will and influence of Catherine Savard.

# Twenty-eight

When Inspector Brun was finished threatening me with prison, we both sat back in our chairs filling the freezing room with warm, acrid smoke. The medical examiner poked his head in the door and muttered something in French. It seemed like a social call, but Brun started asking questions about the Savards in English. The old doctor looked at me, then back at Brun who gestured that the examiner was free to speak. The doctor told us what we already knew, Catherine Savard had died from a single blunt force trauma that cracked her skull, Antoine from a single gunshot wound that entered and exited his liver, spilling toxins into the very blood that was pouring out of him. Regardless of the lives they had lived, there was nothing remarkable about either of their deaths.

The examiner reappeared a few minutes later with second cup of coffee for his friend, the inspector, and a small metal tray. The tray balanced rolls of gauze, angled shears, and a syringe I didn't like the looks of. He said the dressing on my finger needed to be changed and sneered at it like a dirty diaper. He was a thin, older man in brown flannel trousers held up by yellow and navy striped suspenders. He rolled up his sleeves and set to work with the busy energy of a sandpiper. I wanted to tell him to take his time, knowing his usual patients wouldn't complain about being handled like a side of beef. But before I could wince, the good doctor had soaked the bandages in saline, and slipped the old dressing from my badly burned finger. He explained that emergency medics never cleaned a wound well enough and set to debriding bits of charred flesh from my fingertip with tweezers and a small brush like he was setting a watch spring.

When he was done, my finger was shiny and white with a terrible red wound like the belly of a gutted pollock. He'd shelved his English to tell Brun a story while he redressed my finger. When the wound was covered he begged Brun for a cigarette with wordless, probing lips like a giraffe stripping a tree branch. Brun obliged and stuck a smoke in his face, lighting it as they laughed at the punch line of the story.

My left index finger was wrapped tight as a summer sausage and ready for a night on the town with a little bow tie I assumed was a joke. The doctor then squeezed my butterflied eyebrow between his thumb and forefinger, without invitation and said he could put another stitch in it if I wanted, adding it would have to be without the benefit of novocaine. I asked if he thought it was necessary, and he shrugged. On his way out the door, the examiner jabbed the syringe of God knows what into my shoulder and pushed the plunger before I could finish swearing.

Inspector Brun began reassembling the case file when I noticed Adrienne's notes, stuck in the brads, between the pages.

"May I?" I asked pointing to the notes.

Brun considered it for a minute. Remembering I'd seen them before, removed them from the file and slid the notes across the table to me. I thumbed through them like an old yearbook.

"We found Adrienne's bank account, opened using the name and national identification number of the Savard's maid," Brun chuckled. "The maid confirmed she did not open the account, and our expert has compared the signature card to several samples of Adrienne's handwriting."

"And the deposits," I asked.

"Over forty. Each for five-hundred francs exactly." If Brun knew what it meant, he wasn't telling. I had my own ideas.

I flipped through the remainder of Adrienne's notes looking at the addresses scribbled at the bottom of each. When I found what I was looking for, I asked Brun if I was free to go. He said I was but instructed me not to check out of my hotel or leave Paris. I slid the notes back across the table and watched the inspector clip them into the file. Three little letters had stood out on the bottom of the last note. Where Adrienne had spelled out the addresses of her marks, one read only HTL. And I was willing to bet, that HTL stood not only for hotel, but Hotel Lazarus.

This time I approached the Lazarus from the narrow alley in the rear. I recognized the hotel's dumpster and turning the corner, nearly collided with Babby, cooling his heels with the rest of the flies. He jumped out of his skin and tripped when he turned to run. The little rat scrambled to his feet, hissing obscenities and racing for the service door. I caught the door before it closed behind him. The kitchen was empty, but for one chef laboring to fill a large mixing bowl with peeled garlic cloves.

Babby was gone but I didn't care. There was plenty of time to deal with him, and nowhere he could hide. One had only to follow wet alley pavement and the smell of garbage to find rats. And like a rat, Babby could watch others snared, and still return to any dumpster that offered him an easy meal. He would never really go anywhere.

I pushed through the porthole doors and crossed the lounge with my carotids pounding in my neck like kettle drums. Anger contorted my face, jutted my jaw, and hardened my eyes, shutting out light, good, reason, and fear. A few older patrons sat with their espresso and newspapers. Two thin gents postured in the window, looking like English professors in tweeds checkered like the couches in the basement rec-room of St. Agnes. They held pipes with bent elbows and their Turkish coffee failed to cover the burnt resin smell of hashish. No one in this room would dream of giving me a problem.

From the lounge, I could see one of the thin giant's long, pale hands splayed flat on the marble counter-top. One quick step put me in front of the desk. I clapped my left hand over the giant's, waited for the flash of recognition in his eyes, and punched him in the face as hard as I could. I felt the small jag of bone crunch under my fist like the spine of a cabbage leaf, and I knew I had broken his nose.

The Giant folded in half at the waist and landed on his bottom like a toddler. Bright red blood covered his lips and teeth, and tiny droplets sprayed as he cursed me from the tile floor. He called me a lot of things in French, but *son of a bitch* in perfect English; the kid had seen an American movie in his life. The hotel's registry was a padded leather tome with corners like gold epaulets. I flipped it open and turned the velum pages back more than two weeks. I found exactly what I was looking for; Samuel Dile's name and address, Boston, Mass, USA.

I bent down behind the counter, in front of the bloodied but subdued hotel manager and looked him in the face. Even sitting, he was tall, and we were practically eye to eye.

"A young woman came in here a few weeks ago, and asked for this man's address in the States," I held the registry open for the Giant to look at through watering eyes. "Who is she?"

"What makes you think I know?"

"I wouldn't ask unless I knew you did," I bluffed.

He looked at me hard, but without menace. I was close enough to hit him again, and both his hands were busy keeping blood off his suit lapels. And he was a bleeder.

"I don't think you'd risk losing this job for just anyone," I reasoned. "No, you know her, maybe even like her." He grimaced, it was a fresh twist of the knife. "Pretty girl, I can sympathize."

"Enough, I know her," he said, halting his dissection. "Why should I tell you anything more than that?"

Every word that began with *t-h* caused movement in his sunken nasal cavity that threatened to make him sick.

"You know why she wanted that address? It wasn't to return sunglasses or borrowed cab fare. It was blackmail. This man in your book is dead, along with four others."

I could see the two Hash Professors regarding us from the window, neither moved a muscle. They sat frozen, weighing the propriety of action against having their own slender noses broken.

"You give me her name, I'll tell the police I found her myself, keep you out of it." I showed him the credentials I hadn't shown anyone in days. "I'm an investigator."

He hung his head. He knew he was going to tell me. He was just taking a minute to hate himself for it. I'd made a mess of him, and he knew he would wear the signs of it for weeks. He would have to tell the hotel guests something, and would invent a story involving sports, or walking into a door, awash in shame each time he had to tell it. He hated me, but he hated her more for leading me to him.

"Her name is Mina," he said finally. "Mina Tagiz."

The Giant had first seen her, standing alone at a political rally, some group having a giveaway to sell young people on the Labor party. He didn't know her address but knew where she lived. He started to describe it to me, I stopped him, saying I knew where it was, and damn if I didn't.

"When I leave here, don't go calling her. If I find out you tipped her off," I let the rest hang.

"Look at me!" he exclaimed. His hands were painted red, his shirt and tie ruined. "She's not worth this!"

He was right, she wasn't worth this. I had been the one sitting on the ground bleeding, more than once over this girl, and I wondered if the kid could see that in my eyes.

"I'm sorry about your nose. Here," I said, and fished a handkerchief from my coat pocket.

He took it with a quick, polite nod. He wiped his hands clean then applied pressure with the kerchief over the bridge of his nose, which gave him some relief.

"You wouldn't have told me anything if I hadn't hit you, would ya?" I asked.

"No," he said. "Probably not."

I waited with him a moment longer, to make sure the bleeding would stop, and watched his eyes clear.

"You can call the police if you want," I said. "They know who I am, and they'll believe you." I started for the front door. "And do me a favor," I called from the long echoing lobby, "fire Babby."

# Twenty-nine

I took the train to Montparnasse and passed by *La Coupole* already buzzing with waitstaff. *La Boulevarde* didn't seem as long this time. I knew where I was going and cut through the courtyard between apartment buildings instead of walking around the block. As it was before, the door to the building was unlocked. I took the stairs slowly. That time of day the maudlin music of French soap-operas swooned behind more than one apartment door. When I reached the foot of the stairs to the fifth floor, the young woman I had met in the metro station, who took a blackmail payment as Adrienne Savard, who told me her name was Lynae Cuvier after we'd shared a bed, and who the thin giant of a hotel manager had given my client's name and address to, was locking the door of the apartment opposite the dead girl's.

She turned to start down the stairs and froze. Part of me expected her to smile at seeing me again. She didn't. Her face was blank, a clay mask, painted and fired to look like a woman's. Still, seeing her disarmed me and I patted my pockets, searching for my resolve like mislaid car keys. Was I supposed to rush up the stairs and kiss her, or tackle her and call the cops?

She had reinvented herself again, the current iteration looking very uptown. She wore fudge brown cigarette pants with what looked like her boyfriend's blue button-up, crisply starched, sleeves rolled above bangle bracelets. Her hair was slicked into a low ponytail, folded like an omelet, and captured in a tortoiseshell bear trap. I watched her put on a smile that changed to mock reproach for surprising her, to the soft eye-batting of remembered intimacy, and finally the stark realization that I had tracked her down.

"You found me," she said standing at the top of the stairs, forcing lightness into her faltering voice.

"I almost didn't, the name on your mailbox says Mina Tagiz."

She knew there was no name on her mailbox and the smile melted from her face. Still, she waited to see how I was going to play it. I wasn't a cop, and I had come alone, I couldn't very well take her in. We were no longer strangers, she knew I'd bartered with my integrity once, and likely would again.

"Is everything okay?" she asked. I watched her scan the landing and the stairs.

"It's over." I said. "The police have Adrienne's killer."

She covered her heart. "Are they sure?"

"He confessed. Seems he was one of the men the two of you blackmailed. The man you met a couple nights ago at a restaurant." I let her catch up. "He followed you that night, we both did. And if you hadn't lost him, he would have killed you, too."

"There's no telling why he murdered Adrienne," she returned dismissively. "He was probably in love with her."

I told her I doubted it. She was still making like Adrienne had taken these men to bed. She didn't know I had found the club on Cite Pigalle and knew its secret. Or, was there a chance I knew something she didn't?

"They also caught the men who tried to grab you the day we met," I said.

Not a smile, not a nod, not a single visible reaction to what I was saying.

"I thought you'd be relieved," I said.

"They weren't looking for me, they were looking for Adrienne," she reasoned, forgetting the strength of Aziz's grip and the idling black Mercedes that would have been her tomb.

I didn't tell her how Sam Dile had offered me to the mob as a staked lamb. How the Concierge's men were waiting to pounce on whomever appeared to claim the payoff. That gangsters wouldn't care whose name was written on the bottom of a perfumed letter. Or that that day, those men were absolutely looking for her.

"How did the two of you meet again?" I asked as I started up the staircase.

"What do you mean?" she said, motioning to Adrienne's apartment door. "She lived across the hall."

"The other night you said you met her at University, only Adrienne didn't go to University. She ever mention her parents, what they did for a living?"

"We didn't talk about our parents," she refuted. "I didn't know mine, and she wanted to forget hers."

"Adrienne's meetings with Marguerite weren't about blackmail, or any threats," I said. "My guess is she found out her father was carrying on an affair that was supposed to be over. She didn't tell you about that either?"

Her eyes widened as I drew a step closer. She wanted to bolt, but I'd treed her like a cat, at the top of the landing.

"Stop," she ordered while I was still midflight.

I paused to watch her breathe.

"It sounded like a pretty standard shakedown you two had going. Adrienne puts a guy in a compromising situation, threatens to embarrass him, see if he pays up. If he does, you know you got him on the hook, you can ask for the moon. But that's not even the kicker, is it?"

She didn't say anything.

"I figure it was your idea to start the letter writing campaign."

A curl rising from one corner of her mouth told me it was.

"Adrienne had been at this for a while," I continued. "Always the same M.O., ambushing the men in public, taking the same amount off each one. Five hundred francs. A manageable sum, nothing they'd miss. It'd be downright silly not to pay it. Then, over the last few months, a change. The men start receiving letters at their homes, asking for more. A lot more. And unless the payment I handed you was in two-dollar bills, it was damn sure more than five hundred francs."

"And they all paid," she taunted.

"Wasn't so easy for one man, not on a teacher's salary," I shook my head. "He'd never be able to explain the missing money to his wife. When you squeezed him too hard, he decided the only thing he could do was kill the beautiful young woman blackmailing him. But, he made a mistake, didn't he? Only natural to assume the letter came from the same young woman who confronted him on the street. But it hadn't. It came from you, and you alone."

"You don't know what you're talking about," she said and pushed past me on the stairs.

"You asked for too much in your letters because you didn't know how little Adrienne had been extorting," I said as I turned to follow her. "Because the two of you weren't working together."

She stopped on the next landing like she was stuck in mud.

"Did you even know her?" I didn't let her answer. "She had no idea you were blackmailing her marks. No idea you were coming in behind her, trying to cash the same ticket. Neither did her killer." My voice echoed in the stairwell, the accusation seemed to come from every direction. "By chance he runs into Adrienne on the street, after his business with her, but before his appointed business with you. He drags her into an alley and squeezes the life out of her. But it was you who'd asked for more money. It was you he meant to kill."

She moved more quickly now, down the remaining flights, and when we made it to the first-floor landing, the tension in my hands felt as if I'd strangled Adrienne myself. Mina turned to look up the steps as if her fallen meal-ticket was still alive somewhere behind the police-tape on the apartment door.

"Five hundred francs?" she gloated. "She didn't know what she had. I made ten times that, and I did it without sacrificing my dignity or my body."

"No, you sacrificed Adrienne's instead."

She reached into her over-sized purse, black dappled leather trimmed in brown, held in the crook of her arm like she was shopping for turnips, and produced a pair of sunglasses that matched the contraption in her hair. The large, dark glasses were too wide for her face and gave her the alert, predatory look of a praying mantis. I eyed her hind legs in case she had designs on snapping my head off. But, she kept them on the ground and pushed her way out the doors and down the front stoop.

I followed her through the park. I didn't think she could give me the slip in flats. "When I told you Adrienne was dead, you came straight back here, to her apartment, looking for names, addresses, maybe a little black book. You wouldn't have to break the lock, just bat your eyes at the super, say you were retrieving a scarf. But, someone had busted the lock. Someone had already been there. They didn't find the names either. First, I thought you'd doubled back to my place in search of your precious letter. But, when you saw someone had torn her place apart, that someone was getting close, it scared you."

Mina stopped to put a finger in my face. I waited for her to correct me, or yell at me to stop following her, but after a second, we were walking again.

"I found her notes and gave 'em to the cops. The girl liked to keep things in books. I guess we all have secrets, even from our friends."

She tried to quicken her pace, but the thwack of her low heels on the paved walk sounded like a tire with a nail in it.

"You know what occurred to me this morning?" I asked.

"I'm sure I don't care," she snapped, scanning park benches, mindful of who might me listening.

"Of all the things thrown around Adrienne's apartment, there were these big hatboxes on the floor in her bedroom." I exaggerated the size with my hands. "Hatboxes, I thought to myself, but no hats. Like that magenta number you had on the other day."

"She wore an eight, I'm a four," she rasped. "I took the hats. What's your point?"

"Point is, Doll, what are the odds you have more than just her hats in your apartment?"

She looked over the dark glasses to glare at me.

"The only thing I know that the police don't," I said, "is your name, and where to look for those damn hats."

"We were friends," she testified flippantly.

"Without a third party to say as much or a single picture of the two of you together, the cops will punch holes in that like a train ticket."

When we hit the boulevard, I could see her searching the other side of the street for a Samaritan with broad enough shoulders to rearrange my face if she screamed; but my face looked plenty gruesome, and the pilling black felt of my pea coat may as well have been gorilla fur. We were in the wrong part of town for heroics. No one noshing in a café here would dream of laying a glove on me.

"What do you expect me to do? What do you want from me?"

"I want to know why," I said. "Why the accent, why the put on? Why pretend to be Adrienne when collecting the money? Did you hate her that much?"

"Like you said, I didn't even know her."

Her mother's words exactly.

"Is that what this is?" she asked. "Justice for Adrienne?"

If there was justice for anyone, it was too late. But, justice would always be late. It was only ever a consolation, was never restorative where death was concerned, and justice had never prevented anything. Only Birdie Dile was left alive, but Grey and I had seen to it she would never know she was due anything like justice. Marguerite? The man who pulled the trigger was dead, as was the woman who ordered it. Those deaths had little if anything to do with blackmail or the woman standing in front of me. As for Catherine and Antoine Savard, they each lay dead by the other's hand, and were poised to be forgotten by Paris entirely.

"Adrienne Savard was a horrible person," she said. "If you ask me, she got what was coming to her."

"If being an asshole were a death sentence, would any of us be here?"

"You wouldn't," she said. "You've seen her closet, the money she was taking off those men wasn't paying for the kind of clothes in it, and certainly wasn't paying the rent. She didn't need the money. Don't you get it? She did it for kicks. She was mean. It was all a prank to her."

"What was it to you?" I asked.

We'd reach the entrance to the metro. She couldn't decide what the ugliest thing to say to me was, so she turned and disappeared down the unlit stairwell. I followed her down the dark tunnel to the yellowing under-worldly light, fetid air, and mechanical roar of the subway platform.

It could only have ended this way. The lambs had been eaten as they were destined to be eaten, and the wolves trapped as they were destined to be trapped. There were only two of us left, and I needed to know just how much of a wolf she really was.

"Convince me that you knew her," I pleaded.

"I told you."

"Convince me that you were partners. That you didn't know this was going to happen. That you didn't know it would end this way. And that you didn't intend to push Adrienne in front of a bus by making it seem she was behind it all."

"Why does it matter?" she asked.

"Because, I have to know if I can live with what you've done!"

My voice boomed in the empty tunnel. You could see for fifty yards in either direction before a horizon of darkness turned it all black. I didn't know where either path might take us.

"Live with what I've done," she repeated. "Why would you have to live with what I've done? You said it yourself, it's over. You're going back to your life, and I'm going back to mine."

I felt sick, my arms and legs empty, no longer pumping with adrenaline. It was an effort to raise my head to stare into the blaring overhead lights. Anything to keep from hanging it like a scolded dog.

"Oh, I get it," she cooed. "Sweet man." She touched my face. "What could we really have beyond that night in your room? Am I supposed to follow you home to America? Be the boatman's wife? Or are you planning to stay here in Paris -- to be what, my boyfriend?" She laughed an unhappy laugh. "Would you drive a cab, or pour drinks to support us? Could you see me getting a job as a private nurse, or working in a bookstore? Did you think I would cook your dinner?"

Some stupid part of me somewhere was crushed.

"You're a drifter... or at least adrift," she reached out and touched me as if I were a ghost or a soap bubble. "It's written all over you."

She set her bag down between our feet, her arms reached under my coat and wrapped around my waist. With her head against my chest I felt her voice in my bones as she spoke. "Just let me go," she said. "I'm not hurting anyone."

I took her by the arms and held her away from me. "You were right about being underestimated. No man, or woman for that matter, turning to see Adrienne on the street behind them would have thought anything of it, would have never suspected her. And she would never have suspected you. She underestimated you -- underestimated your meanness."

There was a light in her eyes as if she were laughing, but a sneer creased the rest of her face. "Adrienne was beautiful, and evil, and fearless. Once, I watched her stop one of her marks on the street, he was looking all around, you could tell he wanted to hit her. She stepped closer to him, balled his fist up in her hands, daring him to do it. He paid her then and there. She walked right into Chanel and bought a pale blue leather clutch. Adrienne didn't care who she was in front of, much less who was behind her. She never looked back, ...not...once. I guess she should have."

The arriving train slowed to rest behind her. We waited out the hiss of the brake, and the shrill, metallic proclamation of its next stop.

"I played this so wrong I'm facing an obstruction charge. The things I did right are the only reason I'm not behind bars already. I've explained myself to the police, but I'm not waiting for them to decide if it's good enough. In two days I'll be in the middle of the Atlantic. I'm going to give your name to the inspector. You can run and be the one looking over your shoulder, or – "

The bodies rushing off the train divided us like flood waters. She stood in the deluge of strangers as I cleaved my way back to her.

"I think if you explain to the police – "

She dragged her nails down the side of my face. "Explain that to the police."

She slipped away with the current, disappeared behind the closing train doors, and left me alone on the platform with blood on my cheek.

# Thirty

There was a payphone on the street outside the entrance to the Metro. Even if she got off at the next stop and immediately found a cab, she would never make it to her apartment before Brun could have a flatfoot there. Mina Tagiz would face the music or run with whatever costume changes she had in her over-sized purse, and a few thousand in blackmailed francs.

I caught the train headed toward *Les Halles*. My subway car was empty. Wanting to be alone, it suited me. The sway of the train car was consoling, like being cradled and rocked by a pair of giant metal arms. I closed my eyes and waited for the dark tunnel to take me home.

When I reached my hotel, I told Pipe and Sweater I was checking out in the morning, if not sooner. I looked for a train schedule among the rack cards in the lobby kiosk, but they were out. I wanted a train to Fos Sur Mer if I had to lay the tracks myself.

When I turned around, the old man looked agitated. He was waving his hands in a way I'd never seen, like shooing me away from a *souffle*. After a couple of *Monsieur, Si vous plait*'s I got the idea he had something for me. At the counter he produced a light brown envelope and placed it between us like a treasure map. He leaned over the envelope, his nose inches from it, and read "Mih-Key Fay-Fox," his wide, flat finger touching each syllable as he read. He looked at me with a twinkle in both eyes that could have been glaucoma and asked," *Qui?*"

"*Qui.*" I said.

"*D'accord!*" he cheered and pushed the envelope across the counter.

Besides my name, the envelope read Western Union. It was a telegram. I'd never gotten a telegram.

Mickey. Before leave Paris please join friends
for dinner. Lasserre. 17 Ave Ted Roosavelt.
Don't know time. Enjoy.

-Grey

I held the telegram where the old man could read it, pointed to the name

*Lasserre* and asked how fancy the place was. His eyes grew wide and he started a

diatribe in French about *oeufs*. *Oeufs, oeufs, oeufs.*

It's dinner, not breakfast, I thought, "I got it, order the eggs."

He did that thing only the French and Italians do, holding their fingers to

their lips, then blowing them away with a kiss and a flourish of the hand. I

expected him to say something like, *C'est Magnifique*, instead he scurried away to

the little office behind the counter.

He returned with a small, white-haired woman in a green banker's visor, I

presumed to be his wife and bookkeeper. She apparently kept the whole of the

family's English next to a jar of pencils on her desk. Pipe and Sweater gave her

the gist of what I guess you could call our conversation.

*"Monsieur,"* said the older woman, *"Restaurant Lasserre* is a very

prestigious establishment. You are very lucky to be dining there." She looked

uncomfortable and took a moment to preen herself. *"Excuse moi, Monsieur*, it is

also *tres expensive."*

"I'm not paying," I said flatly.

Pipe and Sweater and the Bookkeeper looked relieved and held each other

by the arms. The couple had only dined there once, as an anniversary present from

her parents. I gathered from her story this joint had been around a while.

"Is it the kind of place I need a jacket?" I asked.

"Qui," they replied in unison.

"Well, I haven't got one."

The two bickered in French. It ended in a barrage of slaps to the old

man's shoulder forcing his retreat again into the little office. He reappeared

moments later with a dark colored blazer spread over his arms.

I tried to object. There were still gangsters after me, and I didn't want to get thrown off a building in the old guy's jacket. His wife explained that the coat had been left in the lobby months ago, over the back of a chair, and no one had called to claim it. It looked like any other jacket, so I tried it on. Charcoal gray corduroy, with elbow patches, that turned green and speckled like a bass in the light. It fit like a glove.

The older woman smiled at me maternally, then licked her thumb and tried to rub Rico's knuckles off my chin. She told me the jacket would look nice with a dark turtleneck.

"Well I don't have one – and I don't need one," I said over an admonishing finger.

I told them both, *Merci,* more than once, took the creaky stairs to my room, and solved the riddle of the door knob on the first try. It wouldn't have surprised me to see her – Mina, standing there in the light of the window or curled up on the couch as before. I pressed my face to the bed and search for every lingering trace of her in. Mercifully, while I was out, it had been stripped and fitted with fresh linens. I told myself out loud that she was gone, in case I needed to hear it.

It was hours until dinner, even an early dinner, so I decided to skip lunch and grab some shut-eye. Better to show up to dinner with an appetite than to nod off in my *vichyssoise.*

Avenue Franklin D. Roosevelt, named for the former president of the United States of America, ran right through the middle of Paris, not far from the Arc D' Triumph. It seemed more of an honor to have a street named after you in a foreign country than at home, where every state had a dozen elementary schools named after the man and his fifth cousin.

The outside of Lassarre reminded me of the Savard mansion. It was a two-story brilliant white cube of classical geometry with floor to ceiling windows and weird, knee-high topiary that, excuse my French, looked like a dick and balls.

Ivy had overtaken the building's left side, as well as the adjacent lot, a testament to how long it had remained empty, and what a struggle it was to even exist next to the venerable restaurant.

It was five o'clock. I couldn't imagine international men of means dining any earlier. If I happened to have arrived first, I would be getting drunk at the bar. The inside of Lasserre was lavish. Pheasants groused about tufts of thin grass on the ochre yellow wallpaper, orchids lined the tops of the pilastered partitions like birthday candles, and tall white classical columns kept the recessed ceiling high above our heads.

I hadn't the chance to lament the absence of a bar before I spotted my party, or rather, they spotted me. Two well-dressed gentlemen sitting in the center of the main salon were overtly waving me over to their table. Grey had probably instructed them to look for a sailor who'd lost a prize fight. The smaller of the two rose to greet me with a polite smile, a perfect tie knot, and a single shake of my hand. He introduced himself as George Verdin, he was American. The larger man, did not rise, had likely inhaled his tie, and introduced himself as Hennessey, Franklin Hennessey with a crushing handshake, another fellow American.

Hennessey poured the last of a highball into his trench of his mouth, almost toppling the unsuspecting waiter, when he set the empty tumbler on his tray. Verdin slid his empty martini glass an eighth of an inch to signal for its removal, a caramelized cocktail onion sleeping one off at the bottom. I saw they were drinking scotch and martini's, so I ordered a milkshake. I waited patiently for the humorless waiter to apologize for his inability to bring me a milkshake and ordered a gimlet.

"How do you like the place?" Hennessey boomed. Before I could answer, he continued. "It's supposed to look like the dining room of an old luxury ocean-liner."

"I come here all the time," Verdin chimed.

"Thought you'd feel at home," thundered Hennessey. "So... how 'bout it?"

It took me a second to realize he expected me to answer with some level of authority. "The flora and fauna everywhere had me thinking Noah's Ark."

Verdin tittered.

Hennessey was still looking at me, expecting an answer.

"The Titanic was an ocean-liner," I noted.

"I take it this doesn't remind you of any of the ships you were on," George Verdin said as a fresh drink was placed in front of him.

"No, this is nicer than any ship's mess I ever saw, or any restaurant for that matter. The ships I worked on weren't exactly the Queen Mary. I don't suppose you gentleman spend much time on cargo freighters." We all laughed for different reasons.

Both men were at least twenty years my senior, and obviously very well heeled. George Verdin's thinning comb-over belied his dignity. He wore a dark navy blazer with gold buttons over a pale, yellow shirt, equal parts starch and Egyptian cotton. His club tie was thick stripes of black and green and probably indicated to those who would know, what school he attended or social order he belonged to. His watch was a relic and not a well-preserved one. The cushion-shaped Elgin was bound to his wrist by a calf-skin band several decades younger than the timepiece itself. I imagined he wore it for sentimental reasons, it was the only thing Mr. Verdin had on that looked like it had spent any time on earth before today.

Hennessey was a huge man. He'd played football in college before the advent of the forward pass, measured more than three feet from shoulder to shoulder and sat splay-legged on the dining chair like a sumo wrestler. He sported a full head of white hair that General Patton's barber kept at full attention, and his gold watch looked like the hub-cap of a flying saucer. Despite his size his most distinguishing feature were his eyes. His tightly constricted pupils were grains of lead bird shot frozen in pale blue glacial ice. They were not round, but conical, coming to a keen point at the pupil, and resembled feeding sharks as they swam back and forth over the table.

"How do you two know Andrew Grey?" I asked the obligatory question.

Verdin looked to his companion, Hennessey nodded his assent.

"I export fine food products, cheese, olives, truffles, caviar, and of course wine. A lot of wine. If you've ever gasped at the price of something in a tin or a jar, there's a good chance I'm responsible. Andrew's ships carry most of it to the US and South America," Verdin explained.

"And I send beef back the other way," added Hennessey at a reasonable volume.

My gimlet and Hennessey's latest scotch arrived as did the waiter to take our order. I hadn't looked at the menu, but it was a single laminated plank with about as much writing as a greeting card. I insisted the gentlemen order.

Hennessey ordered the *Duck a L'orange.* The waiter gently reminded Mr. Hennessey that the dish was prepared for two. Hennessey told him it had better be and handed him the menu. Without referring to anything, Verdin carefully ordered the Poached Turbot, Foam *au Poive*, Imperial Caviar, and Sea Potatos smoked over beechwood. I didn't even see that on the menu. It seemed to make the waiter happy and they exchanged verbal high-fives in the native tongue. There were only three of us, but it seemed the *garcon* took my order fifth or sixth. For the blue-collar boy from Boston, with these gentlemen paying the freight, it was Lobster Newburg all the way.

The affable Verdin asked how I'd enjoyed Paris. He made a list of tourist haunts but when I said I hadn't seen any of them, it made any follow-up moot. Hennessey and Verdin looked at each other again, practicing their telepathy.

"Look fellas, I take it this isn't a purely social call," I said. "I hope we don't have to wait for the dessert cart to cut to the chase."

"All business. How do you like that? Grey said you were the right man," Hennessey affirmed and patted my shoulder with a large warm hand.

I didn't think I'd handled this business in Paris particularly well. If I would have done what was asked of me, Mina Tagiz would be dead alongside Adrienne. With their daughter gone, Catherine may still have ordered Marguerite's murder, and maybe the Savards were destined to kill each other. But, Dile might have lived, and he had been my client. I'm new to the hound-dog business, but it seemed the one person who was supposed to survive, no matter the gambit, was the client. He had taken his own life, but that didn't let me off the hook. I wondered what my benefactor had been telling these men.

"It's my son, Mickey," Hennessey began. "He's gotten himself in a little trouble, and I need someone to bring him home."

"Sounds easy. What's the rest of it?" I asked.

Hennessey and Verdin looked at each other a third time. There was no collar-tugging or knuckle-biting, but the tension was palpable. Getting information out of Sam Dile had been like pulling teeth, and I wondered if I was going to need x-rays and a spit cup to get the skinny from these two.

"He *is* my son," said Hennessey, "but he is not my wife's child." Then after a long second, "nor is she aware of him."

Verdin cut in quickly. "Grey assured us you could handle the matter with the utmost discretion."

"My wife knows everyone in my usual employ, lawyers and the like," Hennessey admitted. "Hell, she even knows the investigator I had following her."

A loud mechanical hum put a halt to our discussion. On the ceiling above was an enameled painting, a dozen red-headed maidens with wind under their skirts, playing with ribbon, cornered by four shirt-less, dark-haired studs keeping as many overly-muscled white stallions at bay. A retractable roof split the scene in two and opened slowly on the night sky.

It was a neat trick, and I thought it would have gotten more of a reaction, but my fellow diners were sitting on their hands. Heat was being piped in, around our feet, from somewhere unseen. The night air was balmy, and the men congratulated themselves for wearing jackets. If their wives were clad in anything short of wool, they were frozen solid.

"Robbie's in a kind of rehab facility," the big man continued. "And I want you to bring him here to Paris."

"Going to stay with you and the misses for a while?" I asked.

"Oh, no," said Hennessey. "I leave for Tennessee in the morning. He'll stay here, and Verdin will put him to work when he's ready."

I was sure there was more to that, but the most pressing matter was still at hand. "Where exactly is your son, Mr. Hennessey?"

Verdin cleared his throat. "Tenerife."

"Tenerife?" I exclaimed.

"Yes, it's an island – "

"Oh, I know where it is. Quite a swim from here," I said.

"There's a tramp steamer leaving Fos Sur Mer tomorrow," Hennessey said setting his tumbler of scotch down for the first time since it arrived.

"If you agree to take the job that is," Verdin said somewhat apologetically.

"Of course, he'll take the job," Hennessy boomed. "Grey already said –"

"Robert is a good boy, Mr. Fairfax," Verdin cut in again. "He just makes bad decisions."

Verdin seemed as concerned about Robbie as Hennessey, and I started to wonder just whose son he was. Hennessey felt I'd already been lent to him, like a pair of hedge clippers, and I didn't like it. I hoped it wasn't Grey who made him feel that way.

*Robert is a good boy, he just makes bad decisions.* What a comforting thought. Maybe we were all good boys and girls who just made bad decisions. I think entire metaphysical movements had been founded on less.

I'd heard it argued that we were born bad and life was our chance to get right with God before we died. Others claimed we were born good, it was earthly

219

things that were evil, and you were afforded a measure of dalliance for being surrounded by temptation. If you were sorry, you were forgiven. Simple as that. What mattered was what was in a man's heart. And the only ones who could ever know that for sure, were you and God. And one of you wasn't saying.

Tenerife, huh? Well, my bags *were* already packed.

Printed in Great Britain
by Amazon